THE PLANET OF THE CLEANING BUGS

by

Tony Stefano

PublishAmerica
Baltimore

© 2012 by Tony Stefano.
All rights reserved. No part of this book may be reproduced, stored in a retrieval system or transmitted in any form or by any means without the prior written permission of the publishers, except by a reviewer who may quote brief passages in a review to be printed in a newspaper, magazine or journal.

First printing

All characters in this book are fictitious, and any resemblance to real persons, living or dead, is coincidental.

PublishAmerica has allowed this work to remain exactly as the author intended, verbatim, without editorial input.

Softcover 9781462690909
PUBLISHED BY PUBLISHAMERICA, LLLP
www.publishamerica.com
Baltimore

Printed in the United States of America

ACKNOWLEDGEMENT AND DEDICATION

I wish to acknowledge my friend Dr. Sandra Alfonsi for understanding and knowing how to help me put into words the visions that are in my mind.

Without her help this book would not have advanced beyond the first stage. She has not only painstakingly edited my writing but she has also enhanced its quality. She has guided and taught me how to focus so that I could bring my visual creations to life. Without her friendship and help, this book would not have come to fruition.

Introduction

It's the year 2630. Interplanetary travel has been mastered and people can now visit hundreds of planets within hours or days. Fantastic advancements have occurred in every field of human development. The pharmaceutical profession has discovered medicines that could even cure cancer completely if the disease were not so difficult to control. Scientists have been working with these pharmaceutical companies to create medicines that can change their structures in order to attack the mutations in cancer and slow their development. Bionic limb replacements have become a commonplace solution for limbs lost to war, disease and general escalating violence. Despite all of these amazing advances, mankind has been morally compromised in many ways. All of the planets, including Earth, are rampant with evil and crime.

A corrupt planet called *Everything Is Ours Planet* had already gained control over some planets and was poised to take over the rest of the universe. The planet's inhabitants, called Frights, were one of the oldest intelligent life forms in existence at that time. Once they invented deadly weapons, they became fierce and cruel to each other and after they mastered the art of flight, they spread their evil to other planets, enslaved their inhabitants and set out to conquer the remaining worlds. The Frights had no idea what they were getting into when they decided to subjugate the *Planet of the Cleaning Bugs*, sometimes referred to as the *Bug Planet*. They filled the sky and surrounded it, threatening their inhabitants with destruction if they didn't obey their commands. If people had been watching from another galaxy, they would have seen the Frights go into total shock. A second after the Frights barked their commands, they saw thousands of what looked like huge boulders, actually the Cleaning Bugs, heading straight for their war ships. Two seconds later, the Frights were devoured in their war ships and the smell of their evil filled the air, creating a trail of evil back to their planet. Hundreds of thousands of Cleaning Bugs, like locusts, headed straight to the *Everything Is Ours Planet* where they drained the remaining evil and returned home, leaving the planet *intact* but totally devoid of Frights.

Not very much is known about the inhabitants of the *Planet of the Cleaning Bugs* other than that the Cleaning Bugs communicate by various pitched sounds and instantly pick up any language that they hear for the first time. It has been documented by scientists from other worlds that they are like any other race as far as knowledge goes and that some of the Cleaning Bugs are smarter and more talented than others. At the time that the Frights decided to attack the *Planet of the Cleaning Bugs*, the Cleaning Bugs already had a reputation for cleansing planets until there was no evil life left. Nobody knew what they looked like or where their planet was located.

Because of these rumors and scenarios, some people believe that when the Cleaning Bugs land on a planet, no one survives. Others believe that the Cleaning Bugs allow only the innocent and brave to live. Some think that they do good things but no one knows what. Scientists worldwide are trying to develop methods to catch several of them for experimentation in the hope of finding a way of stopping crime and evil from taking over the rest of the world.

PART ONE
The Planet of the Cleaning Bugs

The First Voyage to *the Planet of the Cleaning Bugs*

Two hundred years earlier, in the year 2430, a spaceship was about to be launched from Earth. It carried ten professional couples, a combination of scientists and researchers, who had been chosen by colleagues and various governmental bodies to make the first exploratory trip to the *Bug Planet*. Each couple was allowed to bring one child.

People just couldn't stay away from the lift-off platform even though the government told them that the launch could be dangerous due to the blast. The crowd packed the space station as though they were at a rock concert. But it was much more exciting than any such concert could ever be. It had been advertised that a new scientific experiment was scheduled to take place on the *Planet of the Cleaning Bugs* and that the best of their scientists and researchers had been chosen to participate. When the scientists and researchers came walking out of the building, the crowd roared loud enough to be heard in the next town. The first one to come out was Dr. Kansas and his wife who was a research scientist. Both were holding their little girl's hand as they walked waving to the crowds. Then came Dr. Drake with his wife Nancy and their child Barbara.

"Mommy, where are we going?" Barbara asked.

"We're heading for a new adventure and going to a wonderful world full of surprises."

"Is that why are all of us are wearing the same type of suit with different emblems representing our countries?"

Mrs. Drake kneeled down to her daughter, held her gently by her shoulders and with a smile said, "You're a very inquisitive girl, sweetheart. Make sure that you stay that way. Remember that questions will always give you some kind of an answer, and if that answer is not satisfactory, you can still ask yourself, 'Why isn't it satisfactory?' That's the good thing about being inquisitive. You'll always have a question which gives you an open mind."

"I promise, Mommy. I will always have an open mind."

Barbara was very intelligent for a seven year old and she wouldn't give up until she got an answer to her question.

"*Now* will you tell me why everyone is wearing the same clothes?"

It just so happened that the inventor of the space suits was standing next to Dr. Drake's family.

"Good morning, Dr. and Mrs. Drake. I am Duke the designer and inventor of the space suit that all of you are wearing. I overheard your daughter's curiosity at work. Would you mind if I answer her questions?"

Both Dr. and Mrs. Drake nodded, "No, go right ahead."

Duke answered Barbara's first question. "The identical clothing shows that everyone is going to travel into space and needs to wear this space suit."

"How does the suit work?"

Duke, showing his pride, was happy to explain it.

"It's quite simple. The suit acts like a barometer and thermometer. If something goes wrong with the person's body, the suit changes colors and allows the individual to know what his symptoms and temperature are and what to do about them."

"Can you explain that better, Mr. Duke?"

"Okay. Here is an example. If someone's body were to start overheating, the suit would show certain amounts of red; the hotter the body, the redder the suit would become."

"Does it show anything else?"

"As a matter of fact, it does. The suit has special curative properties. If any foreign material were to enter into the person's body, the suit would change to a different color, identifying the problem and then it would vibrate in a frequency that would destroy that foreign matter. Each couple is given a color chart of their individual indicators to follow in case of an emergency that the suit cannot resolve. Then doctors who are available will step in to help."

"Thank you so much, Mr. Duke. I'm glad to know that your suits are like doctors who are going to protect my Mommy and Daddy."

"And remember, sweetie," her Mom interrupted, "it's also water, fire and weather proof."

"Come honey," Dr. Drake called to his wife. "We must go. They're waiting for us."

She grabbed Barbara by the hand as she was saying goodbye to Duke and ran to join her husband. Waving goodbye to the crowds, they boarded the ship.

The couples represented ten different countries but they also represented the whole planet Earth. Just before they were to board the ship, the media tried to reach them but the police on duty at the space station held them back. All at once the roaring ceased. The crowd wanted to hear something about the expedition from one of the scientists.

"What do you expect to accomplish once you go to this new planet?" a very persistent newsman yelled.

One of the cops liked the question and said, "Go ahead and get your interview."

"Are you ready?" the newsman quickly asked his cameraman.

"Yes. Come on. Let's go."

"Hello, you wonderful fans of space travel and exploration. This is W.N. News. I am Joey Squeeze. Today, we have twenty brave men and women and their children who are willing to go for the first time to a new and strange world in hopes of saving our planet. It is their mission to colonize the *Planet of the Cleaning Bugs*."

Joey Squeeze suddenly had to take a step back as the crowd started to cheer so loudly that the vibration almost knocked him on his butt. Joey stepped in front of Dr. Crone, another researcher, put a mike to his lips and once again asked, "What do you expect to accomplish when you arrive on this new planet?"

"For one thing," Dr. Crone replied, "we hope that the Cleaning Bugs that we find there will be friendly and willing to help us cure the violence that has plagued our planet for so long."

"Do you know what kind of dangers you will run across?"

"If I knew that, Mr. Squeeze, I would be a psychic or a fortune teller and not a scientist. Please excuse me; we're ready to take off."

Then Dr. Crone looked at the camera and said, "Thank you for your support, you wonderful people of Earth. We will return and all will be fine. We all thank you." Then he waved goodbye as he and the rest of the crew boarded the ship. The lift off nearly burned some near-by spectators as the ship traveled upwards toward a beautiful clear blue sky.

The ten couples, each with one child, left for the *Planet*

of the Cleaning Bugs in the year 2430 and came back to their homes in the year 2436. There are many theories about time and the way it works. Space-time seems to be like a zone where time is in slow motion. A person on Earth sees time in space in the same way as on Earth: one hour is sixty minutes. But that's not the case. One hour in space equals one or two months on Earth. The trip to the *Planet of the Cleaning Bugs* took only a few hours in space-time. Their stay on the *Bug Planet* was a bit more than a year. But for the people of Earth, the researchers were gone for six years.

On the day of their return to Earth, there were so many people gathered at the space station that the army had to control the crowd. Everyone on Earth was anticipating the arrival of the ship with all the data that the colonizing researchers had recorded.

There wasn't a sound to be heard once the spaceship landed and the engines were turned off.

The crowd just stared at the ship. Even though there was no door, a part of the ship began to lower like an electric car window. It was the size of a door and when it opened, some of the crewmembers who were standing inside were suddenly visible to the excited crowd who immediately started cheering. As the scientists and researchers started to descend from the ship, stairs materialized with every step that they took.

It was magical. But it really was science.

The space voyagers walked toward the middle of the platform hand in hand with their partners. Only this time, they didn't have their children with them.

Joey Squeeze jumped on the platform and yelled, "What happened to the children? Where are they? Are they okay?"

A group of well dressed government officials and others

in army uniforms rushed the research team to a lab inside one of the buildings. The couples were separated by country and brought into different dwellings that had a temporary hotel-like set up. But they actually were in a secured government building.

It didn't matter which of the couples the officials asked since it was always the same question.

"What happened to your child?"

Each answer was always the same.

"I can't remember."

No matter what kind of help they got or how much they tried, it was always the same answer, "I can't remember."

General Lean, the army official who was the first to speak to one of the returning researchers, later met with the media. He recounted his conversation with Dr. Crone.

"Tell me everything that happened, Dr. Crone."

"It was terrible on that planet. We are fortune to be alive."

"Were there any life forms on that planet? What did they look like?"

"I'll tell you everything. First of all, when we landed, there was nothing but a colorful desert. We set up camp for the night, which never came because the days on the *Bug Planet* were much longer than we expected. About eight hours later, we awoke and found huge rocks surrounding us and our children gone. Before our eyes could clear, we found ourselves inside a rock, with strange creatures that somehow were draining out part of our energy. Before we knew it, we were ejected out of a long tunnel that looked like a tail. We were all so frightened that the shock from the experience temporarily immobilized us. What made things even more frightening was when we heard this coming from a rock, 'People of Earth! You were not invited to our planet. This is your first warning. You must never return. Only your innocent children will be welcome in the future. If you do not follow our wishes, there will be dire consequences.' That is all I remember. Then we were back on Earth."

All of a sudden, Dr. Crone remembered that the Cleaning Bugs believed that humans seemed to be innocent but only for a certain amount of time and that each human was innocent until he grew up and life took away his innocence. According to the Cleaning Bugs, it was almost impossible to find an innocent grownup. Innocence seemed to belong only to children.

Because of the loss of the children and the warning, travel to the *Planet of the Cleaning Bugs* was suspended.

The Search for an Innocent Child Begins

After that first trip to the *Bug Planet,* it took the leaders of Earth two hundred years to make the decision of what to do in order to solve the problem of evil on Earth. From that time on, the leaders determined that travel to the *Planet of the Cleaning Bugs* would be allowed only to innocent children who were searched for and handpicked by government officials known for their honesty and dependability.

The level of violence had become so bad that something needed to be done. The scientists and the government agreed after examining all of the data from the first voyage to the *Bug Planet* that perhaps enough time had passed to attempt another trip. The good people of Earth were so desperate that they began a search for an innocent child who would travel alone to the *Planet of the Cleaning Bugs.* The government hoped that all of the data was correct and that this time a child would be able to communicate with the Cleaning Bugs and find out if they were willing to help.

The search for an innocent child did not go easily. Innocence was at a premium. It wasn't unusual to see the handpicked officials stop pedestrians in the streets and ask,

"Do you have a child who is innocent and brave?"

"No sir, I don't. But you might want to try my next-door neighbor," was a common response.

It took two years for a child who was innocent and brave enough to make the trip to be discovered. Her name was Jane and she was eleven years old. When the officials found her, she was living on the streets of New York City and eating out of garbage cans. This was a common sight because many children were homeless and forced to live like delinquents and to do evil in order to survive.

Jane's face still had traces of childhood pudginess. Her beautiful large blue eyes still radiated innocence, as did her smile. She always wore jeans that were a bit raggedy from wear and a pair of torn sneakers. Her shirt looked like it came from the dumpster and it did.

Jane had short, greasy black hair, which she cut herself. She looked like she hadn't washed for months and she hadn't, simply because she had to wait for the rains to come before she could bathe. Jane always looked like she had done something wrong and she probably had. She flashed an amazing grin that made her look innocent and guilty at the same time, whenever she was caught by a cop.

At times she stole food and a cop would catch her. Then was she a sight to see! She would look up at the policeman and innocently grin while saying,

"I swear I didn't do it. I'm innocent, I tell you." Stretching her arms out, she would say, "See? I don't have anything."

The cop would laugh and answer her. "It's a good thing that you eat fast and there's no evidence. I'm warning you! Next time you'd better have a way to pay for that apple. Now get out of here."

Jane didn't like to steal but starvation didn't give her a choice. Otherwise, she was an upstanding, very, very poor homeless citizen child.

One day Jane was picking through a trash container when she heard a scream. Lifting her head out of the trash, she saw a girl, perhaps a year or two younger than herself, being chased by some mean looking boys about twelve or thirteen years old. Jane was already toughened by life and very street-wise. She hid behind one of the large trash collectors so that the thieves couldn't see her. The boys caught up with the little girl whom they were chasing. They were about ten feet away from the other trash collector where Jane was hiding. Spike, the skinny thief and Slammer, the already gorilla-shaped thief tried to grab the jewelry that the child was wearing but she was too fast and escaped his grasp. Unfortunately for Jane, but lucky for her, the child ran straight to the other trash container.

Jane could have stayed hidden. But within seconds, many puzzling things flashed through her mind before she reacted to the whole situation. She thought about how she didn't like to see anyone in trouble and that there was something about this little girl that unexplainably touched her heart. First of all, she was very small, one might even say petite, with straight blond hair down to her shoulders and brown eyes that made a great contrast with her light pale skin. Jane noticed that the child was wearing very clean and expensive clothing and she wondered what the little girl was doing in that part of the city.

She must be lost, Jane thought.

Even though Jane was just a child herself, she realized how vulnerable this girl was. Jane's experiences living on the streets where she had to deal with hunger and violence had made her grow up very quickly.

In a flash, Jane suddenly visualized this child walking with her mother and father in a better part of town, either taking a nice stroll or perhaps going shopping. She knew how over crowded the streets and stores usually were and thought that it would have only taken a second for some thugs to grab the child and then demand a ransom. She wondered if this is what had happened. Jane snapped out of her musings. The little girl was helpless and vulnerable and Jane just had to do something. She usually minded her own business but this time, for some unknown reason, she vaguely recalled that something bad had once happened to her and that no one was there to help.

She started thinking about what she could do. Normally, Jane would have had some sort of plan when it came to helping herself, but helping someone else was not exactly in her day planner, so to speak. As the little girl was running away from her pursuers and toward her, Jane came out from behind the dumpster.

"Little girl, come here. Hurry!"

"Help me! Help me!" she screamed franticly, running to Jane. "Those mean kids are trying to rob me."

Motioning with her arm, while urging her to quickly get behind her and stay there, Jane looked at the two thieves and realized that she and her new little friend were lucky because at that time, Spike and Slammer were slow to react and not particularly swift. In fact, Slammer didn't seem to want any part of what they were doing, which gave the girls a bit of extra time. Jane took advantage and lifted the top of the dumpster to see if there were anything there that she could use for a weapon. But she didn't see anything. She franticly looked for a brick or a pipe. But it just wasn't her day until she noticed a few things that could come in handy lying on the ground behind the dumpster's wheel. Jane quickly bent over and picked them up. Unfortunately for the boys, they were too busy to notice any of her movements. Jane leaped forward and stuck a rusty nail in each boy's butt.

"Leave her alone!" Jane shouted at the muggers.

Then she grabbed the girl by her elbow. "Get behind me and run when I tell you to." Jane turned around and took a stance, expecting to fight the two boys. It took her a few seconds to understand that the boys were too stunned to react after getting stuck by the nails. Realizing this, she took the opportunity to escape. "Run!" she shouted and the frightened little girl followed her order. Both girls were almost out of sight when the boys got their bearings. And were they really livid!

"What the hell happened? Did she just stick me with a nail?" Slammer yelled in disbelief.

Spike checked his butt, saw blood on his hand and yelled, "Slammer, look, look. She stuck me too! Please, can you pull out this nail?"

Slammer walked over to Spike and pulled it out.

"Ouch! Thank you," he muttered while rubbing his sore butt.

"No problem! Let's go. They're getting away!"

That was when the chase began. The boys weren't too far behind Jane and the little girl. There was nothing but alleyways and no people in sight. Jane was trying to go where there were people but she made the wrong turn. *Oh! Oh!* Jane realized that they were trapped. She put the little girl behind her, reached into her pocket where she had some of the left over nails, gave several of them to her and kept the rest for herself.

"Take these nails and make sure you hold them tight. If you find yourself trapped, defend yourself. But if you can, just run." As soon as Jane put the nails in the girl's hands, she dropped them, paralyzed with fear.

The boys did not expect what came next.

Jane had a nail in each hand and putting on a brave front, she shouted in her most threatening voice,

"If you boys don't leave us alone, you're going to regret it."

"And just what do you think you and that little half pint can do to stop us?" Slammer asked laughing.

Like an idiot, his skinny partner in crime barked out.

"*Yeh*...you heard what he said."

With amazing speed, Jane began attacking the boys like a tigress protecting her young. She hollered while hitting them with all the force that she had.

"I told you not to mess with us, *didn't I?*"

She really damaged those boys. Blood was coming out of both of them but they were very powerful and brutal and overpowered her - something that you wouldn't expect from such young kids.

But this was not a world for nice children.

One boy had Jane pinned down by her shoulders while the other boy grabbed the little girl's gold necklace and charm bracelet.

"Hey, get away from my daughter," a huge, well-groomed man yelled, coming around the corner and rushing toward them, followed by his well-dressed wife.

The man reached out to grab them, "Come here, you delinquents."

Unfortunately, he couldn't grab either one, but not because he didn't try. The boys ran by him so fast that it seemed like a train had passed. The mother ran over to her child and hugged her.

"Roxy, are you okay, sweetheart?"

Hugging her with great concern, she asked, "Did they hurt you?"

"No, Mommy. This nice girl helped me and I don't even

know her name." She turned around to introduce her to her Mom and saw that Jane was already walking away. She ran to her, grabbed her hand and said, "My name is Roxy. What's yours?"

"I'm Jane."

Roxy pleaded, "Please, please, Jane. Come home with us."

Jane had not felt such closeness since she was five, when her parents were killed in a similar mugging, which she had blocked out of her mind because she couldn't bear the pain. And so she let go of Roxy's hand and ran as though the devil were chasing her. Before Roxy's Father and Mother could thank her, she was gone.

"I wonder why she ran away like that," the Father muttered.

An Innocent Child Is Found

Jane ran for blocks and blocks as tears fell down her face. She tried but she couldn't forget her short adventure with Roxy or the unexpected love that she felt when she held the child's hand. Eventually she stopped running and that was when she saw a newspaper whose headline read: **LOOKING FOR AN INNOCENT, BRAVE CHILD TO GO TO THE PLANET OF THE CLEANING BUGS.** Even though Jane was eleven and lived on the streets, she had managed not to lose her innocence and to keep her positive side. She was perfect for the adventure. She began walking toward the address in the newspaper, anxious to escape from where she lived. Along the way, two men holding a strange looking gadget came up to Jane and asked her to stop.

Charles, a tall skinny man with a thin mustache and balding head, pointed the gadget at her.

Jane's instinct kicked in and she pushed him away. *"What are you doing?"*

Then she walked away quickly, keeping a close eye on them.

The two men caught up with her and flashed their badges.

"There is nothing to fear. Please stop. We just want to test you."

Once Jane saw the badges, she knew that the best thing for her to do was to stop. She did and when they got closer to her, the machine that they were pointing at her began making clicking noises like a Geiger counter.

The other agent with Charles was a short burly man named Jim.

"Look," Jim said with great excitement, pointing to the machine. "The arrow on the gage has never jumped to this hundred percent range before. This is indeed remarkable."

Charles looked at Jane and all he could say was, "This is the child. She is the one!"

"What are you two babbling about?" Jane asked, trying to get a look at the gadget.

The two agents were very emphatic when they told Jane that they were looking for someone innocent at heart to go to the *Planet of the Cleaning Bugs.* Charles knelt down on one knee, looked Jane straight in the eyes and insisted,

"You are the first child to register one hundred percent positive on our gadget which means that you are the innocent child we are seeking."

"Does this have something to do with the headline that I just saw in the newspaper?"

"That's correct, Jane." Jim answered. Then he said, "Truth be told Jane, you are the only one on this planet who can do this job. We have searched the whole world for years and you are the one. Will you do this for your planet and homeland?"

Then he felt compelled to add, "After all, there is no home without a planet."

"Do you mean that I can go to the *Planet of the Cleaning Bugs*?"

Charles jumped in to answer her question. "Yes Jane, but you must understand that we don't know what will happen. We hope that the *Planet of the Cleaning Bugs* will accept you. But there is no way to find out unless you go."

Jane was glad to escape the situation that she had on Earth and she hoped that by doing this, she would perhaps have a better opportunity to live a more productive and decent life. Jane knew that this was a historic occasion and that one day she would be proud of what she accomplished.

"Can we go now?" she asked.

"No," replied Charles. "You're leaving tomorrow. Why are you in such a hurry? Don't you have anyone to say goodbye to?"

"No!" she replied.

"Then you're coming with us. What's your name? You need to be fed, cleaned and clothed. Is that all right with you?"

"I'm Jane. Are you kidding? Of course it's alright." she said with a smile, followed by "You're going to feed me, right? That's what you said."

Thrilled by their discovery, they brought her for the night to the spaceship housing, located next to the launch pad.

She found herself in a beautiful large room, greeted by two women who had come out of an adjoining room to meet her.

"Hi Jane, my name is Molly and this is my sister Holly. We're here to bathe you and give you a change of clothing."

"Thanks girls but I can wash myself. Just leave me the clothes and I'll come out to eat as soon as I clean up."

About an hour later, Jane walked into the dining room, washed and so nicely dressed that she was almost unrecognizable.

She had on a pair of clean, sharply pressed white pants and a shirt like a kaleidoscope whose colors continued to move. Her clothes seemed to have a life of their own. And they did. They were created and programmed to protect her from chemicals and different diseases that she might come across on her travels. They would become part of her space wardrobe.

When she walked into the dining room, everyone stood up and applauded because she was going to save planet Earth. Or so they hoped…

A lady took Jane by the hand.

"Hello, Jane. My name is Nurse-Cure. Would you like something to eat?"

She reacted with a very hungry, "Oh! Yes! Please!"

For Jane and her stomach, the walk through the huge dining room seemed endless. There were people standing in a double line. Nurse-Cure and Jane walked down the middle of it. There were astronauts, scientists, government agents and even the military. Everyone wanted to shake Jane's hand or at least wish her good luck and tell her to have a safe trip. She had to walk half the length of the room before she could even smell the food. When she finally did, everyone stopped and watched her take in a deep breath.

"That smells so good!" she said and then continued walking toward the delicious odors.

Once the food was in front of her, all she could do was stare. She wasn't sure if it was a dream.

"Is this real?" she asked Nurse-Cure who was still holding her hand.

"Oh, it certainly is, Jane. You can help yourself to whatever you want and take as much as you like. I'll even give you a container to fill with whatever you want to take back to your room."

Well, Jane sure was a sight to behold! No one was paying attention at first but then all eyes focused on her

She was oblivious to everything around her but the food.

It was the biggest buffet - and probably the only one, that she had ever seen.

"Oh my goodness, look at the girl's eyes! She wants to eat but she thinks that she's imagining the food. She doesn't believe that it's real," a woman in an astronaut's suit exclaimed.

What she didn't know was that Jane had survived hunger by developing a great imagination. She had been disappointed so many times in her young life that she found that imaginary food never disappointed her. It always tasted like it was supposed to and no one could take it away from her. This situation was too unreal for her to accept so she froze with disbelief and went into her own safe dream world. She did not want this feast to disappear and the depth of her imagination had her mouth watering. In her mind she could taste the golden brown roasted chicken sitting on a platter surrounded by all sorts of vegetables and potatoes. She stared at the moistness rolling down the bird's brown crispy skin. She moved her mouth up and down in a chewing motion. The chicken was just waiting for her to pick up and put in her mouth. But she wouldn't dare. She didn't want to throw away a perfect imaginary meal.

"It's okay for you to eat," Nurse-Cure said softly, handing Jane a plate.

"Are you sure? People have played tricks on me with food many times before."

"It's okay, Jane. No one is trying to fool you."

Then she left the dazed child standing in front of the table.

Jane realized that she wasn't dreaming but the food seemed to affect her in strange ways

Stay right where you are, little birdie, she murmured to herself. Jane still wasn't sure if all that was happening was real but she wasn't about to let the bird escape even though it was already cooked.

Don't worry, birdie. I'm going to eat you very slowly and make sure that I taste every bite.

Well, at least that's what she thought she was going to do.

But as soon as she got within reach of the chicken, her manners went out the window. She grabbed the bird with both hands, took as big bite as she could with her small mouth and as soon as she tasted it, she took a deep breath and then continued eating. Once she was done with the chicken and then the vegetables, it was time for her to start on the sweets.

She began with apple pie and basically took a bite from every kind of cake, cookie or pastry that was on the table.

Kids being kids, she had to dig into the sweets. How can a kid not want to taste every different sweet? Even though her harsh experiences in life had matured her, Jane *was* still a kid…

Jane was done stuffing herself when a woman from a group of scientists and astronauts who had their own trip to make to another world, walked over to her.

"Hello, Jane. My name is Debbie. "Have you had enough to eat?"

"Oh yes, Debbie. I can't fit another thing into my stomach."

"Well, apparently your eyes are bigger than your stomach. You look like an overstuffed puppy." Debbie took her by the hand, walked her to her room, reminded her that it was to be an early morning and told her to have a good rest. She said goodnight to Jane and closed the door.

The change of lifestyle was happening too fast for Jane who was still trying to process everything that had happened to her since she was chosen for the mission. If it weren't for her full stomach reminding her of how much she had eaten a bit earlier, she would still be thinking that all of this was just a dream. Here she was, in a room that to her was a palace, all alone and able to do whatever her heart desired. It didn't take her long to spot her heart's desire. To her left, about twenty feet away was a very tall and wide steeple-shaped window with white shear curtains reaching to the floor. The bright light revealed what seemed to be a fluffy white cloud that promised dreams that no other cloud could claim. She felt herself plopping down on that beautiful cloud while it softly rose and fell with the ebb of its cloudy tide until she was rocked to sleep.

It was the first time for as long as Jane could remember that she had a bed to sleep in. She climbed under the covers, with her stomach full and absolutely no worries.

The following morning at six o'clock on the dot, Jane heard a loud knock on the door. She opened it, and in front of her were Jim and Charles, the two agents who had found her the day before. She later learned that they were actually government secret service men.

"Good morning," they both whispered, still standing by the door.

"Good morning," she mumbled, half asleep.

Charles, with great enthusiasm, began with what he had rehearsed to say.

"Today is a very special day for you."

He looked to his left, in the hallway and then motioned his hand for someone to come toward him. "Jane, this is Lina and Tina."

"Hello," Jane replied. The girls did the same.

"The girls are going to help you get prepared for your trip," Jim said.

Charles and Jim waited in the hallway. The girls went into the room, closed the door and helped her dress. Unfortunately, the girls didn't like what Jane chose to wear on her head and were concerned that they would get fired if she went out like that.

"Please, Jane. We'll get fired if you go out there wearing a pilot's cap instead of the traditional helmet."

"Don't pilots wear caps?"

"Yes. But you're wearing it backwards and you're not a pilot."

"Look. I wear what I want and I wear it how I want. This uniform happens to be cool. Otherwise, I would be wearing jeans and a sweat shirt."

An hour later, Jane came walking out of the room. The two agents were very surprised when she stepped into the hall, wearing a very snug, streamed lined flight suit. It was a perfect fit. Charles looked at her for a second and said, "Cool cap." The two girls breathed a sigh of relief and walked away. Charles was on a time schedule and motioned to Jane.

"Hurry up, Jane. We don't have time to spare. There are a few things that I must explain to you on the way to the platform. Are you ready?"

Jane, who was no longer sleepy, shouted loudly and enthusiastically, "I sure am!"

Charles continued, "You're not going to travel the conventional way."

He asked for her arm and as soon as she stretched it out, he implanted a new micro computerized state-of-the-art device into her wrist.

"How is this supposed to work?" Jane asked.

Jim wanted to explain this to her so he interrupted before Charles could say a word.

Of course this didn't stop Charles from giving him dirty looks.

"Did you ever hear of Star Trek?" Jim asked Jane.

"Oh sure," she replied. "Wasn't that the space show back in the early 1960s where people dematerialized from one place and then materialized in another?"

"That's correct," Jim told her. "But now we have advanced that process so that all we need is the idea of where we want to go. Then we just think about the location and we appear there."

"But what if you're wrong about where you want to go and the place doesn't exist?"

"That's a very good point," Jim acknowledged. "Fortunately, the mind can search an area before the body follows. It's kind of like a mental scout: First the mind, then the body."

Then he explained that the little gizmo on her wrist would make travel choices for her, according to her thoughts. All she would have to do was to think about where she wanted to go and press her wrist on the special spot. Then she would materialize on the exact location that she wanted.

"Are you okay with everything?" Charles asked Jane. "Do you understand everything that Jim said?"

"Yes, I understand everything."

"Good," Charles told her. "Now, I hope that you're prepared for what's coming."

By the time everything was explained to her, they had reached the doors and walked out of the building. The crowd cheered like the Queen of England and all of the world's presidents had appeared. The noise was loud enough for the world to hear and they did, since the event was being televised across the universe.

The launch pad was surrounded by thousands of spectators.

As Jane came through the doors, she heard a Mother say to her son,

"Johnny! Maybe someday you will get the chance to show the world how brave you are. Just like Jane is doing now."

Hearing that made Jane laugh with happiness. She couldn't help herself.

"Thank you, Mam!" she hollered to the boy's Mother. "And don't you forget it, young man!"

Unfortunately, that joyous feeling left her as quickly as it came. She could hear everyone talking about how brave she was and cheering her on her way. They couldn't see that her hope for happiness was gone. Just before she was to take off, Jane heard a familiar voice. It was Roxy hollering her name and trying to get to her.

"Jane, Jane! Please, can I come with you?" She started to run toward her but her father grabbed her arm.

"Let go of me, please Daddy."

"You can't go with her, sweetheart."

Roxy continued to struggle. It wasn't like her but she really seemed to want to reach Jane and so she persisted. Jane didn't know that Roxy's Mom saw how much her daughter cared for Jane and told her husband to let Roxy go.

At that exact moment, Jane saw Roxy finally break loose

from her Dad. Jane dropped to one knee as Roxy ran to her, grabbed and hugged her.

"Please let me come with you," Roxy pleaded.

"You can't! Not this time." Jane kept repeating while Roxy continued to plead.

After a few minutes of tearful goodbyes, Jane felt a strange sensation but she couldn't put her finger on it. She reassured Roxy that she would be back and promised her that the next time, no matter where she went; she would take her on the trip. It was easy to see that Jane was ready to cry but she had to show a brave front. She held Roxy's hand out for her Father, who was right behind. Then she said, "I'll be back."

Jane Meets the Cleaning Bugs

The special platform that had been built for the trip to the *Planet of the Cleaning Bugs* was quite a sight. Known as the Take-Off-Spot, it was cylindrical, about six feet high, flat at the top and about one hundred square feet in circumference. Jane kept looking at the platform and wondering why it seemed familiar. When a panel slid open, forming a doorway into the Take-Off-Spot, Jane recalled what it reminded her of. One day a few years earlier, when she was walking in the streets of New York City, she had seen a Star Trek exhibition through a window of a museum. In the center of the exhibit stood a model of the transporter used on the Enterprise. As Jane looked at the open platform cylinder, she realized that it had the same shape as the transporter that carried Captain Kirk, his crew and other life forms to and from different spaceships and worlds.

When Jane walked toward the platform, an escalator materialized leading up to it. She stepped on it and lights of different colors flashed on and off as the steps took her higher and closer. Once she was on the platform, surrounded by various military personnel and scientists, an array of lights encircled the deck like an energy field, giving it the appearance of a colorful shield.

The world watched while government agents secured the area. It was an amazing sight.

Everyone left the platform except Jane who stood alone in the middle of multi-colored glass-like panels. The only difference from Kirk's transporter was that this new technology made it possible to travel to any part of the universe just by thinking of a destination. Jane smiled at the realization that no type of travel is faster than one's thoughts and that she was about to embark into a higher realm of scientific pursuit.

A second smaller set of panels that were transparent and whose colors kept changing surrounded her. Jane had been told that when that happened, she was to think about and search for her destination and that when one panel turned yellow, she should press the spot on her wrist.

The display of thoughts was amazing to see. Once Jane started mentally searching the universe for the exact location of the *Planet of the Cleaning Bugs*, continuous short sparks of energy light shot out from her entire head, from the point of her chin to the back of her neck and then from one shoulder to the other. The sparks of thought flew out in all directions throughout the universe and moved so fast that they seemed to disappear from sight, like a meteor's tail, miles into the distance. Within a split second, a thin yellow light appeared in the sky, turning the panel yellow and connecting her thoughts to her destination. Jane pressed the button and vanished.

Everything went back to normal except for the loud sounds coming from the cheering crowd who probably thought that earplugs would have been a handy thing to have at that moment.

As Jane was being transported to the *Planet of the Cleaning Bugs*, she was aware of a multicolored, sand-like world, surrounded by odd shaped objects that at times seemed to change form. She marveled at the realization that she was traveling though space without a ship. When she landed and was sure that her feet actually felt the ground, she took a minute to get her bearings. Even though the trip only took an instant, her mind registered it as though hours had passed. When she finally lifted her head, all she could see was colorful sand in every direction. She wondered what had happened to the things that she thought she had seen. Even the rocks that she would have sworn were there only a minute before had disappeared. Not believing that this was possible, she spun around and once more the monument-like rocks appeared in front of her. She stopped and stood still like a statue. A minute later, she looked around and started walking toward what she thought was an unusual rock. It turned out to be a strange creature that resembled a rock. At times its shape changed from round to oval; sometimes it had small and large bumps; other times it was smooth. If Jane had bent down and looked at the rock's base, she would have seen dozens of little hand-like claws that were perfect for digging.

As Jane looked at this rock, something strange happened and she started to have flashes of long forgotten memories and emotions from her past. Suddenly, she was smiling and happy, jumping for joy, laughing like never before and wishing that Roxy were with her. She abruptly stopped laughing when she thought that she saw shadows in the distance.

Could they possibly be the children who hadn't returned to Earth two hundred years before? she wondered.

Jane ran toward them but they disappeared.

"Hello, hello," she repeated. "Are you children here? I've seen you. Please come out."

A very cute girl about her age appeared from thin air.

"Hi! Jane, My name is Christine."

"How do you know my name?"

"Everyone knows you and why you came here. But you still have to explain your purpose to the Bug People." Then she turned around and walked away.

"Wait!" Jane hollered. "Are you one of the kids from our

history books?"

Christine turned back, looked at her and answered simply, "Yes, I am. It's a long story and perhaps we will get to share it, but not now."

Before Jane could respond, Christine disappeared.

Jane checked out her surroundings. She was flabbergasted when she looked toward the horizon because there was nothing there but a colorful desert. Then a meteorite caught her eye as it passed close in front of her. It seemed as if it were as near as the Earth's moon and just as big.

"Oh my goodness, am I going to burn?" she uttered in fear as the sand grew hotter from the passing meteor.

She prepared to press her wrist to return to Earth. But the heat passed as quickly as it came.

Okay. Don't panic, she reassured herself.

"Great. Now I'm talking out loud to myself. Why am I talking to myself? Oh, oh! This is not good. Maybe the meteor did this to me...Where did that child come from and where did she go?"

She scratched her head, wondering if the other kids were with Christine.

It has to be my imagination, she thought.

But she tried calling again. "Hello...Is anyone there?"

She heard a strange sound. When she turned around, she saw a huge, moving, rounded, cave-like mass and what resembled an extra long tongue coming out of it. She was sure that it wasn't there a minute before. Jane didn't know what this tongue belonged to, so she walked toward it very cautiously.

"Are you a monster?" she asked. There was no answer.

Slowly she walked in front of what she thought was a tongue and with the tip of her shoe, she tapped it to see if it was solid or not.

Oh good, she thought. *It's not slimy like it looks from the distance.*

She mustered up the nerve to run her hand along one of the sides, which were curved up high enough to be used as railings.

"Wow!" was the first word out of her mouth. Then Jane again tested the tongue with her foot, stepped onto it and proceeded to walk. She looked into the opening and loudly said, "Whoever built this platform, the woodwork is fantastic. But as for the tongue's design, what were you thinking?"

She paused, hoping for some reaction. When there was none, she sighed in disappointment. Happy that she didn't have to go back to Earth, she continued walking while admiring what seemed to be woodwork and wondering how it could look so wet.

Jane walked along the rock's tongue to a cave–like opening. Entering the rock very hesitantly, she hoped that her destiny wouldn't end up like that of the pirates who walked the plank. Once inside what had become a cave, she heard something slam. The cave closed and she was in the dark. She knocked on the wall. It took a minute and a door started to open. A light was flashing in the air and the sides of all the walls lit up. Then she saw what she was up against: there were hundreds of devilish-looking creatures, clinging to the walls and ceilings like bats. They were about two feet long, had black bodies, with what looked like horns for ears, white angels' wings and dangerous scorpion-like tails. Because of their appearance, they were called Angel-scorps. Dozens were flying around Jane.

A red headed one kept saying, "Stand still, you."

Jane tried to swat it like a fly, yelling, "Get away from me, you ugly bug!"

A deep voice came out of the cave and demanded,

"What's holding things up, Squeak? Why aren't you cleaning the evil out of her?"

"I'm not sure about this one, Boss."

"What do you mean you're not sure? She's trying to hit you, isn't she?"

"Yeah, but she's not mean."

"You listen here, Squeak, you ugly little Angel-scorp. Do what you're supposed to or Sneeze will get promoted and you'll be demoted."

When there were no worlds or individuals to clean of evil and therefore energy on the *Planet of the Cleaning Bugs* was low, only one Angel-scorp was allowed to be energized and have a red head. Squeak was it, for now. Unfortunately, Squeak's head was beginning to turn black from disobeying orders and he was starting to slow down. Squeak could see that Sneeze wanted to be the leader.

Sneeze had an attitude about him and already feeling like he was the new leader, he immediately said, "I'll suck the evil from that girl." His head started turning red with the energy that was being drained from Squeak. Since he couldn't find any real reason to criticize Squeak, Sneeze started blaming him for his allergies. The timing was perfect for Squeak. Sneeze sneezed so hard that he was propelled through the air and slammed into the wall.

Squeak took the opportunity and started yelling, "Okay, okay, Boss."

He quickly told the others. "You heard him, Angel-scorps! Let the Changer come out." Squeak's head turned red again as he retook command of the creatures. A minute later, the Angel-scorps on the walls divided like a door. Sneeze mumbled something and gave Squeak dirty looks.

A huge, very colorful, egg-shaped cocoon dropped and floated toward Jane as though on an escalator. It looked like it was splitting in half but the outside turned out to be the wings and as they spread apart, they revealed a large, butterfly-ladybug-like creature with feet. She started walking toward Jane. There was nowhere for Jane to run, so she stood still.

The Changer glided slowly up to Jane, and in an angelic, hypnotic voice, said, "Don't be afraid."

The Changer's eyes began to open. They were half the size of her body. Once her eyes were completely open, sparkling stars came out and when they were about an inch away from Jane's face, the stars turned into a colorful mist. Jane heard her say in a soft musical voice, "Hello."

By this time, all of the Angel-scorps were surrounding Jane. She was aware of everything but she was paralyzed with fear. The Angel-scorps were ready to attack.

"Hold on," Squeak said. "I have to taste her first."

Meanwhile, Jane was thinking how glad she was that Roxy wasn't with her.

Probably because she was so afraid, Jane suddenly remembered that she once had twin sisters and that when she was five, her parents were killed. Just a glimpse of what she thought might have happened in her past put such fear into her that she immediately forgot everything again. But that momentary insight into her painful past could not be ignored. As young as she was, Jane decided to face her memories at that moment.

It took only a few seconds for her to remember the death of her parents and sisters but in that those seconds, she relived the whole day in flashes.

She heard her Mother's voice call out, "Come on, kids" and then saw herself and her sisters run to her as fast as they could to see who would grab her hand first.

Jane did, of course, and she bragged, "See how fast I am," even though she knew that it was only because she was older, bigger, and faster that she had won.

"Mom, are we going to the park?" Jane asked.

"Yes, we are, sweetheart," her Mom replied. "And afterwards, we'll go window-shopping in the city."

A lot of the day was still a blank until Jane suddenly recalled that she and her sisters had turned into an alleyway and before they realized it, they saw that their father was offering his watch, wallet and money to two nasty-looking men. The men didn't care about those things. Then she remembered that there was some kind of a struggle. She heard gunfire and when she turned toward the sound, she saw her Mother and Father lying on the ground motionless and more than likely dead. Her sisters had disappeared and from that moment on, she was on the run.

For some unknown reason, Jane suddenly came out of her trance-like state and realized that she was no longer in the alleyway but on the *Bug Planet.*

Now that the tragedy had come back to her in some detail, Jane really didn't care what happened to her. Squeak landed on her nose and Jane watched helplessly as the scorpion tail was about to stick into her forehead. She heard a suction noise and "shplat," the tail was on her. Only, it didn't stick her since it had turned into a suction cup. Jane swatted at Squeak but hit her forehead instead. As Squeak's tiny tongue swept across her forehead, she heard the little bugger say, "Yuck, Boss. She tastes good but she definitely doesn't have what we need."

A minute later, Jane was spit out of the cave. She saw that the dome-like opening that she had walked into was actually a huge mouth, belonging to a hideous, lizard-shaped frog. Then, the frog changed its shape into something that resembled a rock. Protruding all over it were carvings of faces belonging to creatures from different worlds.

Jane looked at it and said, "Who are you and why did you try to eat me?"

The rock's eyes opened, bushy eyebrows appeared and from its huge mouth, shaped like a clam, a very deep voice answered, "Hi. My name is Rocky and I'm an Eat and Clean Bug. To be honest, I wouldn't eat you since there is nothing in you that I need."

"Why?" Jane asked, happy to learn that she was safe.

Rocky explained that an Eat and Clean Bug could change its form and size at any time in order to trap its prey, regardless of its size. Once an evil creature entered its stomach through its clam-like mouth, an Angel-scorp would check for the quality and strength of the evil and then a Changer would come out and paralyze the victim. That was when the Angel-scorp would extract whatever evil energy existed. Anyone without evil would be automatically expelled from the cave.

"What do you really eat?" Jane asked.

"We, the Eat and Clean Bugs don't eat food as you understand it. We consume evil since it has powerful energy. We are the protectors of the universe. We go where only evil exists."

"We have very evil people in my world," Jane said. "I was sent to see if I could bring one of you back to help us."

"What can I do to help you?" Rocky asked.

"You can come and eat all the evil people."

"We mostly eat individuals who are 100% evil. Earth still has a chance because not all your people are 100% evil."

"Can't you please insure that chance for us before it's too late?"

"No!"

Jane began crying. "Please, Rocky, the evil is killing us."

She could see that Rocky was becoming uncomfortable.

"What is that coming out of your eyes?" he asked. "Please, stop that!"

But Jane couldn't stop crying. About a minute later, the ground began to shake. Jane stopped crying and rubbed her eyes in disbelief at what was happening. It was as though a herd of hippos was rising out of the water, which was actually colorful sand. And they weren't hippos; they were herds of Eat and Clean Bugs.

From the crowd a loud female voice asked, "What's going on, Rocky? Why is this child crying, Son? We have not seen anything like this in two hundred years. What does she want?"

"Mom, she wants us to eat the evil people on Earth. Everyone I know is running low on energy. We must find food and her planet has plenty. I don't think that she has any but we can taste her and see."

"Now Son, you know we can't eat this little girl. Squeak tasted her and said that she doesn't have the evil nutrients that we need. And as you know, we can't drain a planet until its inhabitants are fully evil or at least 98% worth."

"No, Mom! I really don't want to eat this little girl. I want to help her by going with her to eat the evil people in her world. She says that there are a lot of them."

"This is your choice, Son. But remember that there are things out there that could be dangerous. Since we don't have all of the information that we need here about our own universe, we must assume that there is danger out there, even for us. We know that we are the strongest and hardest substance that exists. But what about what we don't know? That's where the danger comes in. It's better to be safe than sorry. Do you understand me, Rocky?" his Mother firmly asked, showing her concern.

"Yes, I do!" he replied and then added, "Don't worry, Mom. I'm not afraid. I'll eat them all!"

In the background, a very heavy, deep voice said, "Just eat the evil ones, Son and good luck!"

Then his father's deep voice proudly said, "That's my boy!"

"Thanks, Dad. It's nice to hear you say that you're proud of me. You'll be even more proud when I come back with food for everyone."

"Food or not, we love you, Son. Just come back safe."

Then he added, "Watch over the girl. She's special and unusually pure for her age."

"She really is, isn't she?" Rocky murmured with a smile.

"Rocky, this is the first time that you are leaving home. Your Mother and I will keep in mental touch with you. Enjoy yourself but always remember that the Earth people must be the ones to create a relationship with us. We can help them by removing the evil from their planet but it can only be done with their approval and cooperation."

"I know, Dad," Rocky, who was anxious to leave, repeated several times. "I'll be fine, Dad." Then he shouted, "Bye, Mom. I love you."

"Come on, Jane," Rocky urged, impatient to get going.

She looked at the empty desert that was in front of her and right before her eyes, the sand formed a platform of black and white glass.

"How is this happening?" Jane asked Rocky.

"Jane, our planet and all life forms are as one. The elements are at our command. If we can think it, the planet can create it, according to our specifications."

While they were walking to the platform he told Jane that Squeak, the red-headed leader of some of his Angel-scorps, and also the Changer were coming with them since all of them lived inside of him.

"Mr. Rocky, can you explain to me how those creatures are living inside of you?"

Rocky began laughing. "It's really easy to understand, Jane. Those aren't creatures. You must look at them as my blood. Just as you have your own type of blood, they are mine. Each creature, as you call it, has its individual job. For instance, the Angel-scorps and the Changers are like your red and white blood cells. They clean and digest in a different way than any other race in existence that we know of."

"But where are the liquids?"

"Like I said Jane, we're different and there are things and stuff in us that only show themselves when necessary."

"But what about…?"

Before Jane could say another word, Rocky stopped her.

"Jane, if you want to know any more about my physiology, you'll have to take the same twenty-five year course about our physiology as I did. "

"You went to school for twenty-five years?"

"Don't be silly," he replied. "That's just for one course. We go to school for at least one to two hundred years, depending on what we want to study."

"That's very interesting. Just how old *are* you?"

"It all depends on how you understand time and age in our world or in yours. But try to understand that I'm no different than you are, Jane. Just remember that it's my blood and just like yours, it goes where I go."

"Speaking about going," Jane said with a smile, "that's what we have to do now."

Jane and Rocky Travel to Earth

Rocky and Jane were just feet away from the ramp. They climbed up some steps and when they got to the middle of the platform, Jane said, "I hope you're ready for this, Rocky." Then she thought about their destination and pressed the dark mark on her wrist that she had used to travel to the *Planet of the Cleaning Bugs*. In the few seconds that it took Jane and Rocky to travel through space to Earth, she was able to tell Rocky many things that would have taken hours to recount in a conversation on Earth.

"Rocky, you need to know a few things before we land. We are going to a place where very bad people are held and where you will find plenty of energy to feed on."

Rocky's eyes expanded widely in excitement as he said, "Neat!"

Then she hesitated for a minute before saying, "Although the people of Earth sent me to find you and the other Cleaning Bugs, they can be skittish and possibly react poorly when faced for the first time by spaceships and creatures that do not look like humans."

Rocky smiled and looked at Jane inquisitively as she continued.

"Earth people are naturally a very suspicious species so please don't be offended by their behavior."

"Okay, Jane. What is it that you really want to tell me? Just spit it out."

"Can you tell your people not to hurt any of my government people, even if they are pointing weapons at them?"

Rocky laughed at her request. "Is that all?" he chortled.

"Aren't you worried about such things?" Jane asked with a concerned look about his laugh.

"Jane, you don't need to be concerned. Even your atom bombs can't hurt us. You'd kill yourselves before putting a dent in us. Really, you don't need to be concerned. They can point all they want."

By the time the conversation finished, Jane was back on Earth, standing in the courtyard of a prison on the outskirts of NYC, with Rocky next to her. She had mixed emotions about coming back home to the place where she had been found in the streets and recruited to save her planet. But she focused on the work that had to be done to save Earth.

As they materialized in the courtyard, the prisoners ran to a corner of the building. Their eyes showed only fear. Jane looked at Rocky. He was staring at the prisoners and licking his lips. "I'm hungry and they *sure* look good," he stated with great glee. Before Jane could blink, he gobbled up all of the prisoners who were huddled together in the corner. Then he started chasing the ones who were still running, snatching them with his long tongue. Five minutes later, Rocky was ten times his original size and the courtyard was as clean as a sparkling plate.

Jane remarked, "Rocky, you look like you ate too fast and too much. Are you okay?"

He chuckled as he burped. "Give me a few minutes and I'll be fine."

"What's happening to you?"

"Well, Jane, I see that you won't stop asking me until I tell you. Right now, all of the evil from the criminals inside me is being sucked out of them. These guys are really bad. It makes it very hard to separate the good from the evil. I'm having difficulty drawing the evil from them in order for me to do the good that is needed here. You might say that those people are giving me what you call indigestion."

If Jane could have looked inside Rocky at that moment, this is what she would have seen:

The prisoners who were inside Rocky were so afraid that they climbed over and behind each other in the hope of not being seen by the other creatures near them. And when the Angel-scorps parted like a door and the Changer came forward, all of them froze in fear. The Changer grew to twice her size. Her wings spread, her eyes opened and stars began flying over everyone. The prisoners started running again but as soon as the stars burst into a colorful mist, none of them could move a muscle.

Squeak was waiting for the right time to give the order to attack.

Sneeze could be heard trying to instigate a revolt. "What are we waiting for? Let's go, guys!"

A few of his followers were pointing to some prisoners and yelling, "That one's mine!" Then another one shouted to others who were eyeing his meal, "Oh look! He's small but mean. There's lots of energy in him. He's mine! Don't touch!"

They all knew that the meaner they were, the tastier they became.

The Angel-scorps' white wings were spewing out black smoke that was coming out of holes on Rocky's back. Rocky explained to Jane that the black smoke was coming out of the prisoners who were being cleansed of their evil. Every so often a loud sound was heard coming from Rocky, as though he had belched. And once in a while he would hiccup and that was when another sound came from his bottom…

When the smoke faded, the sight was horrifying. All the prisoners had numerous Angel-scorps sucking and draining the evil out of them. The prisoners' faces had turned white and skeleton-like. And even the Angel-scorps were changing from black to white while their heads were turning red and flickering with multicolored lights as they were energizing.

A little time passed. Rocky started shaking like crazy and unbelievably beautiful sounds, made by the Changer as she cleaned, were coming out of his mouth. The sight that followed was amazing. A tunnel-like tail appeared and then opened and most of the prisoners that he had swallowed began walking out with happy, healthy faces. They helped each other and thanked Rocky for restoring them. But some who were 100% evil never made it out. Then something unexpected happened. Everyone stopped moving and stared at Rocky when he started coughing as though he were choking. He took a deep breath and when he coughed, he spit out a boy about nine years old.

Rocky said, "What were you doing in there? You shouldn't be in prison. You're a good boy. Get out of here." Then the kid disappeared from the prison yard.

Given the success at the prison, Rocky and Jane decided to arrange for thousands of cleaning bugs to come the next day from his *Bug Planet* to eliminate evil from Earth. Rocky asked Jane if there were anywhere they could go to develop their plans in private. They walked out of the prison courtyard and into the street where they found hundreds of people who had already heard about what had happened in the prison. She and Rocky waved as the people applauded and then they disappeared into a darkened area near the prison.

"Jane, I'm going to send my people a message telepathically

and tell them that we will come to some agreement as soon as you speak to your people."

Jane reacted instantly by simply putting her lips close to her wrist and talking to the people who were in charge. They were always available to her through the gizmo on her wrist and within minutes, both she and Rocky had spoken to their leaders and an agreement was made.

"Rocky, do you know how long it will take for your people to get to our planet? Do all of them have to think at the same time about where they're going?"

"To answer your first question, Jane, it will only take a couple hours for my people to get here. And no, all of us don't have to think about our destination at the same time. Do you remember what the men explained to you before you came to us? Like you, all we need is the idea of where we want to go. Then, we just think about it and we appear there. And in order not to end up in the wrong place, our minds can also search an area before our bodies follow. But we do not need your gizmo. It's built into each one of us and we use it when we fly our space ships."

Rocky took a deep breath and a good look at his surroundings and then continued.

"Well, when someone travels in the universe, it's almost an instant thing, depending on how fast the individual thinks about his destination. Even though the traveler is going at hyper speed through space, he will be mentally traveling at whatever is considered normal time for each individual planet. When you and I traveled to Earth, you were holding onto me so that we could travel at the same time since *I* don't have the particular Earth technology that you were given. Believe it or not, we can travel in our ships almost as fast as you can conjure up and arrive at your destination. And it has the same drawback as your method of travel – you have to think in order to travel and if you get surprised or have a headache, you can't think as fast as you should and your trip is delayed. The same principle applies to our spaceships. The difference is that in our ship, we have all the comforts of home."

Jane started clowning. "Well, I guess your ships better not get any headaches!" They burst into laughter.

Rocky continued laughing while responding, "I don't think anyone is having any headaches today."

The Cleaning Bugs Arrive on Earth

Rocky told Jane to look up toward the sky. She raised her head and what she saw made her mouth drop. It was a beautiful yet scary scene. Some of the Cleaning Bugs' spaceships were bigger than anyone could fathom. They were hovering over every city on Earth, not just where Jane and Rocky were standing. Everyone across the planet stared into the sky, gasping and jumping when one of the ships appeared.

The spaceship hovering above Jane and Rocky carried herds of Cleaning Bugs. As it drew closer to the Earth, two of the bugs started to talk.

"Look at planet Earth," Gugg said to Hangy.

"Oh, yeh," Hangy replied. "I can feel the evil energy that is coming from all the evil people. I can't wait to taste them. I can almost smell them."

"Take it easy, Hangy. Remember, we can only eat the ones that we're told to eat, so don't just attack as soon as we land."

"Ah! Alright," Hangy sadly agreed as his tail stopped wagging.

Meanwhile, as Jane was staring at the approaching ships, she saw that there were Cleaning Bugs floating down like rain. They landed on streets, on buildings, in parks. And they didn't move. They just looked around and feel for the evil that was in the air. Then, all at once, when given the telepathic signal, dozens of them attacked. Once a Cleaning Bug sensed the evil, it began its job.

The people on Earth were afraid. They did not know that the Cleaning Bugs were not a mean race and they did not understand that the Cleaning Bugs could have devoured their planet within hours, if they so chose. Rocky and Jane were surprised when they looked around and found themselves surrounded by all sorts of weapons as though Earth were already prepared for war. It was obvious that the military as well as the people were nervous. And if their looks didn't show it, then the weapons that they had prepared definitely did.

Jane reassured Rocky. "Please tell your people not to be concerned about my people. They have been told about your mission and that no matter what happens, all of you are friends to Mother Earth."

Then she added with a wink and a smile, "We always seem to be prepared for war even when someone brings us roses."

"We're not concerned," Rocky answered confidently. "Our bodies consist of the strongest and hardest material known in the universe. Why do you think we can clean any planet, no matter what kind of evil or weapons they may possess? Besides, sweetheart we don't think that your planet will attack us. We can also sense the good that is in your planet."

Rocky and Jane were so busy talking that for a minute they weren't aware of all the people who had gathered around them or even of what was happening. When they finally looked around, they realized that everyone was staring at the sky, which had suddenly turned dark. Everyone waited for something ominous to occur but instead the sky turned sunny. They started to wonder what would happen next. This unsurety put fear into them. But they acted as if there were nothing wrong. Before long, a shrieking sound pierced the air, with a deafening effect. No one could hear for a few seconds. As if that weren't bad enough, emotions went into overdrive because more spaceships appeared like magic just as the city turned dark at midday. Then all at once, bright multi-colored lights burst from one particular ship and lit up the entire city. Seeing something larger than a city hovering over them was more than most of the people could digest.

"I thought that they were supposed to save us," a woman near Jane said to her husband while holding her child protectively in her arms.

"Why isn't the military shooting them down?" the husband asked his wife belligerently.

She had no answer but their child, who had heard what his Father said, surprised his parents with his next words.

"But Daddy! If they get shot down, they would smash the whole city into a pancake."

His father's smile had never been so big. He looked at him with great pride.

"Son! What a great point! I'm very proud of you for being so aware and clever."

The Mother kneeled down, hugged and kissed her child and then told him, as only a beaming mother could,

"Do you see how good it is to read and educate yourself? You're only eight and you already think like a smart grown up!"

Almost every military man who was watching this scene as it repeated itself around the planet could be heard asking the same question,

"Shouldn't we shoot them down?"

The response was always, "Only if we wish to die."

It took only three days for planet Earth to be rid of most of its evil. The Cleaning Bugs were allowed to go into prisons and neighborhoods known for their criminal activity. At times, they could even grab evil individuals off the streets. However, Earth's government made it very clear that they could not touch anyone in a military or official uniform, thereby leaving many evil individuals untouched. Since the Cleaning Bugs had limited time and certain restrictions, it wasn't a complete job but *it was* what Earth wanted.

It seemed as if Earth were now a happier place. It didn't take long before the word on the street was that people wanted a celebration to thank the Cleaning Bugs. And what was great about all this was that the Cleaning Bugs also wanted to thank Earth for reenergizing them and becoming their space friends.

The Celebration

While the cleaning was still taking place, there were leaders from both worlds making plans in another part of the city on how to go about celebrating the destruction of evil around the world.

Anyone who has ever seen a royal wedding has a good idea of just how big an event it is. Well, it doesn't hold a candle to what was going to happen across planet Earth.

Rocky spoke to Jane about helping with the arrangements for the celebration.

"Jane, our world leaders really want to celebrate this success. My family wishes to provide the place. Can you arrange this with your government?"

"Tell me their plans and I will convey the information to the necessary people."

Rocky told her that they wanted to hold it in a spaceship and explained how it would be done. Because the Cleanings Bugs were able to change their own forms at any time, they also created the technology needed to do the same to their ships.

All the details were worked out and a few days later, there was a huge celebration in honor of Jane and Rocky.

It looked like the entire city had come out for this occasion. In addition to the marchers and spectators, the grounds were full of military personnel. Workers started preparing for the parade. They put up barricades and did whatever was required to get the parade started. The set up took several hours and then the parade got under way.

Everyone was waiting with anticipation to see the

spaceship. A small ship floated down from the huge ship that was hovering above the city. It was worth the wait. Since the spaceship could turn into any shape, it created its own marvelous design. Everyone's eyes filled with admiration as it touched down in the middle of a spacious park.

The ship was amazing to watch as it changed its shape. When it landed, the ship started to grow. It stretched sideways until it was a quarter of a mile wide and its length extended for two miles. The ship rose until it could hold fifty floors. It was the largest mechanical structure that the humans had ever seen. What they didn't know was that it was also a living entity.

The Cleaning Bugs made sure that there would be enough space for the celebration. The inside of the celebration area spread from one end of the spaceship straight through to the other. The inside of the ship was where the official government celebration was to take place. The ship's floor looked as if it were made of marble. On each of the ship's sides, people could see the walls with multiple individualized compartments that resembled windows. As they glanced into the compartments, they could see different life forms working with the Bug People on various types of projects.

Balloons floated in the air, mingling with the tantalizing smells of grilling food.

Within minutes, kids could be heard asking different questions that most of the time even the parents didn't know how to answer. They were as surprised as their children when they saw how the Bug People changed forms, trying to fit into the Earth's world.

The Bug People wanted to pay homage to Earth and all of its creatures. They thought that if they took on the form of their favorite Earth animals or bugs, or even some of their parts, they would be paying them a compliment. Some made people look twice while others put a smile or a laugh on the happy faces. In a few instances, people couldn't react in any other way than to just stand and stare, wide eyed and with their mouths open in disbelief. And there were a few combinations that scared the heck out of everybody but only for a few minutes because the Bug People, once they realized that something was wrong, were very fast to change their appearance since they did not want to scare anyone.

Sometimes, they got a kick out of hearing some of the kids' remarks.

"Mommy, look. That Bug looks like a man but he has ears that are larger than his head!"

"Don't stare, sweetheart. It's not polite."

Another child yelled, "Ouch! Why did you hit me?"

"Why did you pull my tail?" a rather distressed Bug replied.

One child was just plain rude to a little girl with beautiful, long red hair who was standing in front of him. He persisted on pulling it even after she told him to stop.

The little girl was very patient and put up with that boy's abuse for a few minutes. Then she did what the boy, his parents and the people around her never expected, especially from such a perfect looking, well-mannered little girl. She turned around and faced the rude little boy. A second later, the kid and everyone within ten feet of him jumped back with screams. The little girl had turned into a horrible combination of a giant spider, snake, and scorpion. No one could understand what had just happened. They didn't know that this was one of the few Bug People that could change into any non-human shape and also imitate a person perfectly. When it saw that everyone was scared, it instantly turned back into the little girl and said,

"I'm sorry, I'm sorry. I didn't mean to frighten the rest of you…only that nasty kid. "

Then it looked at the little boy and scolded him,

"You shouldn't be such a nasty little boy. Pulling hair hurts. See?"

In a flash, the little girl tugged on the boy's hair and then as the boy yelled, "Ouch!" the girl turned around and continued to watch the parade as if nothing had happened.

The end of the day was approaching. The parade was finishing and the leaders of both worlds were standing next to one of the ship's front doors. At first even the Earth's officials were skeptical and concerned about walking into the very strange spaceship. They were afraid of being abducted by the aliens, even though they had been told that the Cleaning Bugs were their friends. Because of this fear, the Bug People that were going to be involved with or seen by the public had to change their appearance to resemble something human. Their new looks weren't perfect but they had to do.

The formal celebration had already begun.

The visitors were kept out of the structures by what looked like glass walls that at times changed colors. Some sections were see-through; others were solid but made to look glassy. Only, all of them were actually a force field that served as the ship's entrance.

By now, all of Earth was celebrating the removal of evil. Everyone was free to participate in the parades and the streets were filled with thousands of joyous people. But because of the size of the crowds, there were legal and security concerns and safety measures had to be put into place. Only news media, officials from both worlds, and selected government families could enter the spaceship. This would be the case in every city of the world.

Only those with invitations could enter the spaceship. There were a lot of military personnel at hand. The eighth of a mile force field held twenty entrances into the ship with a guard on each side. The limousines and long governmental cars were dropping off all sorts of dignitaries. Some of the most popular were scientists who wore special jackets advertising the drugs that they had discovered and the companies that made them. But the main dignitaries who arrived at the entrance of this beautiful ship were the two heads of state, each representing their world. They exited the specially made armored vehicle, which was more like a limousine bus since it had to carry secret service agents for both men, official government personnel and handpicked journalists. The other news media were climbing all over one another for a clear shot of the only two different planet leaders whom they would probably ever see during their lifetime.

The head of planet Earth, known as Leader John, was an impressive, husky, six foot five man, wearing the customary white shirt, black tie and gray suit. The head of the *Planet of the Cleaning Bugs,* named Kreckcore, was another story. The crowds fell silent as they watched a tall but massive silver figure appear, step and then float out of the car and over to Leader John. As soon as Kreckcore stood still, loud mellow music filled the air and the crowd started to cheer. A small round stage suddenly rose up from the middle of the ship's floor and lifted the two leaders about ten feet into the sky.

A microphone appeared in front of Leader John. He stepped toward it, stuck his face almost into it and began to speak in a firm and determined tone.

"Ladies and Gentlemen, we are blessed because good has come to replace Earth's bad. I wish to thank our new friends, the Cleaning Bug People, for consuming most of the evil of our world. Please welcome the person to whom we owe our gratitude. Ladies and Gentlemen, here is the leader of the *Planet of the Cleaning Bugs*, Kreckcore."

Still draped in a silver sheet-like material, making him look like a very tall silver Casper the Ghost, Kreckcore floated forward and gave his opening remarks.

"People of Earth. You saw us take on different shapes when you first met us during the parade and celebration. I would like you to see our true form so that you will not fear us but rather accept us for what we truly are."

A second later the silver material floated toward the sky and disappeared, revealing a rock that resembled the well-known stone statues of Easter Island.

"Thank you, citizens of Earth. I hope that you are not too offended by my appearance and just in case you are, I hope that this one is more pleasant for your eyes to behold."

As he spoke, he took on the form of Leader John. Some of the crowd began to laugh; others weren't sure what to make of it. Then Kreckcore changed back into a large stone shaped like a human, just a few inches taller than John. The crowd cheered with excitement.

Leader John put the mike to his mouth and closed the ceremonies,

"Thank you all very much for coming and honoring our guest. We must leave now and continue our negotiations for peace and freedom from all evil."

The crowd applauded as the stage slowly sank down and

once again became part of the ship's base. The two leaders waved to the people as they walked through one of the entrance doors and into the ship.

As soon as they were in the ship and the doors closed behind them, John froze with amazement at the sight of what he had stepped into and unable to move forward, he looked straight ahead for a while. Then he lifted his head. When John looked up, he saw many levels of rectangular glass rods, connecting one side of the ship to the other, all with different kinds of creatures walking through them.

It was hard for John to believe that he was now in a spaceship. He was totally mesmerized by his new surroundings and Kreckcore could see that John needed a bit of help before they could continue their dialogue.

Kreckcore put his arm on John's shoulder.

"Come, my dear friend. Let me show you a different view."

In front of them was a walkway covered with red carpet. People from each world were lined up on both sides, ready to greet the leaders. Kreckcore escorted John onto the red carpet.

At the end of the walkway was a surprise that would make John very happy.

Once they reached the end of the crowded walkway, a glass sphere appeared ten feet in front of them. The sphere disappeared but the huge base that it had been on remained. They stepped on to it and immediately a protective guard railing surrounded them as the base slowly began to rise.

John was fascinated and amazed by the different views as the base started to rise. At first he saw peoples' shoulders and heads. Before long, he saw only heads that seemed to extend toward the horizon. As he rose higher, he could see different groups of people from both races listening to speeches. There were different kinds of pamphlets all over the place. Set along the celebration area were rows of benches for people who might need to rest. When the base reached the fifth floor, John could see some of the massive Cleaning Bugs lined up on both sides of the ship. He also noticed how much smaller his men were in comparison to them. John was glad that the Cleaning Bugs were on Earth's side!

Kreckcore was enjoying the reaction on John's face as they were lifted to the tenth floor.

"What do you think of our ship?"

"It's a marvel of ingenuity. Everything is so well organized and there never seems to be any kind of disagreement or insubordination. The inhabitants, in conjunction with the spaceship, are like one well-oiled machine."

John paused, looked at Kreckcore, and then asked.

"Is everything in your world as large as your ships? And if so, why can't we see anything through our telescopes? Your cities must be the size of one of our small states."

Kreckcore once again put his hand on Leader John's shoulder and said gently,

"My friend, you can only enjoy the beauty of my cities in person and up close. We cannot be seen from afar because our cities are underground where we prefer to live."

"Does your ship look like anything else in your world?" John asked.

"I would prefer to bring you to my world rather than describe it. Unless you will see one of our crystals before you leave our ship."

He paused and looked straight ahead as if he were looking

at one of his cities and with melancholy in his voice, he whispered. "Only the eyes can be the true beholder of the beauty that is my city."

Then he finished with, "Perhaps you can make time to visit."

"I would be honored to visit your world when time allows it."

Then they both just looked at the people who were honoring them.

John was surprised when he saw how large the quarter of a mile really was when he viewed it from a height of ten floors. Then he noticed that he could see all the way along the two miles to the other side of the ship. John stood there motionless and tried to take it all in. Kreckcore stayed nearby and kept John company while he enjoyed this new adventure. John saw additional sections set up for different events along the two miles. There were many speakers and almost everyone was wearing some kind of an official uniform.

John couldn't get over his amazement at the size and design of the ship's technology. Looking down from the tenth floor at the crowds, John was hoping that the Cleaning Bugs all around the world were experiencing Earth's different cultures at their best just as he was experiencing their marvelous culture.

This fantastic marvel of a ship was only a dream for John when he was a kid. But now that it had become a reality, all he wanted to do was walk amongst the crowd.

John put his hand on Kreckcore's shoulder.

"What do you say we join the crowd?"

As the base slowly descended, John felt wonderful seeing how the two races could mingle even though it took a bit of a visual and intellectual adjustment by both sides. Once Kreckcore and John finished their descent, they joined the crowds and walked down the street where they overheard bits and pieces of conversations.

"Look, Mommy!" an army child cried out, pointing into one of the levels of the see-through floors in the spaceship.

"What are those creatures?"

His mother looked up and saw that there were several creatures shaped like greyhounds but standing on two feet like men. Their arms were twice the length of their bodies and they had thick sculls and finely sculpted faces with long thin snouts. They were passing some kind of equipment back and forth and their long arms came in handy when they had to stretch to twice their already long reach for sphere-shaped objects on the shelves.

"What are they doing?" the child asked.

"I don't know, Son" she replied.

It just so happened that there was a Cleaning Bug next to them who overheard the conversation and hurried to give the answer.

"They are collecting energy spheres, which are just like those things that you call batteries."

"Thank you very much," she replied. "That's very informative."

Then her son grabbed and pulled on her arm

"Mommy, Mommy. What does informative mean?"

She bent down to his level to explain.

Kreckcore found this behavior interesting until he realized that John was not in sight

Right away he thought that John must have come across one of the crystal life forms from his planet that was on display. He backtracked about a block and sure enough, John and many other people were surrounding a mesmerizing piece of living material. They didn't want to take their eyes away from its beauty. It was a multi-colored crystal that changed colors while it flickered as if it had lights of energy coming from within it. A few minutes passed and then the crystal lit up like a flashbulb. When everyone's eyes cleared, they saw dozens of different crystals made up of all kinds of rocks, minerals, and semi precious stones. Then a large hologram appeared showing a section of their world that only had fields of crystals.

The hologram was so perfect that everyone who was staring at it would have sworn that they were on the *Planet of the Cleaning Bugs.* John felt as if he were standing in a cave that had crystals that were hundreds of feet long hanging from the ceilings. Some were very thin; one reminded him of the Empire State Building whose picture he had once seen in a history book. Only this one was upside down. Then the Hologram moved around, giving John the illusion that he was floating. In front of him there appeared a pathway that eventually led him out of the cave and into this new and wonderful world.

John couldn't take his eyes off of the crystals that shone in the fields ahead of him. There were crystals made of gold mixed with silver and platinum. Some were tin with lead, gold and iron. Then there were thin diamond crystals that behaved like a volcano. Only instead of lava, it spit out gold, steel and copper and such jewels as sapphires, rubies and diamonds. John was focused on one diamond crystal as it spit out a giant ruby. He suddenly saw that it was headed straight for him. John was too shocked to think or to move as the ruby sped like a bullet toward his head and was just inches away from hitting him.

Kreckcore grabbed John's shoulder and John reacted like anyone would in his situation… he ducked.

When he realized that he was actually in the ship celebrating with everyone, he looked at Kreckcore and immediately asked, "Is that what your world looks like? It's magnificent. I would love to visit it."

The two leaders continued walking and greeting different delegates and officials from both worlds. There were soldiers from both races lined up on each side of the ship, keeping guard.

Since this was a special occasion, rules and protocols were loosened, even though there were security precautions in place.

The Cleaning Bugs like any other race liked to enjoy life.

One particular Cleaning Bug called Hrrroo was standing guard but wanted to join in the celebration. Every once in a while, when the opportunity presented itself, he would gracefully accept it, as long as it didn't cause him to leave his post.

This was one of those opportunities.

A little girl glanced up at Hrrroo, completely unaffected by his size or appearance. He was huge and stood at his post like one of the Stonehenge rock statues. He slowly started to take on a more human form, change his appearance a bit and then finally return her glance.

"You don't seem to be afraid of me like some of the other kids," he stated softly and then added, "I'm glad. Can you tell me why you picked me to look at?"

"Well," she sighed. "You look a little like my friend in Chicago whom I just visited." Then she added sadly, "I miss her."

Hrrroo changed his appearance again to look even more like the girl's friend. He adjusted his body's composition so that he could move. Then he bent down on one knee and said, "I need to practice my mind reading. Is this what your friend looks like?"

He barely finished altering his appearance, when she flung her arms around his neck and kept repeating excitedly,

"Jacky! Jacky!" Then she pulled back from the rock and said, "Oh! Thank you so much Mr. Bug for letting me see my friend again!"

By this time the little girl's mom had finished talking to a friend. She turned to her daughter and greeted Hrrroo. "It's nice meeting you."

Then she took her child's hand, said goodbye and walked into the crowd.

When the conversation was over and the girl and her mother had walked away, Hrrroo went back to his comfortable rocky body and stood at his post tall and proud.

The two world leaders started to wrap up the celebration.

The celebrations that were going on worldwide were another story. Given the time zones and distances covered and the number of people involved, these celebrations were scheduled to last a week.

Kreckcore walked John to the door that they had entered through at the beginning of the celebration.

"I will leave you here. I must attend to some things but we will see each other tomorrow."

They shook hands. Kreckcore left and John did the same.

The two leaders spent the entire next day together in a conference room where they met to discuss intergalactic political issues and to form an alliance with the Cleaning Bugs before Kreckcore had to leave for his planet.

PART TWO
Towards the Planet of Stolen Property

Jane Learns the Truth

On the day the Cleaning Bugs were scheduled to leave, it seemed as if no one had a minute to spare.

The Programmers worked feverishly to reprogram the spaceship so that it would return to its regular shape in time for lift off.

As this was happening, the rest of the Cleaning Bugs were working at what needed to be done.

If they weren't loading pieces of luggage, then they were pushing buttons or pulling levers to insure a safe take-off.

Many of the Cleaning Bugs took time to say goodbye to their new human friends. It was a very emotional and happy day for both races. Jane and Rocky were standing by the ship talking until it was time for Rocky to leave.

Before long, they heard a voice coming from the ship.

"You have five minutes before the doors close."

They spoke for a minute longer and just before the doors started to close, Jane asked anxiously.

"Can you tell me anything about the kids whom I'm pretty sure I saw on your planet?" The doors closed. Rocky disappeared from sight. Then Jane heard Rocky's voice as it faded in the distance.

"If you want to know, I'll show you the next time...."

The crowds backed up, expecting to see a big blast as the ship lifted off.

But boy were they surprised when not a single sound was heard as the ship rose and disappeared into the heavenly body of space right before their eyes.

Jane was ready to go back to the alleyways of New York City but before she could leave, she had a crowd of reporters bombarding her with questions. All sorts of job offers were flung at her and she didn't know what to do. Suddenly, she saw Roxy's Mom and Dad coming toward her from the crowd but without Roxy.

Roxy's Father greeted her.

"Hi Jane. Do you remember us? We're Roxy's parents. I'm Frank Regain and this is my wife Judy."

Jane was strangely confused. Oddly enough, even though she thought that she was listening to Frank, her mind had drifted back to the *Planet of the Cleaning Bugs* and she had started to recall things about her family that had unexplainably come back to her while she was there. What Jane didn't know was that there were minerals in the planet's air that had affected her mind, causing her to mentally relive any part of her life that happened to come into her mind. Lost in her memories, Jane didn't really hear anything that Frank said to her.

Frank could tell that something was wrong.

"Jane, Jane," he hollered while shaking her. "Are you okay?"

Startled, Jane came out of her stupor and stammered,

"Oh! I'm so sorry, Frank. Where is Roxy? Please, please tell me. Where is Roxy?"

Frank and Judy took Jane's hands and went to sit with her on a nearby bench. Jane's heart was pounding hard as Frank told her that about a week ago strangers had come to his house and rung the doorbell and that when he opened the door, there were three men with their badges extended. Frank stopped, looked at Jane and tried to prepare her for the story that was to follow. He explained to Jane that he needed to recount the entire conversation so that she would understand everything that took place. Jane was now paying close attention to what Frank was narrating.

"Good morning, Sir. I'm Agent Asnel and this is Agent Brie and Agent Bra. Would you mind if I come in? I have some very personal news that concerns you and your child."

"She's in her bedroom sleeping but please come in and have a seat," I answered in an uneasy tone.

"You boys wait out here for me," Agent Asnel told Brie and Bra.

"This is my wife Judy. Would you like me to get Roxy?"

"Oh no, please. This is not something she should hear right now. You will need to tell her in your own way."

"Sweetheart," I softly asked. "Can you bring in some cake and coffee and then sit next to me?"

"Yes, of course."

Judy served us and then sat next to me. After a few minutes, I looked at our guest and asked impatiently,

"What is this visit about, Agent Asnel?"

"There is no easy way to say this, Mr. and Mrs. Regain. It's a very long and difficult story. When we discovered Jane as a candidate for the trip to the *Planet of the Cleaning Bugs*, our agents needed to find out where she came from. In our search to identify her, we discovered that a few years earlier, a Dr. John Kaczynski and his wife Theodora were robbed and killed in an alleyway. They had their three daughters with them when they were attacked. At that time we did not know their identities. Two were twins. One was supposedly killed. Unfortunately, we couldn't verify her name or her death because at that time we weren't able to find her body. The other twin was definitely kidnapped but we were never able to identify the kidnappers. The third child who escaped turned out to be Jane. While investigating Jane's background, we learned that the names of her twin sisters were Lisa and Roxanne."

"Oh my goodness," Judy gasped. "Our Roxy is one of the twins!"

"Do you know what happened to Roxy's twin Lisa?" Judy and I asked at the same time.

"Well," Asnel replied. "It's not good news but at least it's better than nothing."

"Do you know what happened to her?" Judy impatiently asked again.

"Somehow, Lisa ended up on a planet called *Stolen Property*."

Judy was satisfied for the moment about Lisa but needed to know something about her adopted daughter's biological parents and siblings.

"Did you learn anything about the Kaczynski family? Where did they live? Were they New Yorkers?"

So many questions came tumbling out that Agent Asnel had to interrupt Judy in order to tell us what he had discovered during the investigation."

As Frank stopped his narration, Jane looked at him, stunned by what he was telling her. He and Judy held Jane's hands tightly as he continued his story.

Agent Asnel told us that Dr. and Mrs. Kaczynski had just moved to New York from Nebraska. They found a nice apartment in a doorman building on Wall Street. But it was not the same New York as one might remember seeing in twentieth century history books. By this time, Wall Street, Chelsea, and Greenwich Village, just to mention a few well-known neighborhoods, were blocked off areas. Each one was like a separate community, surrounded either by fences, gates, walls or all of the above. Everyone had to be checked before entering a new neighborhood. The Kaczynski family lived in one of the best.

One of the things that made it so was that there was a park. By this time, everything was owned by private corporations in conjunction with the government. The parks at that time had become prime territory. You had to be pretty rich just to buy a ticket for a walk in any park.

Dr. Kaczynski paid the five hundred dollars for his wife, three kids and himself to enter and walk in the park for an hour. It was a beautiful Sunday morning. The small park that was next to the Hudson River was very well kept. There were flowers and small trees sectioned off from the reach of passers-by. The rose buds had developed into the size of watermelons and had opened to twice the size with an aroma that traveled for blocks. Tulips, gardenias, daisies and many other flowers made this area look like the botanical gardens. Unfortunately, if anyone wanted to see butterflies or other insects in addition to the flowers, tickets were needed for an indoor tour and reservations had to be made weeks in advance. Since this was a spur of the moment decision for the Kaczynski family, they only saw the flowers. But the time spent enjoying their sight and smell made it seem like they were in a park back in Nebraska. The peacefulness of the experience gave them the illusion that everything was fine and for a while they forgot that they were in New York City. Actually, they had no idea of what it meant to be in New York City.

Unfortunately, no one was immune to the criminal element.

Mrs. Kaczynski walked away from the flowerbeds and headed toward the railing overlooking the Hudson.

"Come, children," she called, stretching her hand out. Theodora was standing next to the railing looking over the Hudson River across to the Statue of Liberty and Hoboken.

"What is it, Mommy?" all three hollered as they started running toward her, forgetting that their Dad was just showing them the flowers about twenty feet away.

As they were running toward her, she asked, "Isn't the Statue of Liberty beautiful?"

Their Father couldn't believe how similar all three children were.

Watching them run to their Mother was an endearing sight. As they got closer to her and farther away from him, he noticed how athletic and competitive they were with each other. It was a strange sight to see such aggressive young girls in pink fluffy dresses, racing and grabbing each other to see who would reach their Mother first. Strength was a good thing to have in the world that they were about to experience.

Dr. John watched his wife and kids play for a while and then noticed the time.

"Come on, Sweetheart," he said to his wife. "The hour is almost up. And if we want to see more of the city, then we need to go."

"Let's go, children." Theodora said. She playfully grabbed Roxy and Lisa's hands but had to walk almost twenty feet to get Jane who was back at the flowers, staring at them. She was two years older than her sisters and not as attached to their Mother.

"Come on, Honey," John said to his wife when she and the kids were next to him. The kids skipped their way out of the park with their parents watching them closely. Even skipping became a competition for the girls to see who could jump higher. Of course Jane, being older always won, making the challenge more between Lisa and Roxy. Once they were all together, they left the park.

Walking along the streets of New York and window-shopping was a mesmerizing experience for the entire family. They had never seen such a variety of shops in Nebraska. One window had a display of all sorts of toys.

"Mommy, Mommy. Daddy, Daddy," seemed to be the only words that came out of the kids' mouths.

Jane pointed. "Can I have that bike?"

Then it was Roxy's turn to point. "I want that game!"

"Daddy, can I have that doll house?" Lisa asked as she pulled on her Daddy's sleeve.

"Kids, we're only window shopping today, so stop asking for things. We can shop another day. Let's see what else the city has to offer. Okay?"

All at once the kids dropped their heads and sighed, "Awe, all right," giving him looks that would make any parent cave into their demands.

They walked for a few blocks. The girls began getting restless and once again started to skip. They were about ten feet in front of their parents.

"Wait for us," their Mother yelled and they did wait. What was to come next would change all of their lives forever.

The end of one building was about three feet in front of the children. Next to it was the opening to an alley that was five feet wide and thirty feet deep. Then there was a wall with another building attached to it. Roxy looked into the alleyway and saw a toy car big enough to ride.

"Look, look," she hollered to her sisters in excitement. All three children ran into the alley.

Their Mother shouted, "Stop, stop."

She and her husband were only a few feet behind them. By the time the kids reached the toy car, their Mother and Father were right there.

"Don't you ever do that again," their Mother said in a scolding manner as she grabbed and hugged Lisa and Roxy.

"Jane, you should know better," her Father said.

Unaware of the danger, Lisa and Roxy began to struggle with each other, each one trying to be first into the car.

"That's not yours," their parents said as they each reached to grab a child.

That's when the nightmare began. A loud bang was heard behind them. All five of them stopped what they were doing and turned toward the sound that came from the direction of the entrance.

The wooden gate that they hadn't noticed before slammed shut.

"Well, well, well," a big scroungy bearded man smiled. "What have we here?"

Dr. Kaczynski stepped forward.

"Get behind me, Honey," he anxiously said to his wife. Then he told the kids, "Stay close to your Mother."

"Look, fellas," John said, taking off his watch. "Here, take my watch." Then he reached into his pocket, pulled out his money and said, "It's all I have. Take it but please don't hurt my children or wife."

A short, round and very creepy guy stood next to the scroungy man.

"Hurt your children?' he laughingly bellowed. "Don't be silly. They're worth way too much for that."

The two men advanced toward them.

"Everything will be okay," the Doctor reassured his wife and kids who were crying and holding on to their Mother. But he knew better.

Dr. Kaczynski had heard about men who stole children for a living and realized that he had to fight. He took a stance and prepared to fight and die for his family. It was the worst situation that any family could be in and oddly enough what happened next was also his proudest moment.

Standing next to him was Roxy, with her fists prepared to defend her family.

"Sweetheart, what are you doing?" He asked Roxy. "Stay with your mother."

"No, Daddy," she proudly said, with confidence and a growl toward the thieves, "They need to be taught a lesson."

Laughing hysterically, Creepy said,

"Isn't that great! She's a fighter. The gladiator ring will pay plenty for her."

"Let's go, Creepy," Scroungy said very impatiently, smacking him on the back.

Creepy reached for Roxy. The Doctor and she backed up, to get closer to the others.

When Creepy advanced again, the Doctor punched him in

the face but that only made Creepy fall back a few feet.

Standing in front of Lisa and the rest of the family, he began,

"Please, I don't want any trouble. Just take what I have."

"Oh there's not going to be any trouble," Scroungy answered very seriously and in a rush.

"And don't worry, we're still going get everything." He pulled out a gun and shot him.

His wife screamed and almost flew at the gunman. She was shot and fell dead as soon as she began her attack.

"Hurry up and grab the girls. I'll get this one," Scroungy screamed at Creepy as he reached for Jane. She ducked and kicked his kneecap.

Jane ran like the wind as the two men gathered their senses. It only took them a few seconds but before they could reach her, she had managed to open the very large gate and to escape.

The crooks were so busy trying to catch Jane that they didn't notice that Lisa had smeared herself with her parents' blood and had the intelligence to even tear a hole in her blouse so it would look like the bullet had also hit her. Lisa told Roxy to play dead but Roxy couldn't do it. The men were on their way back and Lisa had no choice but to play possum.

Roxy was stunned and could only cry out, "Mommy, Mommy."

Scroungy grabbed her and told Creepy to get the other child lying under her father.

Creepy went to pick up Lisa but she was limp and lifeless.

"Hey man," Creepy hollered, "The bullet went right through him and killed the kid. Do you realize how much money we just lost?"

By this time Scroungy had put Roxy into a laundry bag. "Forget about her. Here take this one."

He dropped Roxy and looked out into the street to make sure that there was no one there so that they could get away. Let's go."

Scroungy repeated through gritted teeth. "Let's go."

Creepy went to pick up the laundry bag with Roxy in it.

"Stop moving, you little rat." But Roxy wouldn't stop. "Hey, boss. She's still crying and moving around."

Scroungy closed the gate. "Put her down," he said, "don't open the bag but let her stand up." Once Scroungy could see where her head was, he tapped her on the head with his gun, just hard enough to knock her out but not to hurt her too much.

"See," he said with a big grin, "no more crying."

"Good move," Creepy said. He picked up the bag, opened the gate and they walked out of the alley, never to be heard from again.

Agent Asnel stopped to take a breath. Before he could continue to tell us anything, Judy interrupted and impatiently asked,

"What happened to Lisa? Where is she now?"

"I'm sorry, Mam, but my men and I have been working since midnight and we must take a break and eat something."

"Please Agent Asnel," Judy pleaded. "We know how these things work. If you leave now, we'll be lucky if you're back next week. We must know today. Don't leave us like this."

Agent Asnel had a daughter of his own and just couldn't leave.

"Can you wait a minute?"

He opened the door. "Agent Brie, Agent Bra. Why don't you boys call it a day? I'll finish up here."

"Yes Sir," they both replied and then left. Agent Asnel closed the door.

While this was happening, Roxy sneaked back into her room. Her mother was headed in her direction and she didn't want to be discovered eavesdropping. But she kept her eyes and ears open.

When she turned around, Judy was next to the kitchen.

"What would you like to eat, Agent Asnel?"

"Whatever you have will be just fine, Mam."

She returned with some sandwiches for Agent Asnel and me. She was too nervous to eat.

Once everyone was seated, Judy started a conversation so her mind wouldn't think about what was to come.

"Do you have any children, Agent Asnel?"

"Yes Mam. I have one daughter."

"Are you looking forward to having more?"

"I wish that we could have a dozen but we're not allowed to."

"What do you mean? You're not allowed to?" she asked in surprise.

He had taken a bite from the sandwich and swallowed it almost without chewing.

"Well, Mam. Anyone who works for the government is only allowed to have one child. People who don't work for the government are allowed to have up to three children, as you must be aware. Even those who work for private corporations that are affiliated with the government can only have one."

He realized that Judy was becoming anxious. He sipped some coffee.

"This is excellent coffee. And the sandwich is superb. Thank you so much. This is just what I needed." His plate was empty and so was his cup.

"Would you like some more?"

"No thank you, Mam. I'm sure you're anxious to hear the rest of this hard to take story."

"We would greatly appreciate that, Agent Asnel," I said as he handed Judy his half empty plate.

"Please don't start the story until I return."

Judy took the plates into the kitchen and returned within ten seconds.

I was sitting on the couch, my arm extended to grab Judy's hand.

"Come on, Sweetheart, sit."

As soon as Judy sat, she asked Agent Asnel.

"Do you know who Scroungy and Creepy are?"

"No one knows their true identity. They're only known as Scroungy and Creepy because that's exactly how they look and what they are."

"Let him continue, Honey," I told her.

"Right after the tragedy, life took a positive turn for Lisa and this was when fortune and luck changed for her. About a block away from the alley where Scroungy and Creepy exited, stood the man who turned out to be Lisa's trainer for the arena and her guardian angel. His name was Astro Jackson and he turned out to be a well-known man in the criminal underground. He was aware of the tactics that Scroungy and Creepy used to make money. He also knew that they were very sloppy with their work and that he needed to check for any mess that they may have left behind. When he opened the gate to the alleyway, what he saw was bad enough to cause even a man of his dubious profession to have a painful emotional reaction to such a horrific scene."

Agent Asnel waited a moment for Judy and me to digest what he was telling us and then continued.

"Astro Jackson was an odd looking man who wore a long raincoat, a large hat and sunglasses in order to disguise himself. He resembled an old-time 1960s private detective. His face looked like a boxer who had been hit by a Mack truck many times over. His ears were so long that they seemed to be flattened and glued over half of his skull. No one would believe that he had never been hit in his life. No one was ever fast enough. Astro Jackson was a retired gladiator fighter. Very few gladiator fighters ever lived long enough to survive, let alone retire. Astro was in the arena for one hundred and one years. He was very large and wide and weighed at least five hundred pounds. His longevity in the arena, speed and strength came from the fact that he was born on the *Mine, Mine Planet,* where the life span is much longer and body density is much heavier than on Earth. When Astro Jackson walked into the alleyway, he was not just sickened by what he saw; he was also flabbergasted and amazed by the events that would take place. He saw the child Lisa crying while trying to cover and protect the bodies of her mother and father.

Lisa was not aware of her surroundings. While she was shaking her parents, blood sprayed with every movement that she made and she kept crying, 'Daddy, Daddy, Mommy, please wake up.'

Astro had never shed a tear in his life until now. He was surprised as his teardrops fell. They looked like sharp, dense nails of water and as they hit the ground, they cracked and chipped the sidewalk. As he slowly walked toward Lisa, she seemed to come awake, noticed him and stopped crying. What she did next not only surprised Astro, but it endeared her to him to the point that he found himself wishing that he had a daughter just like her.

When Astro took another step toward her, she jumped up into a fighting stance and growled, 'You come near my parents and I will kill you.'

Astro stopped in his tracks. He stared at her while she was standing there in her bloodied pink dress looking like no animal that he had ever seen. She was so young yet she had such a raging fury. He couldn't help but notice how special she was. He immediately saw the potential of her fighting skills. She had a rage that matched the fierceness of her heart. If the way that she looked at him didn't convince him of that, the way that she attacked him certainly did. She charged at him head first with such speed and anger that when she rammed into his brick-like stomach, she knocked herself out. He gently picked her up and carried her out of the alleyway. Then he made plans to take her to the *Mine, Mine Planet* where she would be safe."

After a brief pause to drink some water, Agent Asnel continued.

"The first thing that Astro did after he rescued Lisa and recognized her fighting potential was to give her an arena name. He called her Flower Stinger because in his eyes, she was as delicate as a flower with a deadly emotional stinger hidden inside. Astro understood the force of that well hidden stinger the very moment when Lisa attacked him. He also knew that if he took Lisa to the *Mine, Mine Planet* at such a young age, she would become dense and hard enough to be the first outsider to fight in their arena with a native gladiator. He was aware that he was taking a big chance with her life and that she could die on that planet because of its different environment and density. But he believed that the advancements in technology and chemicals would give her a better chance to survive these changes and that her anger over her parents' death would give her the sharp edge needed to prevent her from being killed in the arena."

Once again Agent Asnel paused, took a deep breath and then went on.

"The last thing we heard about Lisa was that Astro Jackson was training her on the *Mine, Mine Planet.* We believe that when Lisa is a teenager, she will be sent to the *Planet of Stolen Property* for her first professional fight. She may already be there."

"Aren't you going to do anything about it?" Judy interrupted with great concern.

"There is nothing that we can do, Mam." Agent Asnel told her. "The only thing we can do is to bring you the information. If you wish to do anything about it, we can't stop you. It's not a problem for the government. And it is not a problem that we know how to solve."

"Thank you very much, Agent Asnel." I said and then added, "May I ask one last question?"

"Of course."

"Why did it take so many years for this information to get out?"

"Well…Astro Jackson is a very private and mysterious

character. On his planet he is one of very few people who can own an island. No one has ever stepped on that island without his permission and anyone who tried was never seen again. There is a rumor that he has creatures that protect him with their lives. One in particular, who is the most powerful and thousands of years old, is his one and only magical friend."

"Who is this friend?" Judy interrupted in anticipation.

"We're not sure, but we believe that it is someone or something that was somehow born or created on his island. I'm sorry, Mam but I don't have any more information, and I really must go."

"Thank you so much. We really appreciate your visit. Would you please keep us informed if you hear anything else?"

"Definitely and we will do what we can, Mr. and Mrs. Regain," he added as he left.

When Frank finished the story, he stared at Jane. The girl was so involved in what he was saying that it took her a couple of minutes to realize that Frank had stopped talking. That was when she saw that she was still on the parade grounds where the celebration had been held. When Jane understood Frank's story fully, the cloud lifted from her mind. She became very anxious and bombarded Frank with questions, which she immediately wanted answered.

"You said that Agent Asnel told you that Lisa was on the *Planet of Stolen Property*. But you still haven't told me why Roxy isn't with you."

"Jane, the only thing we know is that when Judy went to wake her up, Roxy was gone. Judy and I think that Roxy must have listened behind the door and heard everything that Agent Asnel said and that she snuck out then to find a way to go to the *Planet of Stolen Property* to rescue her sister."

Jane thanked Frank and told him that she had to find both of her sisters and bring them back safely. She paused for a minute to think and suddenly remembered that she had heard some bad things about this planet.

Jane turned to them and asked, "Will you help me if I need something?"

Frank and Judy could tell from the look in her eyes that she was determined to find Roxy and that there was nothing that they could say or do to stop her. There was only one thing that they could say to answer her request.

"Anything you need or want."

"Then I'll be back."

The next thing they saw was Jane's back, a block away. They looked at each other in amazement at how fast she was moving.

Jane Searches for Her Sister

Jane found a bench on a side street and sat down to collect her thoughts. She realized how tired she was and that she needed to sleep before making any decisions. She went to a shelter that she knew from her previous life on the streets of New York and spent the night there. The next day she set out to locate some men who could help her get to the *Planet of Stolen Property*. As she was walking in the city, Jane's attention was drawn to the Bull Barn Bar when she heard a lot of commotion coming from that direction. As she peered through the front window, she caught a glimpse of what looked like a man trying to win a bet. Her curiosity was aroused and she approached the door. That was when she heard a young man challenge four guys to a fight.

The guys didn't like his bragging and challenged him to back up his boasts.

"You can't beat the heck out of all four of us," one of the four men barked. We're professional fighters. Are you sure you want to fight all four of us at once? You know you can't win."

"Here's my money. Where's yours?" is all that the young man said.

Jane walked into the bar and headed toward the young man who seemed familiar to her.

She looked at him for a while but it wasn't until she spotted the skinny guy, with the nails in his head, standing near him that her memory slowly started to work.

Then it was as if she were right back in the city years ago, sticking the same two kids in the butt with nails.

Time certainly seemed to have aged them a bit since she last saw them. Although they were teenagers now, their physical appearance was very different than when she first encountered them perhaps five years ago in one of New York City's alleyways. Jane walked over to a friendly man and asked if he knew the name of the fighter and the skinny guy who was with him. He nodded yes and told her both names.

She wasn't surprised when she heard the name Slammer. It fit the fighter perfectly. Jane noticed that he had grown to twice the size that he was when she first saw him. She was sure that he and the skinny kid named Spike had been genetically altered over the years. Slammer was about three hundred seventy five pounds, six foot tall and strong enough to pick up two oxen.

About six months earlier he had gotten into a bar brawl and destroyed the Bull Barn Bar. Bobby Joe, the owner told him if he ever did that again he wouldn't be allowed in the bar. Well, it looked like Jane would be fortunate enough to witness the second destruction of the same bar.

This time Bobby Joe started acting tough with Slammer.

"I told you before, you big gorilla, if you break up my ba...."

Then there was a choking sound.

Slammer had grabbed Bobby Joe by the neck and while holding him off the ground at eye level, he growled, "What did you just call me?"

Bobby Joe's arms and legs were twitching and kicking while he was stammering,

"I'm sorry."

Slammer put him down and mumbled grudgingly while

trying to be a good guy, "I accept your apology."

"Thank you for not killing me," Bobby Joe kept repeating. Then he got a look in his eyes and a grin on his face as though he were up to something.

"I'll tell you what, Slammer. If you can pick up two bulls at once, you won't have to pay for the damage. If you can't, you will have to pay me double.

Slammer agreed. "But if I pick them up, I get to walk away with the bulls." Bobby Joe laughed, believing that no one of his species could pick up a bull, let alone two and so, he agreed.

No one had ever been challenged to pay off a bar tab by picking up a bull, let alone two. Word got around quickly. Slammer was known for his strength. Within a half hour, Bobby Joe's bar was full to the brim with customers and paying spectators. The challenge was already making him more money than Slammer owed. But not more than the bulls had cost him.

Bobby Joe jumped up on the bar and hollered at the top of his voice.

"The show is about to start. Now all you lovely drunken people shut up and let the man prove himself."

The crowd immediately became as quiet as a mouse. There was an amazingly large round bar counter with a custom made platform built right in the middle for Slammer to stand on. It was narrow and about three feet off the ground. Slammer stood on it like a gladiator ready for the fight. The bulls stood on either side of the platform. There were harnesses on them so that Slammer could pick them up. The floor that was around the bar counter was especially built for these sorts of occasions. It was made of a special material that could look like whatever one chose. The sight was amazing.

While Slammer was preparing, Bobby Joe was taking side bets while praying. He knew that if he lost, the bar would be shut down and the guys he owed money to would also shut him down.

The crowds were climbing on top of each other, stretching to get a better look at Slammer and the bulls. Spike was near by the whole time. Slammer told Spike to keep his mouth shut. He knew that if Spike started to talk too much, especially with what Slammer was trying to pull off, things would never work. Bobby Joe called for quiet. Once there was complete silence, Slammer began his lift. Slammer didn't like being a thief, so he learned how to be a good showman and in a way, an honest con artist. 'How can that be?' you might think. Well, he was a bit of a show off but he never showed his full capability. But this time, it seemed as if he had finally met his limits.

Each bull was especially bred by Bobby Joe at his indoor farm, to be twice the size of a normal bull. They were really huge. Each one weighed three tons.

Slammer started his lift. The crowd gawked with their mouths open as he struggled to succeed. The bulls' harnesses tightened until the bulls started snorting from the uncomfortable pressure. They looked like Suma wrestlers who were being pulled up by their loincloths. The bulls were barely off the ground when Slammer dropped them. The entire place shook. Some of the customers even fell over and hit the floor. A few seconds passed in silence followed by various sounds of disappointment. Bobby Joe went bouncing around from customer to customer trying to collect on his winnings. But when he went to collect from one of the well-known and powerful gangsters, this monster of a man said, "Hold on a minute. Look," and pointed to the platform where Slammer was standing.

Billy Joe turned around and saw that Slammer was going to try to pick up the bulls again.

"Hey, you can't do that," he began yelling.

This monster of a man known as Mountain grabbed Bobby Joe by his head. His hand was so big that it looked like Bobby Joe's head was the size of a baseball.

In a deep voice Mountain said, "He gets three shots at this. Do you have a problem with that?

"Oh no, Sir. It's okay with me. Besides you can make a higher bet if you like."

"You better not be pulling anything, Bobby Joe," Mountain said.

A gasp came from Bobby Joe and the crowd, as Slammer appeared to have lost a bit of his footing trying for the second lift. Once again he barely got the bulls off the ground but did not keep them up for the required ten seconds. This time the crowd became very rowdy and it looked like it was going to get out of hand. Mountain jumped from the second floor balcony onto the platform like a huge bat. It was amazing and frightening to see such a large man so fast and light on his feet. When he wanted to be heard, he was heard.

"Shut your big traps, you mugs. The man gets a third try. Anyone got a problem with that?"

The crowd almost simultaneously roared, "No, Sir!"

Then to everyone's surprise he put on the biggest smile they had ever seen and said, "I have a special table set up for betting."

He pointed to it and hollered, "For every bet you make,

there's a free drink."

About five minutes later, Slammer gave the signal to Bobby Joe and Mountain that he was ready for his third and final try to pick up the bulls and hold them up for the full ten seconds. Bobby Joe caught a look that Slammer and Mountain shared, which made him think that they were up to something. He couldn't prove anything and he wondered if it could just have been his imagination. Besides, he realized that there was nothing he could do even if they were up to something. And the lift was about to commence.

Bobby Joe took the microphone near him and announced, "Ladies and gentlemen. You are about to witness a man who is already legendary for his strength attempt something never before done. Can this possibly be the end of a legend? Or can it be the beginning of a superman-like hero? So far, a man you all seem to know has failed two tries at lifting six tons of bull. If he fails this time, his reputation will be tarnished and he will have to pay his tab. When people mention his name, perhaps he will even be labeled, 'He's full of bull.' However, should he succeed, he will be a legend forever and will not have to pay his tab."

It was so quiet that they could hear a pin drop. The lights were shining on Slammer and the bulls. This was when Slammer really shone as far as showmanship was concerned. Just bracing himself for the lift had him sweating like he was in a sauna. What the crowd didn't know was that there was a heater underneath him. He looked like a lobster that was ready to pop. Anyone could see that there was no way for him to lift those two bulls. The harnesses were getting taut and Slammer's veins were popping out of his neck from strain. The crowd went into a frenzy, making side bets against Slammer. With every bet that was made, Mountain gave away drinks like they were water and most of them were. He was a happy man. He knew something that no one else did. How could anyone in the bar possibly know what was in his mind? Slammer could be seen straining and groans and snorts could be heard as the bulls were lifted three inches off the ground. The crowd was dead silent until he stumbled and almost let the bulls hit the floor. A huge gasp was heard. Then....dead silence. When the crowd saw that he caught his footing, the side bets were bringing in cash by the millions. Many people were going to go home rich that evening and Mountain knew that he was going to be one of them. The free drinks continued, as did the bets. Mountain never looked happier.

Slammer had barely raised the bulls up to his shoulders. His final success or failure was only an arm's length away. All he had to do now was to lift the bulls above his head and hold them there for at least ten seconds. Then he would get to go home debt free and rich.

Slammer grunted forcefully as he jerked the bulls to the sky. There were all sorts of reactions - some good and some awful. However, there was one thing that everyone joined in on: the counting of the seconds. People could be heard for miles. Anyone walking the streets of the city would see and hear pedestrians standing and counting to the rhythm of the crowd in the bar. The pedestrians stopped counting when they heard "ten" but the crowd in the bar continued counting.

"Are they still counting?" a woman walking with her husband asked.

"Oh, yeh," he replied and then added, "Slammer must be showing off again."

After the count to fifteen, the roar of the crowd could be heard for miles. Slammer got off the platform, walked over to Bobby Joe and said,

"I don't owe you a thing and those bulls are coming with me."

A few muscle-bound bouncers who worked for Bobby Joe tried to stop Slammer but they didn't have a chance, especially with Mountain standing next to him.

Slammer walked away with the bulls, as the bar crowd watched in awe.

After all of this was over, Jane went outside so that she could hide and follow Slammer when he came out.

Once he was out of the building, she followed him until he met up with Mountain. They both were just about the same size. One could even say that they almost looked like brothers.

"Here you go," Mountain said to Slammer as he passed him a suitcase full of his winnings.

"Thanks, Mountain. It's been a long time. It's good to see you again, my friend."

"It's good to see you too," Mountain replied.

He paused, looked at the bulls for a minute and then asked, "What are you going to do with those bulls?"

"I can't take them with me. I figured that the butcher shop would be my next stop. Now that I'm rich, I don't need the bulls. Do you want them?"

Mountain was pleasantly surprised when he heard that.

"Are you kidding? Bobby Joe is going to go nuts when he sees me with them. Slammer, I really enjoyed how you conned Bobby Joe into believing that you couldn't lift the bulls and I really appreciate your generosity in giving them to me. If you ever want to do something like this again, just let me know.

"Oh, by the way, Slammer, be nice to that admirer who's been following us. I believe she has her eye on you."

Slammer replied, "I saw her hiding behind a building a while back. Spike and I ran into her when we were still kids. She's harmless. I must admit though, she's a real toughy. She's the only one whoever drew blood from me and my partner Spike."

"It seems like you might have your hands full with that one."

"Nah! She's one of the good guys, just like you and I are trying to be."

They looked at each other and burst into laughter at the idea.

Slammer thought that it was a shame that he couldn't actually let Mountain know that he really wanted to be one of the good guys and that he just acted like a bad guy while doing good whenever possible.

Then he thought, *After all I shouldn't ruin a perfectly bad reputation.*

After their good-byes, they went their own ways.

Slammer was at a time in his life when he wanted to change his ways. Now that he and Spike were rich, they could do just that. In any case, it turned out to be a lucky day for Jane. At least that was what she was hoping.

Slammer turned to go back to the bar where Spike was waiting for him. Before he walked ten feet, he stopped in his tracks. Jane came out from behind a building, stood in front of him, looked into his eyes defiantly and said,

"Do you remember me?"

"I sure do! Everybody knows you by now. You're very

famous."

"I asked if you remember me not if you know me from the newspapers. Do you recall when you and that skinny toothpick friend of yours tried to rob a well dressed little girl?"

Before she could finish, Slammer answered,

"I'm sorry Jane and so is my friend Spike. We often talked about you. You are the reason we got out of crime as soon as we could. Sticking a nail in our butts made us think about our crooked ways and how pathetic you made us look that day. How can I thank you for that? In a way, it saved our lives."

Jane couldn't believe what she was hearing.

"You mean you will help me if I need it and I won't have to stick another nail in your butt?"

Slammer couldn't stop laughing. He loved her right away just for her spunk and bravery. Then and even now, she was like a kitten threatening a mean pit bull.

"Jane, I am in your debt and so is Spike. Whatever you want or need, we will be there for you. Spike and I always talked about doing good to make up for the bad that we have done and you are now giving us another opportunity to grow. For some reason, you seem to bring the good out in people, especially in me and well, all you have to do to Spike is grab his nose and he'll follow."

Jane and Slammer went back to the bar for Spike. Slammer opened the door for Jane and they walked over to Spike who was sitting at the bar talking to some locals.

Slammer put his hand on Spike's shoulder. "Hey Spike!"

"Hello, Slammer," he quickly replied with excitement.

"Say hello to Jane. Do you remember her?"

"I sure do."

Then, as if he had waited a long time to say this to her, he apologized, almost gasping out the words.

"I'm sorry for being so mean to you and that little girl."

"Spike, that little girl turned out to be my sister and she needs our help. You're going to make up for what you did, aren't you?"

"I guess so. If you say so…" Then he looked at Slammer and said. "You already agreed to this, didn't you, Slammer?"

"You sure know me, buddy. Of course we're going to help her."

They raised their glasses and drank to a successful rescue.

After their drink, Jane spent a few minutes telling Slammer and Spike about the situation. For the first time, they learned the name of the little girl whom they had attacked so many years ago. Spike and Slammer started talking about rescuing Roxy, Jane's sister. While they didn't know many of the details, they were already preparing themselves for this new adventure.

This gave Jane a chance to observe her surroundings. She found herself looking closely at Spike. He was about six foot six and weighed one hundred and ten pounds. He had different size colored nails in his head. Spike didn't have these nails when Jane first fought with him.

She interrupted Slammer and Spike.

"Spike, I would like to speak with Slammer. Do you mind?"

With a big smile he replied, "Yes I do, but you can anyway." Then he went and sat with some friends at another table.

Jane looked at Slammer and the first thing out of her mouth

was, "Why does Spike have nails in his head?"

Jane found Spike's story fascinating. She learned that the nails helped him communicate with other worlds and that Spike was a Nail-ion who originally came from the *Brain Planet*. She was amazed to learn that every Nail-ion has a body and brain but that the brain is actually a separate entity that resides in its body's head. Each brain has its own name and personality. The body and the brain have to understand each other at the same time. The different size colored nails in their heads provide this way of mutual understanding and communicating. The brain, not the body, controls the world of the Nail-ions. Sometimes the brain finds that its body doesn't listen to it. Spike was a perfect example of a Nail-ion body that constantly defied its brain. Spike's brain was about one inch in size. This little creature inside Spike's head was named N.I.T. (or Nail-ion Intellectual Technology). N.I.T. looked like an inkblot that changed form and was able to float. When N.I.T. was sitting in Spike's head, its eyes were focused on whatever Spike was seeing at that moment. N.I.T. had two huge, round white eyes that looked like windows. When N.I.T. wanted Spike to do something, its tentacle-like hands would reach for and press different colored spots on the inside of Spike's head. Of course, that didn't always work. Spike lived in his own mind, which was very small. N.I.T. was always busy computing distances and other geometrical figures, not noticing what Spike was doing, until it was time to work, or too late to get his body out of the trouble he put them in.

Jane was listening to Slammer. Then her mind drifted off and she began thinking about Slammer and Spike from years ago. No wonder the boys hadn't stayed down when she hit them the first time they ran into each other. She could only assume that they were already developing different types of strengths and even unknown powers at a young age.

Then it suddenly dawned on her that she needed to get a crew together and in a hurry if she wanted to rescue Roxy before it was too late.

Let's see, she thought. *So far, there is Slammer who can pretty much do anything. I need his strength and his know how when it comes to fixing the ship, should something go wrong. If I'm lucky, I'll run into my friend, Ragrezy. That will solve my problem of looking for a mechanic.*

She thought a bit more and realized how weird it was that Spike, the least serious and most likely to say and do the wrong thing, was the best suited to be the computer analyst, the flight navigator and the advisor to the captain and that she just happened to be the captain! Then, she wondered if she should be concerned that N.I.T. might lose control of Spike. After all, even though the brain had the knowledge, if N.I.T. couldn't manage Spike and his actions, then she would lose two crewmembers, Spike and N.I.T., in one shot. She understood that this was not the time to worry about such things. She still had two more crewmembers to find. It was time to leave Slammer and Spike and start looking for the others. Jane called Spike away from his friends and said goodbye to Slammer and him.

"I'll meet both of you later. I still have to find at least two more crewmembers."

Then she left the bar. Jane knew that she needed a gunner and that Franky would be the perfect person for this job but Jane still had mixed emotions about contacting him. She had gone out with him a while ago and he had broken her heart. Her common sense outweighed her emotions and she decided to speak to him. He was the only man she knew who was great with all sorts of guns. She started looking for Franky in different bars. She found him in a bar surrounded by dance girls who watched goo-goo eyed as he showed off how well he could handle his gold revolvers. Franky was a young, good-looking, tall, muscular fellow with broad shoulders, black hair and brown eyes. As far as the local girls were concerned, he was very cocky but still quite a catch.

For a moment Jane's memory flashed back and she recalled her feelings when she first caught him sharing a soda pop with another girl in a different bar. Jane realized that this was childish but at the time, she was hurt, child or not. But these memories were for another time. Now she needed to put this in the past since she was about to ask him if he would help rescue Roxy.

She walked up to him and with a bit of sarcasm said, "Hello, Franky. I see that the girls know that you can twirl your gold revolvers. But, tell me, can you handle a real man's gun on a battle ship?"

Then two of the dance girls interrupted, "Tell her you can handle any gun you want, Franky."

"All right, you two," Jane told the girls. "Take a walk. My friend and I have some catching up to do."

She grabbed the stool next to her, moved it a bit and sat next to Franky at the bar. Jane watched the girls leave and then looked at Franky in a very businesslike manner.

The first words out of her mouth were, "Franky, I'm going to make this simple. I need to rescue my sister from the *Planet of Stolen Property* and I need a crew. You're the best gunner around. So are you going help me or not?"

With a big smile on his face, he quipped, "How could I refuse such a charming proposal and the opportunity to catch up?"

"This is not about catching up, Franky. This is a business deal and you owe me."

She explained the situation to him and they rapidly came to an agreement. And it was all her way.

After recruiting or rather manipulating Franky into helping her, she got up from the stool and said,

"I have to find a friend of mine named Ragrezy. You know where to meet me."

"Wait a minute, Jane. Why don't I tag along, just in case?"

She looked at him and thought, *It's just business and why not? Trouble could show its ugly head at any time.*

She was almost at the exit when she turned, while still walking and said, "What are you waiting for? Didn't you already invite yourself?"

They exited the bar and walked into the street. Jane told Franky that Ragrezy and she were childhood friends and that she had not spoken to him since her parents' death. Jane figured that Ragrezy would be in the tavern near the local train station. It was a good place to make business deals.

The train station was across town. Jane hailed a cab, told the driver where to go and in a short time they arrived at their destination. Franky and Jane were surprised to see that the train station was made up of two buildings.

The bigger building had a large painted wooden sign that read "Train Bar Tavern."

Next to it was a much smaller and run down building whose hanging crooked sign said, "Train Station." The building looked like a Wells Fargo post office, where horse-drawn stagecoaches used to stop for a few minutes to drop off mail and passengers.

The tavern was busy. The door was open and Jane could feel the excitement in the air. There was an unusually large number of big men sitting around, prepared for some kind of action. But what kind of action was yet to be determined.

Curiosity about what was going on was driving Franky crazy.

"Excuse me," Jane asked a burly man who was entering the bar. "What is everyone so excited about?"

"Oh, you must be new around here. Men have been competing all day long and this is the last competition for the day and for the championship."

Franky started to ask "What competition?" but before he could get the two words out, the man rushed into the bar like he couldn't wait to get a piece of the action.

Jane and Franky followed the burly man and when they got into the bar, which was much larger than it appeared from outside, they saw the reason for all of the excitement. A huge banner hung across a section of the ceiling. It read *The Great Train Put Together Competition.*

Jane stopped and looked around the place. She spotted Ragrezy at the bar just as two guys sat down next to him, one on each side.

"Look, Franky," she pointed, "There's Ragrezy."

They walked over but when they were close enough to be within hearing distance, Jane grabbed Franky's arm and stopped him dead in his tracks.

Jane mumbled, "Here comes trouble."

"What's wrong Jane?"

"Those two guys are about to make a *big* mistake. They don't know that Ragrezy sometimes gets out of hand and can't control himself. He hits things that aren't supposed to be hit."

They both fell silent, listened and observed Ragrezy as the scene began to be played out.

"Hey, Craig," a man called out to his buddy while pointing to Ragrezy.

"Have you ever seen an uglier face? What's with those nostrils that look like oversized eye sockets? Is he going to blow his nose so he can see better?" They burst out laughing very loudly and obnoxiously.

Ragrezy had seen these two before when the guys tried to start fights with competitors so that they would be disqualified for fighting or injured in the fight. Their aim was to make sure that certain strong competitors couldn't compete. Ragrezy immediately understood that he was their next target.

Ragrezy thought that the man who was standing to his right laughed too abrasively. He wanted to beat the crap out of him but he knew what could happen when he lost his temper. Ragrezy also didn't want to be disqualified. Because of this, he tried to avoid such incidents whenever possible. It just so happened that the guy started calling Ragrezy insulting names such as Metal Head, Ugly Parts and Rust Bucket. These were fighting words to a man who had mechanical body parts.

Ragrezy was still okay with the name-calling, but he wasn't sure for how long. The two bullies couldn't provoke Ragrezy to fight until one of them grabbed his shoulder. That's when Jane saw Ragrezy's arm turn into a giant hammer and smash the bully's head through the countertop and into the floor. Jane and Franky were amazed when they realized what had just happened but they continued to walk toward him.

"Holy molely!" Franky laughed. "That guy's not getting up for a while."

The people who were watching made a pathway for one of the judges to get to Ragrezy. A very tall thin man wearing a judge's robe stood in front of Ragrezy, pointed to the body that was on the floor and asked,

"Did you just fight with this man?"

"Nope," was all that he answered.

"Okay," the judge replied and started to walk away.

But Jake, Craig's friend, said, "He should be disqualified from the competition because he just hit my friend on the head with a giant hammer."

The judge stopped, looked at Jake and said, "Did your friend swing back?"

"No," he answered.

"Then it doesn't count. This was a slaughter, not a fight." Then the judge walked away.

Jane didn't know that Ragrezy had been bionicly and chemically transforming himself since he was a teenager and that he had acquired a few "upgrades." This was how he was able to change portions of himself into tools when he had to fix something or gain an extra arm that could pop out of any part of his body when he needed it.

Ragrezy heard a familiar voice say "Hi there!" He turned around and saw Jane. His arms opened as she ran to him and they hugged with great affection.

He grabbed her by the shoulders, lifted her up about a foot into the air, stretched out his arms and held her in front of his face so he could take a better look at her. She was dangling at the end of his arms like a rag doll. He put her down and with a big, toothy smile, said,

"Where *have* you been? *I've missed you.*"

"First, let me introduce you to my friend Franky."

They looked at each other. Franky put out his hand to say hello. Ragrezy did the same.

"I've heard about you, Franky. Are you as good a shot as I've heard?"

"I don't know what have you heard," Franky answered, waiting for a compliment.

But before Ragrezy could say anything, Jane grabbed him by the arm.

"Please, Ragrezy. I don't have much time and I must get to the point. I need your help. And you *will* help me."

At that moment, they heard the train station's whistle. The first call for the competition to begin had sounded. Ragrezy started to walk toward the back of the tavern. There was quite a crowd building up both around and in the tavern.

Jane followed Ragrezy and Franky followed Jane.

"Can't we talk about this after the competition?" Ragrezy asked.

"Can't we do it during the competition?" Jane responded.

"I don't think so, Jane."

Jane and Franky were right behind Ragrezy.

"Just how *big* is this tavern?" Franky asked.

And just then, the second whistle sounded

A minute later, people stopped moving. Then a loud creaking sound, like a door opening, drowned out the noise of the crowds. Everyone stood still as the back of the building started to rise. A light began to show along the building's sides and floor as the tavern's back wall started to lift like the back door panel of a van. Once the tavern's wall was lifted, the crowds rushed out, anxious to see the event that they were waiting for.

Jane and Franky found themselves still in the tavern, too surprised to react to what had just taken place. They needed a moment to take it all in.

Ragrezy had disappeared and the crowd was outside, hundreds of yards away from them.

They looked at each other and slowly walked out of the tavern. The sight was magnificent. In the distance there were mountains whose beauty was enhanced as the red sun dropped behind them. Jane and Franky stopped, turned and looked to their left where they saw train tracks with trains that had been retired decades ago. Even further to their left were trains from century ago. It was a very private museum that had been abandoned for hundreds of years.

By the time they walked down to where the competition was supposed to take place, it was over. Ragrezy came over to Jane and Franky, carrying two trophies that he had just won. One was for assembling the train's engine and the other was for winning the race around the mountain with the train engine that he just put together.

A minute later, when he was standing in front of them, he asked, "Okay, Jane. What is it that you wanted to talk to me about?"

She explained her plans for rescuing her sister and asked him to join her crew.

Ragrezy was a man who enjoyed adventure and he immediately replied, "Yes."

Jane knew that she couldn't have found a better mechanic. She told him that she would call and see him as soon as they were ready for lift off.

It took Jane more than a year to assemble her entire crew and to get ready for the trip to rescue Roxy. She gathered some unusual and odd-looking individuals as crewmembers to take the trip with her to the *Planet of Stolen Property*. Jane knew that many of the people and different life forms on that planet would be very evil because they were a mixture of bionicly and chemically produced life. She realized that the only way that she would have a chance of beating her odds for failure would be to find Rocky and ask him for his help. In this way, he could suck the evil out of the All-for-One-Man, the owner of the *Planet of Stolen Property*. Once that happened, things would change for the better. At least that was what Jane hoped.

The day of their scheduled take-off, Jane told everyone to meet her at midnight so that they could lift off on time. Unfortunately, the adventure was already starting out with problems.

Spike was in the ship with Slammer.

The papers aren't here, Spike kept repeating to himself while rummaging in every nook and cranny of the ship.

"What's the matter?" Slammer asked. "Just get on the tube and tell them that were going to lift off."

Spike stopped moving.

Slammer had seen this happen before and mumbled, "Here we go again."

N.I.T., the brain inside Spike's head, popped out of his ear, hung onto one of Spike's nails and started talking to Slammer.

"Slammer, I want you to keep a close eye on this skeleton

of a body that I'm stuck with. If you see Spike playing or hitting his head, check for any nail that might have loosened up and tighten it."

"Okay, N.I.T. but you have to get better control of him from the inside of that head of his. You are his brain, aren't you?"

"Don't rub it in. Spike's body was defective from the start. I can only control 90% of him. The rest never kicked in and so he does his own thing. Now will you help me so I don't have to keep popping out of this skeleton head?"

Slammer thought how cute this ink spot of a brain was, with its two huge white eyes, but he still preferred to talk to Spike. In order for Spike to start moving, this time N.I.T. had to go back into his head.

Slammer agreed to keep a closer eye on Spike.

"Okay, no problem."

Then he added, "Will you please get back into his head! I don't like to see him like that."

"Why not?"

"Because he looks like he's dead."

As N.I.T. flew back into Spike's head, he looked at Slammer and mumbled, "That's not a bad idea."

Slammer felt that he had to comment on that. "I know you don't mean that but you sure sound like you hate him."

N.I.T. popped out of Spike's ear and flew straight for Slammer's head of hair, grabbed it and like a monkey, swung onto the top of his nose and looked him in the eyes.

"You know I love him. But really, would *you* choose that skeleton for your body?" he answered, pointing to Spike who was now bumping into the walls like he was drunk. And in a flash N.I.T. was back inside Spike's skull.

Spike stopped walking into things and immediately said to Slammer,

"We can't get the clearance to lift off without the proper documents."

Then he added, "You know, I really believe that this ship is fast enough and has enough gadgets to take off before we can be stopped."

"What do you suggest, Spike?"

"Why don't you go outside and see if Jane is in sight?"

"Okay. But I have a bad feeling. You stay where you are and be ready for a fast takeoff."

As soon as he stepped out onto the platform, Slammer could see Jane, Franky and Ragrezy in the distance walking toward him. Everything seemed too quiet for Slammer. He could feel that something was wrong. The large open area with buildings here and there gave the place an eerie and dangerous feeling. Slammer saw shadows coming from the buildings and waved for Jane to hurry up and look behind her. She didn't even have to look. She realized that something was wrong. Jane immediately started running with the rest of her crew following right behind. Chasing them were Bobby Joe and dozens of government agents who seemed to be popping out of nowhere.

Bobby Joe started running toward Jane while hollering,

"Hold the ship. Don't let it leave!"

He knew that if Slammer left, he'd never see him again. Bobby Joe was not about to let Slammer leave with his winnings and he was still mad that he had lost his two bulls to Slammer.

Jane, like a natural leader was the last to enter the ship. By the time the door closed, she and the crew were strapped in their seats, ready for takeoff. Within seconds, the tip of the rocket ship was covered with government men. They had their weapons pointed at the crew, warning them not to touch the ignition. The crew wasn't sure if the enemy bullets could penetrate the ship's glass since they weren't regular ammunition but technologically propelled nanobot bullets. There were a lot of threats and shouting.

Jane pressed a button and when she looked up, the G-men were now yelling, "Look out," as they were swept off the rocket ship by things that resembled windshield wipers. Franky pushed the ignition button and they were off. Once they got into space, the ship went into hyper speed. It took about an hour to arrive on the *Planet of the Cleaning Bugs,* their first stop on the mission to rescue Roxy.

The hour passed, as if it were seconds. When the *Bug Planet* was close enough to see, everyone stood and looked out of the control room's glass windows. From the distance the *Bug Planet* looked like a world made up of a desert with dunes. As they got closer, they could see the sand move as though it were an ocean. Every once in a while, a wave seemed to develop eyes that searched the horizon and then vanished as fast as they appeared. It was as if a large rock-like whale had popped its head out of the sand ocean to see what might be flying around within its reach.

"Are you sure it's safe to land?" Spike asked Jane and then added, "Won't we sink? There's no land, only sand that moves."

"Don't worry," she reassured him. "The planet is as solid as a rock. Only the Cleaning Bugs can move that freely in the sand."

Spike looked for a place to land. There was none in sight.

"Where are we going to land?" Spike asked Jane.

Jane wanted to tease Spike a bit. So, with a bit of a giggle she said, "Are you worried that we might crash, Spike?"

A bit unsure how to answer, Spike gasped, "Don't talk like that."

"Easy does it Spike. Rocky and I have already communicated and he has already prepared everything. Why don't you look down again, Spike?"

"My goodness, Jane! How did you do that?" Spike reacted with amazement in his voice.

"Look," pointing to a smooth glassy platform, "That wasn't there a second ago."

Their landing went smoothly. Rocky's Mother and Father, plus local residents, greeted Jane and her crew with enthusiasm when they came out of their ship. Jane went by herself to see Rocky. Her crew watched her walk about fifty yards when all of a sudden a rock as big as a building rose out of the ground. Her crew was happy to stay near the ship because going into what looked like a rock was an experience that they felt that they could do without…especially when the rock turned out to be an alien creature. When Slammer saw an opening appear and what looked like a large tongue come out, he prepared to run to Jane's rescue.

But before Slammer could budge, Rocky's father, as if he were a ghost, appeared next to him.

"There's no need to be concerned, Slammer. My son loves Jane and would protect her at all cost. That's my son's tongue, as you Earthlings call it, that you're looking at. That is how we let our guests know that it's okay to enter inside our body. Each one of us is equipped with the same type of tongue-walkway and inner working system."

Jane once again found herself admiring the ingenuity of this walkway. It reminded her of the first time that she had entered it. Back then she was afraid but now she looked forward to seeing her new yet old friends that resided within Rocky's body.

When Jane finished walking the length of his tongue and entered into Rocky, she was greeted by everyone like a long lost friend. Squeak was especially happy to see Jane. They greeted with hugs, sniffs and licks. The hugs were from Jane. Squeak had to sniff and lick Jane because he hoped that some evil from Earth had rubbed off on her and that he could eat it as a source of energy. After their initial hellos, things changed a bit when she asked him if he were willing to help her rescue her sister. Squeak became hysterically happy and quickly said "yes." A second later he realized what he had just agreed to and seemed to hesitate until Jane mentioned how good those evil creatures on the *Planet of Stolen Property* would taste. After that, Squeak gleamed bright red at the thought and jumped with joy. Now, all that Jane had to do was to get the okay from the Changer. Jane knew that she would have no problem with her because she liked adventures and cleaning up evil. Jane walked over to the Changer, which almost looked like a huge colorful egg. Jane stared up at her for a few seconds and then shouted, "Hello."

Just as the Changer started to open up and reveal herself, a soft sweet voice came from within and said in a melodious whisper, "Hello Jane. It's so good to see you again."

"I'm happy to see you too."

Jane watched the Changer for a second as she was opening and then continued. "I've thought about you often, about your beauty and that hypnotizing voice of yours. And how caring you were when you extracted evil from people who still had some good in them."

The Changer gleamed a bit brighter because of the compliment.

"Thank you. You know that whatever you tell Rocky, you're also telling us. But I would like to hear it for myself."

"Would you like to help me rescue my sister?" Jane asked.

"You don't have to ask such a question. Did you ever doubt that I, or any of us, would ever say anything but yes? Yes, yes of course we will help you. Besides, you know where to find good tasting evil."

Once the Changer answered Jane, everyone was ready to go.

The only problem was that Rocky wasn't thrilled with what Jane told him he would have to do if he wanted to help her rescue Roxy. The idea that he would have to shrink small enough to fit into Jane's pocket was a bit humiliating for him but he got over it when he thought about the delicious evil meals that they would enjoy.

"You be careful," Rocky's Mother told him while they were saying their goodbyes. His Mother didn't want to let him go. But Rocky, even though he was hundreds of years old, was still a young man as far as his Mom was concerned.

He tried to reassure her and said,

"I'm not a kid now, Mom. I'm a provider."

"Yes you are, Son," she proudly told him and then kissed him good-bye on his cheek.

Meanwhile Rocky's Father was talking to Jane.

"Jane, there is something that I want you to do for me and my planet. In return, you will be protected from evil."

"What is it, Mr. Rocky? Whatever you need is okay with me."

He told Jane to place her hand on his head. As soon as she did, she grinned from ear to ear.

"What was that wonderful feeling?"

"Jane, I have just given you the power to do what no other creatures in the galaxy other than us can do."

"You gave me some sort of power?"

"You could say that, but I really only enhanced what you already have. Jane, you can sense evil and good in a way that no one has been able to for as long as we have existed. Besides my race, you are the only one who can feel and then identify someone or something 100% evil. Because of this ability, if you encounter complete evil, whether it be a planet, ship or person, all you have to do is think of *us* and that person, place or thing will vanish from wherever you are and come straight to us. We will drain all of the evil and be energized."

"What will happen to what's left after you drain the evil?"

"There's never anything left when it's total evil. It disintegrates like dust in the wind. Only an empty planet remains," Mr. Rocky answered quietly.

Once all of the plans for the trip were made, it was time to leave. There was no need for a big send off. Jane thanked Rocky's parents for letting him come with her and waited for Squeak, who had a big grin on his face, to say his goodbyes.

Rocky, with Squeak and the Changer inside him, shrank in size and floated into Jane's pocket as she entered into the spaceship where the crew was waiting.

Once inside the ship, Jane found a spot where everyone could see each other.

"Hey boys!" she shouted.

"A friend of mine, who will soon be yours as well, is with me and I want to introduce you."

Slammer looked around and exclaimed. "Nobody is with you! Jane, did you get hit on the head by a rock?"

"That's very funny," Ragrezy commented and then snickered sarcastically, "What are you saying, Jane? Is your friend in your pocket?"

Everyone started laughing. They had heard about the Cleaning Bugs but didn't know a thing about them. The next thing that came out of Jane's mouth freaked them out.

"Look down, guys. Here's my friend and our newest participant in the rescue," she said as she put something on the ground.

They stopped laughing. They thought that perhaps the aliens had done something to her.

Franky walked over to Slammer and Ragrezy. Spike quickly joined them. They were watching Jane very intensely. They didn't know what she would do or say next.

Franky, unaware of what he was doing, started talking, almost to himself

"Did she just say that the rock that she took out of her pocket and put on the floor is her friend and that he is going to help us rescue Roxy?"

"I hate to answer that," Slammer replied. "But I think that is what she said and that she means it."

Spike added in a questioning manner, "It's just a rock, right?"

"Look fellas," Jane began. "I wanted to tell you about Rocky but you never would have believed me. I figured that it was best for you to see for yourselves."

"See what?" Spike shouted.

She pointed to the rock, "my friend Rocky."

The guys looked at each other. "Has she gone to the cuckoo birds?" Spike asked.

"The only thing cuckoo in here is you, Spike. This is Rocky. He is a Cleaning Bug and one of the sons of the planet's leader. He is also one of the *Bug Planet's* representatives. I am going to tell him to reveal himself. So, don't freak out."

They looked at the rock for a minute.

"Nothing is happening," Franky commented.

"Okay," Jane urged. "Rocky! Come on and show them who you are."

Everyone just looked at the rock and just as Spike was about to say something, everyone but Jane nearly jumped out of his skin.

They stared at Rocky with their mouths open, unable to move.

Jane's crew had no idea about the type of powers that the Cleaning Bugs had. They didn't know anything about their ability to fly or to communicate telepathically. Now they were about to witness something even more amazing.

Two seconds before, they were looking at Rocky and seeing only a rock. Suddenly, that rock swelled and then popped up to the size of a big doghouse. As if that weren't enough to freak them out, they heard a voice coming from inside of it.

"We would like more room, Rocky."

All four crewmembers jumped back another time when Rocky popped up again and became twice the size.

Rocky opened his eyes and mouth. As his tongue rolled out, the Changer floated out of his mouth with Squeak sitting on her shoulder.

"Say hello to Rocky," Jane continued.

"This is the Changer and on her shoulder is Squeak. He's an Angel-scorp."

Rocky was greeted personally by every crewmember.

Slammer, Ragrezy and Franky immediately wanted to play with Squeak. They asked Jane at the same time, "Can I have that toy?"

Squeak heard what they said and immediately flew to Jane's shoulder, hid behind her ear and whispered, "You're not going to give me to those three guys, are you?"

Jane started laughing. "Of course not, Squeak. You're not mine to give and if you were, I would never do such a thing. It would be like giving my own blood away. Isn't that right, Changer?"

"You're absolutely correct," the Changer very studiously remarked.

"You're not kidding," Rocky commented. "They're my blood supply and nobody gives my blood away!"

Then he rolled up his tongue with the Changer on it and carefully closed his mouth. Squeak stayed near Jane.

"Don't worry, guys," Jane said reassuringly. "The Changer will come out if we need her."

It took about ten minutes before the ship could leave. That was all the time they needed to bond and become like a family. They finally lifted off and were on their way.

When the ship was already far away, Rocky's Mom and Dad started communicating telepathically with each other about how beautiful the ship looked from afar. This was their normal way of talking to each other. They remarked how, with the background of the dark universe as a canvas, the beauty of the ship's shiny silver, falcon-like shape was enhanced even more. And just when Rocky's parents thought that it couldn't get any prettier, a group of shooting stars passed by, leaving behind sparks of flames to embellish the beauty of a ship that was already beautiful.

Jane and her crew were approaching the planet *Krim*, a place known for hiding criminals. She knew that Slammer used to stop there to get maintenance supplies when he owned this particular spaceship which at one time had more breakdowns than a break-dancer whom she had once seen on the streets of NYC. Now that it had been remodeled and Jane didn't have to find parts for repairs, they could pass by *Krim* and continue on their course toward the *Planet of Stolen Property*.

When they passed *Krim*, Squeak noticed that Spike was starting to slam his head against the walls. Squeak flew to Jane to find out what was wrong with Spike. Jane told him not to worry.

She turned to Spike and asked, "What's the matter with you?"

Spike tried to answer but could only stutter.

"Jane… the…the…the"

N.I.T realized that Spike was too overwrought and couldn't talk because of the threat to their safety. N.I.T. popped out of

Spike's ear and told Jane that a spaceship was about to attack them. Because N.I.T. had to warn Jane and the crew, he didn't take the appropriate steps to make Spike motionless before appearing. The result was terrible: Spike was stumbling into things like a bug that had been sprayed but not killed.

Just then Spike wrapped his arms around Jane and hung onto her neck.

Jane grabbed Spike by the shoulders, held him out in front of her and quickly said, "Spike, I know what's wrong. Just stand still."

As N.I.T. prepared to fly into Spike's head, he said,

"Jane. Spike has some loose nails on his head. As soon as I get back into his skull, tap his head gently against a wall and the nails will automatically tighten up. Then I can once again have some control over his actions."

Once Jane tapped Spike's head against a near-by column, he hollered. "Franky! Slammer! Get ready for battle. Jane! Pirates are going to be on top of us in five minutes."

Now that Spike was functioning again, Jane released him. He immediately ran straight to the control panel and programmed the ship to maneuver out of the way, if they were attacked. Jane was looking out of the ship's control room window at the *Krim* battle ship as it approached. She wanted to avoid the ship but knew that it would be impossible and that her crew would have to outsmart the enemy if they were to avoid the Krims' attack. After all, those monsters were known for robbing and killing. Their battleship was many times larger than Jane's, with a sharp pointy design that made it look very sinister.

Jane was staring at the ship when over the intercom she heard a voice say, "I am Captain Scuz, the ship's commander."

Jane told Franky to put the Captain up on the screen. It wasn't long before his enormous body appeared there. Scuz was six foot four and weighed about four hundred pounds. He was ugly. His large round head was covered with uneven, short, spiky, greasy black hair. His features were severe and twisted. And his beady black eyes and thin pale lips didn't help his appearance.

Captain Scuz looked at his screen and saw Jane sitting on the captain's chair. He and his crew did a double take and started to laugh. Captain Scuz was still laughing when he said, "Okay, the joke's over now. Take that child away. I demand to speak to the captain."

Jane stood up, introduced herself and then said very defiantly, "What do you mutts want?"

The captain looked at his crew and spoke to them in their language so Jane wouldn't understand.

"Those dumb Earthlings have a child for a captain. How stupid of them and easy for us!"

Then he answered Jane in English, "I'll tell you what I want, you arrogant little pipsqueak. I want whatever you have, of course,"

"I can't agree to anything until I speak to my adviser."

She turned around and called Spike over to her. Jane put her hand on his shoulder and pulled him toward her so that she could whisper her instructions.

"I know that you love me but you have to smack me."

Spike looked at her with disbelief and said, "What?"

Jane was about to repeat her instructions when without any warning, Spike smacked her, sending her reeling back a foot.

Slammer and Ragrezy didn't understand what had just

happened but they trusted Spike and Jane and so they did not take any action against Spike. However, they wanted to attack the Krims' ship but Jane stopped them with an almost unseen motion of her hand. Her crew didn't know that Jane wanted to make Captain Scuz even more confident than he already was and let him think that she was incompetent and that he could conquer them with almost no effort.

And it was working. Captain Scuz was bragging to his crew how easy things were because he was in charge. Then he pointed to the screen.

"Look at that. She has a scarecrow for an adviser. This is easy picking. Let's have some fun."

His idea of fun was scaring other species to death whenever possible. If that approach didn't work, he and his crew would torture and rob and then kill them.

Scuz wanted to scare Jane and began getting belligerent.

"Hey! You! Captain Squirt."

Jane stood up and looked at him and his crew.

Scuz pointed to some buttons on his control panel.

"Do you see this red button? If you don't do as I say, I will press it and all of you will disintegrate."

He paused, turned to his crew and continued talking. Jane knew that with his ego he needed an audience. Scuz went on and on and when he finally finished talking, his crew glanced at one another, as if to say, "Thank heavens! He finally shut up!" While Scuz was threatening her and talking to his crew, Jane pretended to be scared, giving her crew time to get the upper hand.

Scuz looked at the screen and said,

"Jane, I see that you're scared and this makes me happy.

Because you're a kid and you're afraid, I'm going to make you this one time offer: Give us everything that you have. If you don't, we'll torture you first, take everything that you've got and then blow you up."

Jane took a deep breath and replied. "I have a much better deal for you, if you're willing to listen. I have a chest full of treasures from the *Mineral Planet*."

Scuz had heard about that planet and realized that very few people knew about it, where it was or how to reach it.

"Will you accept my offer?" Jane asked with an attitude of not caring, hoping to throw the captain off track.

"What if I just torture you until you tell me where the planet is?"

"Let me put it this way. If you don't agree with my offer and you're going to kill us anyway, then we will blow everything up and take you with us."

"You Earth children just don't care, do you?"

"You give us no choice, Captain Scuz. Besides once you see what is in this treasure chest, you will never want for anything else again. Do we have a deal?"

With much skepticism Captain Scuz agreed.

Jane instructed her crew to act normally and go about their routine. She ordered Spike to land on the bay of the Krim's battleship. Spike got on the intercom and asked Scuz to open the bay so that they could dock. Scuz didn't trust Jane so he demanded that she and her crew stay in the control room where he could keep his eye on them. Jane turned off the sound and told Franky that when she yelled, he should pull down the lever next to him and stay there.

When Scuz realized that the intercom was shut off, he

started jumping up and down and screaming. He threatened Jane that if he couldn't hear her in the next thirty seconds, all deals would be off and he would kill them all. Jane turned the sound on and said that something had gone wrong with the intercom and then apologized.

Slammer, Franky, Ragrezy and Spike all knew what to do.

When their ship docked, Jane knew that if she timed it right, they would still be able to escape. When the ship's door opened, Slammer carried out a chest of treasures and put the chest on the ground. Scuz and his men were about fifty yards away from Jane's ship, standing on the entrance of the landing bay. When Slammer got close enough, he kicked the chest right at them. The Krims were so surprised that they didn't have time to react. Slammer broke into a run and headed inside his ship. As they were shooting at him, the chest exploded into a cloud of smoke. The RoxyResk's take off was timed just right. When the smoke cleared, the ship had already shot out like lightning. The RoxyResk, with Jane and her crew aboard, was out of sight when Jane suddenly remembered what Rocky's Dad had told her before she left his planet. It took her less than a second to identify all of the Krim evil and telepathically transfer the information to Rocky's Dad. Before Scuz realized that the smoking chest also contained a few timed explosions, Rocky's Dad and a group of the Cleaning Bugs were in the Krim ship where they happily shared a Krim appetizer. They left as quickly as they came and then the Krim's battle ship blew up.

Jane and her crew were far enough away that the blast didn't affect them.

"That was a smart plan you had,' Franky told Jane.

"Yeh, they never saw you coming, huh, Jane?" Spike

commented.

"Nice thinking," Ragrezy said to her.

Slammer picked up Jane, put her on his right shoulder and said to the crew,

"Three cheers for Jane."

As the cheering started, Rocky flew out of Jane's shirt pocket, with the Changer on his back and shouted three times, "three cheers for Jane." A second later, he returned to her pocket as if nothing had ever happened.

"Thank you fellows! Keep in mind that it was a united effort. So, three cheers to all of you from me." They congratulated each other and bonded a bit more.

A few minutes later the crew heard Jane's voice on the intercom.

"Let's get the hell out of here!"

An hour later they arrived on the *Planet of Stolen Property*.

It wasn't so easy for Jane and her crew to get the okay to land on the *Planet of Stolen Property*. For safety reasons, they first had to dock on the Space Interrogation Center where the planet's Administrator checked their papers and collected various fees. It took a couple of minutes for the Administrator to reach the web cam and when he did, he saw Jane looking at the screen and waiting for him. He stepped in front of the web cam so that Jane could see him. She saw a large man with long black hair and eyes that at times changed their shape and structure.

Jane was surprised when she heard him say her name.

"Hello, Jane."

Her immediate response was, "How do you know me?"

"Everybody knows you, by now. Don't you realize that this is a small universe?"

"Not for me," Jane replied. "Now tell me. Who are you?"

"I'm called Zinngy. I'm the man who is going to check your papers, so you'd better be nice. Scan me a copy of your paper work and take care of your fees." All of this was done electronically and only took a minute. Once everything was straightened out, Jane looked at Zinngy and said,

"I don't know what you've heard about me Zinngy but I would sure appreciate it if you would tell me where I could find my sister Roxy."

"I don't know Jane but for the right price, I will allow you and your crew to search the planet."

She had no choice but to keep it friendly and scanned "under-the-table" money just for the Administrator's pockets. Even though she had just been "legally" robbed, she waved goodbye and with a big forced smile said, "Thank you, Mr. Administrator" and headed for the planet.

While descending toward their destination, Spike tapped Slammer's arm and pointed to something.

"Do you see those mollusk-like buildings? Don't they look like upside down squid and their windows like the squid's suction cups? Even the dark smoke spouting out of the tops of the buildings resembles their inky waste. Boy, you can even see various types of life forms residing there."

Spike paused, waiting for an answer and when he couldn't wait any longer (which was less than two seconds,) he anxiously asked.

"Well, can you see what I'm talking about?"

Slammer had already seen what Spike pointed out. "Yes, I

saw it," and then he gestured and said,

"Do you see that area over there? It's about ten thousand miles away from what you were looking at. That part of the country is mostly marshes with willow trees hiding all sorts of native animals and some that aren't originally from this particular planet. Do you see that beast chasing that herd of animals?" Slammer asked.

Spike glanced toward it and wanted a better look. He asked for a pair of binoculars.

"Here, use mine," Ragrezy said. "I've seen this before."

"Thank you," Spike replied. Then he looked through the binoculars and started talking.

"Ragrezy, look at those beasts run!" Spike said, showing his excitement and enthusiasm for this new experience.

Then he turned toward Slammer. "Hey, look! Those beasts are the size of elephants and they have six big bull-like horns, strategically placed on their heads for maximum damage."

By this time Jane, Franky and Rocky had seen the planet and found the conversation between Slammer, Ragrezy and Spike more interesting.

Spike was in the middle of an observation when the trio turned in his direction.

"Did you also notice how their trunks resemble scorpions' stingers?"

Jane couldn't resist and asked, "Do you know if their trunks are poisonous?"

To everyone's surprise, Rocky, who was now in a corner and still shrunken to the size of a small rock, suddenly grew to five foot and answered in a very knowledgeable voice.

The Planet of the Cleaning Bugs 129

"They are very friendly animals and yes, their snouts squirt and spray deadly liquids, but only when they are provoked."

"Hey, Spike." Ragrezy asked. "What do you think they're running from?"

"I thought they were playing," he replied.

"Why don't you just keep looking?"

Spike continued looking and still only saw the beasts running.

He started to put the binoculars down but Slammer told him to give it another minute.

"I sure ho...." but before Spike could finish the word "hope," he dropped the binoculars and jumped back a foot or so.

"Did you see what just happened? What the heck is that creature?"

"It's a Beast Snapper," Ragrezy volunteered. "You just witnessed an event that is rarely seen."

A bit shaken, Spike said, "First, all I saw were beautiful wild beasts running and enjoying life. The next thing these poor beasts knew was that they were running on what seemed to be ground but turned out to be the open mouth of a flat clam-like animal. Then, I saw one half of something slam down and immediately start eating the beautiful beasts. This thing that you call the Beast Snapper looked like a small mountain when it closed its mouth but as it was chewing, it seemed to just disappear into what was really the ground."

Before anyone could answer Spike, the RoxyResk approached the planet and a round landing platform lit up. They were excited to see where they were going to land. From the sky they saw many landing pads. Each one had a different color to help the ships to identify which one was theirs. From the distance, the movements and the heat that were produced from and around the platform made the landing spots look like different colored rings of fire. Their landing pad was a bright light blue. Since they were still very high and looking down, they could see that the *Planet of Stolen Property* was a mess. There were dome-covered cities scattered throughout the planet and they all looked like scrap yards. However, there was one bright spot on this ugly planet and it was controlled by the All-for-One-Man. Most of his city was like Las Vegas, bright and alive, with lots of lights and crime. Its dome was made out of a special glass that never got dirty or broken.

Jane could see his whole city, divided into four distinctive sections, with a landing circle in the middle. This was where all outsiders like she and her crew would land.

"Jane!" Spike shouted, from the control section of the ship. "I have Agent Sachee on the screen."

Jane walked over to the screen so that they could see each other. Showing a serious side, Jane said,

"Hello, Agent Sachee. I was led to believe that we could land and that you would provide the proper arrangements for us so that we can visit your lovely planet for a bit."

"Of course, of course, my child."

He looked at the paper pad that he was writing on and told Jane,

"That will be fifty thousand dollars to cover landing taxes and one hundred thousand for the landing itself with a week's worth of parking."

Slammer straightened up and puffed out his chest, ready to beat Sachee into a tax coma. Jane signaled him to behave and said,

"But we're only going to be here for a day or so."

Jane, in her own way, was protesting with looks and showing her disapproval of how this planet did business. She didn't like being robbed again but there was no other way. In order for her to avoid the aggravation of such an injustice and to be able to cope with it, she started thinking of the cost as the price of a ticket for the admission to a new adventure and all that it had to offer.

All of a sudden, she found herself smiling, paying what was necessary and thinking of how lucky she was that Slammer had gotten rich and that he didn't mind helping her to make up for the wrong that he and Spike had done to her a few years back.

Once all transactions were finished, the RoxyResk landed and everyone got out. Now all they had to do was decide where they wanted to go. Spike had grown very fond of Jane and wanted to stay close to her. He realized that she had a plan and plans usually brought trouble. Spike wanted to be there so that he could protect her. Of course, he knew that wherever he went, Slammer would follow He also realized that Slammer would protect them both, making him a hero. At least that's how he liked to look at it.

"Where you are going Jane?" Spike asked.

"Don't you mean...where are *we* going?" she replied.

This put a big smile on Spike's face and the faces of the other three crewmembers.

Jane continued, "Let's get a cab. I booked rooms in a nice hotel across from this landing station."

The next thing she heard was Franky calling her. She

looked toward the street and saw that he was standing next to a cab, holding the door open for her and the crew to get in.

"Take us to Bright Side Lane," Jane told the driver. Five minutes later they were getting out of a cab and entering a luxurious hotel, at least for that part of the outer city.

"This is an expensive place, Jane. How can you afford it?"

"Oh, that's easy, Spike. I'm spending your money."

He just looked at her and said, "I have money?"

"Yes, you do. Slammer made sure of that. You're very rich now."

He jumped happily and very excitedly said, "I saw a chocolate store in a magazine. Can I have it?"

"For what? You can't run a chocolate store."

Spike looked at Jane. "I don't want to run it. I want to eat it."

Franky, Slammer, Ragrezy and Jane found it funny and laughed aloud. Spike didn't get the joke.

Then Jane said, "Franky, I need to go and see someone. Why don't you and the crew check into your rooms? I'll be back later."

The *Planet of Stolen Property* was controlled by the All-for-One-Man, a disgusting creature made up of three separate evil characters. Everyone feared him because of his three different personalities and their powers. Mr. Evil was a tall, thin man with a mustache, a top hat and a long raincoat. Mr. Happy was a bit shorter, huskier, and always laughing and playing tricks on people. The third, Mr. Brain consisted mainly of a head, with barely a body, arms, or legs. Most of the time, all three would be contained in the All-for-One-Man who usually had the features of Mr. Evil because this was his dominant personality. Every once in a while he would actually show his three separate but physically connected entities. The All-for-One-Man truly exemplified multiple personalities. One minute, Mr. Happy would be laughing while drinking with a friend; if he didn't like what he heard, Mr. Evil would pop out, shrinking his body to two thirds of its size. As Mr. Evil started beating the hell out of his companion, Mr. Brain would pop out and try to reason with both of the other two personalities. It was strange to watch as one body divided into three and then came back together when the problem was solved.

The All-for-One-Man designed his city like an apple pie cut into four slices. There were four distinctive towns, each with its own purpose. The first was Happy Town, where creatures came to re-experience childhood memories and childish dreams. The second was Evil Town where Hell showed its fury. The third was Brain Town, where geniuses came to compete in mental games and plot their takeovers of planets and moons, or just about anything that could make them money. Finally, there was Economic Town, where world business was dealt with, industrial services existed and parts for spaceships were found and repairs done. The outer perimeters were protected by walls. The middle of the city was circular, like the mound of apple that could be seen in the center of the pie. This was the section where spaceships landed and voyagers boarded or exited the spaceships.

Visitors could enter the different towns of the All-for-One-Man's metropolis through the outer, middle part of that circle. The entire center of the city was surrounded by a beautifully sculptured, twenty-foot high wrought iron fence. People were amazed the first time they entered through the gate. Who wouldn't be when the gate would change shape and say, "Here's your pass. Now where is your ticket?" The four towns were divided by a three hundred foot wide water way. The outer part of each town stretched for miles. Anyone looking down from the sky could see the distinctive separation of each town and with the lights on at night it looked like a twenty-five mile, multicolored fruit pie sliced into four segments.

Jane and her crew had the night off to do whatever they wanted. The guys wanted to start their search for Roxy the next day but Jane couldn't wait until then to begin looking for her sister. She wanted to do something now. Jane wasn't a selfish girl and so, she figured that whatever she was going to do shouldn't interfere with her crew's night off. She took a few steps and Franky gently put his hand on her arm. Ragrezy and Slammer were nowhere in sight.

"Jane, I'm really sorry about that big mistake I made. Are you still mad at me?"

"Franky. That was a while ago. I'm not mad at you. You're my friend, aren't you?"

"Of course I am and that's why I want you to know that you shouldn't go anywhere alone. This is a dangerous planet."

"It's okay Franky. I'm a big girl now."

Franky told her what he knew about the city. But before going his own way, he had to ask,

"Jane, are you sure that you don't want me to come with you? This is a very dangerous place."

"I know," she answered, "that's why they call it Evil Town."

Jane needed to go to the meanest part of the city on her own. She didn't want to be considered or looked upon as a female. She was the Captain. Evil Town was where she had to go and that was where she was going. She didn't need any man's protection. She did her own butt kicking.

She thanked him for his concern, told him to have a good time and then she started to leave.

Squeak came flying out of Jane's pocket and clung to her neck.

Before leaving the ship, Jane had taken Rocky out of her pocket. They agreed that he should stay and watch the ship. But then Squeak hollered, "Let me out" and Rocky opened his mouth. Before Jane could react, Squeak was in her pocket. He looked at Rocky and said, "I want to go with Jane." Rocky knew that Squeak wanted to go with her for the company and adventure and that of course, he hoped that she would run into some evil people or creatures for him to feed on.

"I'm coming with you, right?"

"Of course," Jane replied. "Remember, Squeak. I promised Rocky and the Changer that I would take good care of you. We have a bit of a walk until we get to Evil Town. Now tell me, what's on your mind?"

Once Squeak started talking, he continually described the varieties of different flavored evil. Walking to Evil Town was in itself a danger. While Squeak was babbling on, Jane realized that she also needed to be aware of her surroundings and of what was going on. She told Squeak to get back into her pocket and to be quiet. About five minutes into their walk, Jane began feeling as though she were being followed. She turned around and to her surprise, Slammer, Franky, and Ragrezy were right behind her. Jane asked them why and they said that they wanted to keep her safe and help her find Roxy.

Slammer told Jane that Spike and N.I.T. also wanted to join them later. But first they had to decide where they would spend their free time.

"The last time I saw them, N.I.T. was swinging on different

parts of Spike's face, trying to convince him that he wanted to visit Brain Town while Spike kept repeating that he wanted to go to Happy Town. I wasn't going to hang around until they came to some compromise, and so, here I am."

"Do they know the time that they have to be back at the ship?" Jane asked.

"Spike has never missed a deadline," Slammer commented. "N.I.T makes sure of that."

When Jane, Slammer, Franky and Ragrezy arrived at the gate of Evil Town, they weren't sure of what to do because the gate was locked and there was nobody there. All four of them turned to see if there was some other way in.

"Now what are we going to do?" Franky asked. But before anyone could say a word, they heard a voice behind them say,

"You can show me your papers and then be on your way." Then the voice grumbled impatiently, "Hey, let's go. Can't you see that I'm busy here?"

The voice paused until Jane and her crew turned around. Their faces showed their surprise at what they saw. It was like magic. One minute there was just a huge, rounded, locked, wrought iron gate. The next minute, there was a magnificent looking guard standing there. He was about seven feet tall and strangely enough, he was made out of the same material as the gate. Next to him was a wrought iron table that had a wrought iron computer sitting on it. Jane and her crew didn't know how to react so they just stood there and stared.

About ten seconds later the guard shouted, "Let's go. I don't have all night. Can't you see that being a gate is a twenty four hour a day job? Now hurry up."

Jane and her crew didn't know what to say and so they

showed their IDs to the guard who unbelievably was also the gate. After everything was checked out, the guard who was the talking part of the gate wished them all good luck. Squeak popped out, landed on her shoulder and asked Jane what the guard meant by "good luck." She told him that he just wanted them to have fun. She didn't want to tell him that what the guard really meant was "good luck coming out alive." The guard turned back into the gate, opened for them to pass through and then closed.

When they were about five blocks into the town, they ran into a local youth gang having their own kind of fun. They surrounded Jane, Franky, Slammer, and Ragrezy. One of the thieves stepped up and said, "Give us your money or you're dead." While this was happening, Squeak was trying to get Jane's attention to tell her that he was hungry and that each one would make a good meal. Jane was too busy trying to figure out how to get out of this mess to pay attention to Squeak and so she ignored him. She and her crew were prepared to fight. They formed a circle but they were outnumbered four to one. Jane's circle was shrinking with the slow advancement of the gang. Squeak finally had enough. He flew off Jane's shoulder and grew to five times his size. Before anyone knew what happened, Squeak was feeding on the leader of the gang. The rest of them never ran so fast. When it was all over, Jane and the crew looked at Squeak with surprise and admiration and said, "Nice going!" Jane hugged and kissed Squeak and his head began glowing with happy colors. Jane asked Squeak what happened to the gang leader that he sucked up.

"Don't worry, Jane. When we get back to the ship, the Changer and Rocky will restore all of my meals."

"I don't understand what that means."

Squeak got serious. "It means that he has been shrunk to a microscopic size. I will be using his evil energy, and when I get back to Rocky and the Changer, all three of us will finish the process of cleaning him up. If he can be helped, he will be returned to his home without any recollection of what happened to him. In this way he can start living his life, Evil Free." As soon as Squeak finished explaining this, he returned to Jane's shoulder and went back to talking about how good the guy he just swallowed tasted.

Jane thanked Squeak for answering her question and they continued on their way. During their walk they saw a place called the "Put It Here Malt and Soda Bar." There were many types of malt bars in Evil Town. Some had characters belonging to the era of gangsters, others to motorcycle gangs. The "Put It Here Malt and Soda Bar" combined country western music, gambling, drinking, and sometimes even fighting. Jane walked in first and everyone's eyes were fixed on Squeak who was now wrapped around Jane's neck.

Some big guy, surrounded by his bully buddies, asked Jane if she wanted to sell the odd-looking creature. She told them that he was part of her team and not for sale. When she tried to walk away, he blocked her path and said, "I'm willing to pay you for him." He realized that she wasn't going to part with him easily. Once again, in a meaner tone, he said, "Look here kid. Take my offer because that thing around your neck is going to be mine, one way or another." Squeak undraped himself from Jane's neck and hovered near her ear, as he whispered.

"Jane, go ahead. Give me to this guy so I can surprise him. He has plenty of evil food in him."

"I would love to Squeak but now it's about the principle of

the thing. I don't let anyone bully me around."

"What did that bug just say to you?" The big bully asked Jane.

"He said that you would make a good meal." Then she added, "Did you just call him a bug? He doesn't like that and neither do I." Then she stepped closer to him and punched him in the stomach. The guy didn't budge. In fact he even started laughing, Jane was now so mad that she flew toward his face and punched him in his throat. He fell back a couple of steps. The blow didn't faze him much except for the embarrassment that he felt as his buddies started laughing at him. The big bully stepped toward Jane.

"You shouldn't have done that. Now…no more Mr. Nice-Guy!"

He reached out to grab her but she wasn't worried. When he was an inch away from her neck and anxious to snap it, Slammer grabbed his arm and flung him across a table and into a wall. This started a fight that lasted a while. Slammer was pulverizing this bully while Ragrezy was doing the same to his buddies. Franky and Jane were fighting other bullies side by side and holding their own. With everything that was going on, no one noticed that the crowd in the bar was thinning out as though people were vanishing, and they were.

Once everything was over, Jane saw why the place was emptying out. Squeak was having the time of his life sucking up all those whom he felt were evil and making them disappear. Jane picked him up, shook him and told him that he had to stop doing that.

"There won't be anyone left to question if you eat everyone in here."

"Oh. I'm sorry, Jane. I was very hungry and I was just

trying to help. Besides when I get back home, they will be better creatures and I will have provided some energy for my planet."

The owner of the "Put It Here Malt and Soda Bar" looked around his bar and told Jane that she and her crew weren't welcome there anymore.

Meanwhile, in another part of town, N.I.T. was holding onto Spike's hair like it was a rope and swinging back and forth from his ear to his nose.

"Look, you ignoramus," N.I.T. said impatiently, while perched on Spike's nose. "We're going to Brain Town first! How can I be happy if I don't win the *Alpha One, The Brain Game* Competition? All I want to do is play one game. After that, we can spend the rest of the night in Happy Town. Okay?"

"Okay," Spike muttered, putting his enthusiasm for going to Happy Town on the back burner. Then, almost like a warning he added, "You'd better win the first game because I'm not staying for a second one!"

Spike didn't have the patience to sit through a Brain game but promised N.I.T. that he would do his best.

In order for N.I.T. to play the *Alpha One, The Brain Game*, he needed to get back into Spike's head, through a hole under his ear. Spike began to get jittery right away and started complaining.

"Why is it taking so long for you to join the competition?"

N.I.T. simply said, "Shut up!"

Spike walked to the Entertainment Center, where the competition was being held. He sat in a corner, looking very out of place with his spiked head and jittery manner. After a few minutes of fidgeting, Spike asked.

"When is this game going to start?"

N.I.T. once again popped out of his ear, sat on Spike's nose, looked at him and said,

"Weren't you supposed to behave yourself?"

A second later N.I.T. jumped in excitement as he heard the announcement for the game come over the intercom.

"Hurry, hurry," N.I.T. told Spike as he flew through his ear, back into his head.

When N.I.T. heard his name called over the loud speaker, he had to act fast. He sat on the chair of Spike's mind and took control of his body.

N.I.T. needed to maintain some decorum and dignity and so, Spike suddenly became very dashing and quite a sight to look at, distinguished and calm, in his tuxedo and top hat.

The crowd cheered as he entered the walkway leading to the stage area, which was filled with famous "brains" waiting for the competition. N.I.T. had a hard job ahead of him. He had to win the game while controlling Spike and making sure that he behaved himself.

Crossing the walkway while crowds were cheering gave Spike a good ego boost. But when N.I.T. saw whom he was playing against, he made sure that Spike was serious.

N.I.T.'s competition was a lady called Mrs. Complex. She was an impressive looking, giant-like woman, almost six foot five, with very broad shoulders and webbed hands. Her whole head looked like that of a dolphin, her entire scull was made of transparent material and she had the eyes of a woman. The really great thing was watching Mrs. Complex think. Besides having wall-to-wall computers in her head, she also had creatures. These multicolored, ant-like bugs jumped from place to place in her scull as sparks of various colors appeared. And when she spoke, everyone could see her mind at work.

N.I.T. bowed to Mrs. Complex, told her that she looked nice and wished her good luck. Before N.I.T. could react, Spike told Mrs. Complex that he had every intention of beating her. N.I.T. popped out of Spike's ear, grabbed his hair and began swinging back and forth, smacking his face. He told him that if he had to come out of his head one more time, he wouldn't get to go to Happy Town. Then N.I.T. returned to his place in Spike's head, made Spike apologize for his behavior and then pull out the chair for Mrs. Complex. She thanked him and wished him good luck. The time had come to begin.

The announcer began to explain the rules of the game over the loudspeaker.

"The object of *Alpha One, The Brain Game* is to make money. But that's not the important part. It's the part that would make someone say, 'Keep the money. I just want to play because when I win the game, I will have the honor of being called the Brain,' that is, of course if he is given the chance to play."

The announcer continued after a melodramatic pause.

"Each player gets to spin the wheel twice. The first spin is for a letter and the second is for a number. Each word must start with the letter that the arrow lands on in order for the word to have a money value. And the number will be how many words must be used in the sentence, before time runs out, which in this case is a minute. Each sentence must make sense. For example, if a contestant lands on the letter M and the number eight, he has to create a sentence with at least eight words, each beginning with the letter M. If he succeeds, then each word is worth $1,000. If the sentence has some words that do not begin with an M, these words have no monetary value and the words that begin with an M are only worth $100 each. If the contestant merely calls out random words beginning with an M, each word is worth only $10."

N.I.T., being a real gentleman, made Spike say that Mrs. Complex could go first.

The competition between them was so fierce that when it came to the final spin for each of them, they were even in the amount of winnings. This was the last play. N.I.T. reminded Spike to behave himself and not do anything stupid to cause them to lose the game.

Mrs. Complex spun first for a number and came up with a nine. Then she spun for a letter and got a W. She had one minute on the clock to create a nine or more word sentence. All of the words had to begin with a W.

She said, very confidently, "What will William want Wednesday when Wanda wears Wendy's wig?"

The crowd stood up and applauded her for once again surpassing the required number of words starting with the assigned letter W. Mrs. Complex knew the rules. If a player surpassed the required number of words starting with the letter, the extra word doubled in value. There were nine words at a thousand dollars each, plus two thousand dollars for the tenth word. That added up to Eleven Thousand Dollars!

It was time for Spike to take his two spins. Everyone was so quiet that the wheel could be heard spinning. He landed on the number eleven. Then, he took his second spin and the letter H appeared. Spike was about to say something but he froze and could only look straight ahead where a girl named Lolly was standing. The audience couldn't tell if Spike were thinking or paralyzed. Lolly was a brain groupie who loved smart people and would attend every brain competition. This was the first time that she ever saw anyone from her planet play the Brain Game. When she noticed Spike staring at her, she instantly fell in love. The same thing happened to Spike.

The room seemed to have disappeared for them. N.I.T. popped out of Spike's ear, stretched out and held on as if he were a sail. Lolly's Brain N.A.T. (short for Nail-ion Analyst Technician) popped out of Lolly's ear and imitated N.I.T.'s behavior. When their eyes made contact, a bolt of lightning flew across the room. Everyone in the place was stunned as N.I.T. and N.A.T. floated in slow motion toward one another. N.A.T. introduced herself. N.I.T. stood motionless, like a lovesick puppy.

People started looking at each other, not understanding what had just happened and asking one another if Spike were okay. The loud speaker announced that there were thirty seconds left on the clock. Then, the voice added sarcastically, "Will our challenger lose his mind? Or can he save himself?" When N.I.T. and N.A.T. heard the announcement, they flew back into their own bodies. The time kept ticking away. Lolly wished that she could help Spike but it seemed as though no one could. There were just fifteen seconds to go on the clock and Spike was still not mentally all there. When Lolly heard the last ten-second count down, she began to cry. Spike noticed that right away. Then, he heard the announcer count down five seconds, four seconds…Spike understood but was mesmerized by the fact that Lolly had a N.A.T. Then N.I.T. took control and Spike had to show off. Before the announcer could get to three seconds and counting, Spike jumped up out of his chair, stood on his head and shouted out these words, beating the three-second count.

"Harry hollered: Henry! Hurry! Help Harriet! Helen has

her hanging hoops, hiccupping Happy Hanukkah. Henry, have Hilda help her!"

Everyone's face registered shock. Mrs. Complex was truly perplexed at how quickly Spike had come up with that odd but still legitimate sentence. It not only surpassed whatever she had done but it made on impression on her. N.I.T. was ecstatic because he really wanted the admiration of the brilliant Mrs. Complex.

Just as the announcer pronounced Spike the winner, Lolly was by his side. All she wanted to do was to stick to Spike like crazy glue. This was the best thing that could have happened to him. He looked into her eyes and before she could react, he grabbed her by the hand and started rushing past everyone, shouting over and over, "We're going to Happy Town. We're going to Happy Town." Lolly had to run in order to keep up with Spike. The two of them left the Entertainment Center hand-in-hand and headed for Happy Town. Once they arrived at its entranceway, the wrought iron guard collected their fee and the doors to Spike and Lolly's paradise opened.

For Spike and Lolly, love at first sight was not a simple thing. Both bodies and both brains fell in love at the same time. It was easy for Spike and Lolly to spend time with each other.

However, N.I.T. and N.A.T. were kept separated as long as they were inside their bodies.

And yet, they were still able to communicate, through their own individual visual cortex screen.

Looking for a place to go, Spike and Lolly passed a malt bar that had computer games set up for kids to play. Some people went there to identify planets to visit and others to plan crimes that they wanted to commit. The latter had to communicate with their partners in crime on other worlds and what better place to do it, than in a computer playground? But mostly kids who enjoyed playing games hung out in that malt bar. Some did homework; others wrote novels while simultaneously playing their favorite game. Most brains, like those that lived inside Spike and Lolly, also loved playing in that establishment. This time it was Spike's turn to go where he wanted. When N.I.T. told him that he wanted to play with the computers, Spike immediately hit himself on the head with a hammer as his way of saying "no" to N.I.T. A second later, Lolly hit Spike on the head and asked him if it helped any.

"Actually, I could have done without it," he replied.

Lolly hit him again and said, "Well, I hope that one helped."

"Much better, thank you," Spike said laughingly.

They continued walking and Spike kept telling Lolly that she would love where he was taking her. They passed a few soda and malt bars. Every once in a while, N.I.T. popped out of one of Spike's ears and told him to make up his mind and pick a place. N.I.T. was annoyed because he could have been playing with the computer all this time. N.A.T. came out of Lolly's ear and agreed. As soon as Lolly pointed to the Nail-ion Malt Bar and Club, N.A.T. jumped back into Lolly's head and waited for Spike to grab her hand. She could see that Spike wanted to make her happy and in his enthusiasm, he grabbed and practically carried her across the street to the malt bar. At that moment, Lolly realized that he really was the simple genius-idiot that she thought he was.

With a big smile she said, "Let me thank you for that trip to this malt shop." Spike thought that he was going to get a kiss. And boy did he! She "kissed" him over his head with the biggest hammer she could produce and then told him not to pull her again like that.

Lolly was very giddy when she saw the huge Nail-ion Malt Bar and Club. Lolly, like Spike, was a Nail-ion and she knew that this malt bar catered to her people. It was a place where wishes and fantasies could be granted and fulfilled for the right price. It didn't cost much - just a smile and a thousand dollar admission fee.

The whole building was shielded by invisible vibration walls that let the patrons see but not hear what was happening on the other side. Fine art painted on the entrance doors matched the beauty of the red canopy that had silver enhancements on its borders. Through the doors and past the coatroom, there was a large dance floor whose beautiful cherry wood shone under the lights. There were tables to the left, set up for all sorts of games. Patrons could play cards, monopoly, chess or whatever their hearts desired. To the right of the dance floor were soda fountains and counters with stools where people could sit and be served food and drinks.

The back part of this bar and club was a bit of an eye catcher. Just picture looking into a club where, in the back of the room, there were tiers of marble steps stretching across the width of the wall. It looked like a stage. Now imagine a six-floor building, where each floor was about a foot and a half high. This was where the tiny Nail-ion Brains, one to two inches in height, hung out and kept their eyes focused on their bodies. Nail-ion bodies on the loose without their brains were known to damage themselves. They walked in front of trains or cars. They jumped into water because it looked like fun and then either drowned or were eaten by some creature swimming around them. Sometimes, the Nail-ion bodies just stood still until someone told them what to do. Every once in a while a Nail-ion would find himself being chased for robbing a bank or something equally stupid because someone told him to do it. The Brains stayed close by, watching their bodies, ready to act if they saw something alarming through the invisible vibration wall.

N.I.T. and N.A.T. said goodbye to Lolly and Spike, told them that they would be keeping an eye on them, and suggested that they behave themselves. N.I.T. and N.A.T. flew up and down the building and decided to land on the third floor balcony. The entrance to their part of the club was a bit unusual. The doors were made of gold with silver accents. The red carpet leading to the dance hall integrated with the wooden floor. N.I.T. and N.A.T. made sure that they sat where they could see Spike and Lolly. Spike looked up at N.I.T. and N.A.T. Because of the invisible wall, he thought that their two brains were so close to the edge of the building that they could fall off.

A Maitre d' with a tuxedo took them to their seats. Their waitress resembled a starfish. She wore a uniform that looked like one from the fifties. Her glasses were almost as big as she was, making her blue, blood shot eyes look like saucers. While she was taking their orders, she hiccupped a lot. As N.A.T. and N.I.T. were making their choices, the waitress pulled up a seat next to them and told them to take their time. She stretched her head toward their table. As her head dropped like a hot potato, she was out like a light and snoring like a bull. Two bouncers came from the back, grabbed the sleeping waitress and flew away. Another waitress appeared as fast as lightning. She looked like the other one but without the bloodshot eyes.

"Hi! My name is Candy and I will be serving you. Are you ready to order or would you like a minute?"

"Please bring us two ice cream malts," N.I.T. replied. They

held hands and waited for their ice cream malts to come. N.A.T. pointed to the artwork next to where they were sitting. There was an entire wall of carved picture frames, holding sketched artwork, suspended in mid air. "What a marvelous sight!" she said and then called N.I.T.'s attention to another wall made up of dozens of separate rooms. Each room had a different design. Some were the style of the Roaring Twenties; others had Walt Disney themes; some were French Victorian.

Let's leave Spike and Lolly for now to enjoy themselves and their newfound friendship.

The rest of the crew wasn't so fortunate. Jane, Slammer, Ragrezy and Franky were getting closer to finding out where Roxy was but they were also getting closer to danger. Jane was questioning the irate bartender while Slammer, Franky, and Ragrezy were about to get into another fight with some drunk. Jim, a man with a mustache, cane, and a top hat stopped the fight. Jim told Slammer that he had seen him fight in Bobby Joe's Bar.

"How would you like to make some real money fighting?" he asked.

Slammer replied, "No."

"Why not? How hard can it be? Besides, it's good exercise."

Jim told Jane that if she could get Slammer to fight just once in the ring for him and win, he would tell her where Roxy was and let her have twenty percent of the gambling take. They came to the agreement of thirty percent and that he would give her any help that she might need in order to find Roxy. Jim took Slammer to the fight ring which was in a building next to the one where Spike and Lolly were. Slammer knew that when it came to fight rings, gambling and a kidnap rescue, danger was almost always guaranteed.

It was going to be a couple of hours before Slammer was scheduled to fight. Jane decided to go to a local hangout to ask if anyone knew exactly where Roxy was being held. She found a soda bar called the Space-Em-Out Bar and Grill. It was a very popular bar, filled with many odd looking and spaced out patrons. Jane recognized a burly man named Give Me who turned out to be an old garbage-picking buddy from the streets of New York. She asked him if he knew anything about a girl named Roxy. He had never heard of her but added that there was a rumor about some new warrior girl who would be fighting in a city called the Sphere of Tears, located on the *Mine, Mine Planet*. Jane knew that this warrior girl wasn't Roxy but she thought immediately about her other sister Lisa.

Slammer's fight was about to start so Jane joined Franky and Ragrezy ringside. The place was futuristic and bright, as though the sun were illuminating the beauty of the ring. The ring was held in the sky by an invisible force field and remained still while the entire inner room rotated around the fighters, so that the spectators could have a complete view of the fight.

They hugged Slammer and wished him good luck. Jane saw what was in the ring and told Slammer that he didn't have to do this. He looked at her and said "Aw! Don't worry. He's just a big pussy cat." Then, under his breath, he muttered, "A really big, ugly pussy cat." Slammer looked at this monster of a beast, named Bullhorn and found it funny and even a bit ironic that only a short time ago he had won a bet involving two bulls. This beast had a baboon-like face and a long, brilliant red snout with yellow and blue stripes. His head was a little larger than that of a bull and his horns were much longer and thicker than those of any bull that Slammer had even seen. It didn't surprise Slammer that the beast had a bull-like body with legs as thick as those of a bull elephant. But, the oddest and most dangerous parts of this opponent were his four octopus-like tentacles, each one with a five-fingered claw-like hand that was powerful enough to puncture steel. Normally, such a beast would be feared but Slammer was finding it hard to be afraid of something wearing pink and blue striped leotards.

A see-thru, cylinder-like door-less elevator lifted Slammer about a hundred feet into the air and placed him onto a stage, which was surrounded by an invisible wall that was actually a force field. What Slammer saw did not make him happy. Bullhorn was dancing around in circles like he was already the champion. Bullhorn had never lost a fight and this gave him his prima donna attitude. Slammer entered the ring, prepared for a difficult fight. Unfortunately, he was right. The first thing that happened was that Bullhorn swiped him with one tentacle and his claw-like hand slammed Slammer clear to the other side of the ring. It was strange to see him stop in mid air and then slide down face-forward against this invisible glass with his arms stretched out trying to break his fall. It just so happened that when Slammer's face was plastered against the glass, he could see that the evil part of the All-for-One-Man was sitting next to a girl who could easily have been Roxy. Slammer tried to get Jane's attention by waving his arms. He wanted to make her look at the girl who resembled Roxy. He suddenly couldn't do anything because Bullhorn had wrapped all four tentacles around him and had started swinging him around. Then he threw him to the ground and tried to stab him with one of his horns.

Slammer was starting to feel the strain of the fight and he realized that if he didn't win soon, he would lose. He knew that he needed to find Bullhorn's weak spot and so he tried a few different moves. Slammer continued fighting but his efforts seemed too little too late. Bullhorn knocked him unconscious. Or so everyone thought. While the crowd cheered, Bullhorn raised his tentacles toward the sky, showing off for all of his admirers. Bullhorn began his winning signature dance and sang his victory song.

> YOU THINK I'M MEAN
> YOU THINK I'M PRETTY.
> I'M FULL OF BULL
> I HAVE NO PITY
> YOU FIGHT WITH ME
> I'LL BEAT YOU SILLY

The broadcaster was about to enter the ring to announce Bullhorn the winner when the unexpected happened. Slammer jumped up from the floor, grabbed Bullhorn by his left tentacle and began rubbing under his arm with lightning speed. Before Bullhorn could swing his tentacles at him, he dropped to the floor asleep like a baby. No one knew that all one had to do was to rub Bullhorn under his arm to make him fall asleep, just like a crocodile does when rubbed on its belly.

Slammer looked out into the audience and saw the All-for-One-Man dragging the girl by the arm as he headed into another building. Slammer hollered to Jane but she couldn't hear him over the crowd. He found a way to jump from the stage, located Franky and Ragrezy and waited for Jane to join them.

Slammer, very anxious to continue the chase, immediately asked his two pals, "Did either of you see the girl that the All-for-One-Man was forcing to go with him?"

Jane was just feet away and she heard what he asked. As she ran past them, she shouted out, "Yes, yes. She's my sister. Come on before they get away!"

"I guess that means she's Roxy," Ragrezy shouted as he saw Slammer dart after Jane. He immediately followed Slammer, with Franky right behind him. They continued their search to find Roxy. There were many buildings for the All-for-One-Man to hide in and little time to look in all of them. Jane got a glimpse of Roxy and she and her crew ran toward her. The All-for-One Man was just standing there motionless and waiting. They were about ten yards away from him when his men ambushed Jane and her crew.

One of the thugs actually thought that he could jump on Slammer and knock him down because they were the same size. He didn't know that Slammer was many times stronger than he and that he was a professional fighter. Slammer had the thug on the floor before the guy could blink. At the same time that he threw him to the floor, Slammer grabbed the thug's buddy and tossed him into the air. Slammer was throwing hoodlums around like they were as light as popcorn. Ragrezy was doing the same, just not as many or as quickly and Franky was exhibiting some pretty good knife fighting techniques. Jane, acting like Benny Ha-Ha the chef, was slicing and dicing those thugs closest to her with her dagger. The fighting went on for a while. The All-for-One-Man was enjoying himself so much that he just stood there, holding on to Roxy and acting as though he were directing the action.

"Come on you, go to the left!" he shouted. Just then one of his thugs fell backwards, almost landing on him. This gave Roxy the opportunity to grab the thug's weapon. Roxy freed herself and immediately started fighting. Jane was surprised when she saw how well her sister could handle herself.

While the fight was going on, N.I.T. and N.A.T. were still enjoying themselves in the club and watching Spike and Lolly through the invisible wall. N.I.T. and N.A.T. were totally unaware of everything that had happened. The waitress brought their ice cream sodas. Life was pleasant. There they were, just sitting back, enjoying ice cream and discussing whatever their hearts and brains desired. They had eyes only for each other and were almost oblivious to what was going on around them. It was their way of taking a break while policing their bodies. Unfortunately, this time they were not particularly successful…

Lolly and Spike were dancing when they felt the building shake. They looked at each other as if their being together was giving them that wonderful shaky feeling. A minute later, there was a huge noise. This time, the dance hall and building shook more violently. Before anyone realized what was happening, Slammer came running through the walls like they were paper. Jane was following right behind, holding onto her sister Roxy. Squeak was wrapped around Jane's neck and Franky and Ragrezy were right behind them. Slammer saw and grabbed Spike, who then grabbed Lolly. They went flying, holding onto each other for dear life as Slammer propelled them through the air.

N.I.T. and N.A.T were in the club, looking into each other's eyes, unaware of everything but themselves. Slammer sped by them unnoticed, followed by Jane, Roxy, Ragrezy, Franky, Spike and Lolly. It took some time before the two brains realized that their bodies were missing and that the bar and club now had a big hole on each side of the room, made by Slammer and his friends as they ran through the walls while rescuing Roxy. Invisible wall stitchers were repairing the holes, as N.I.T. and N.A.T. stared. It took them a minute to realize that their bodies were in trouble. N.I.T. and N.A.T. flew through the obvious exit hole where they found Jane and her crew running from the All-for-One-Man and his gang. Lolly and Spike were flying like kites, with Slammer's arm serving as the string. When N.I.T. and N.A.T. saw how close Mr. Evil was to catching Lolly and Spike, they flew straight into their heads. Once they were safely inside, it only took a second for Lolly and Spike to free themselves from Slammer's arm and run by everyone, yelling "See you at the ship."

Slammer, while still running, saw that Jane, Roxy, Ragrezy and Franky were almost next to him. He immediately told Roxy to follow Spike and Lolly, which she did without questioning his instructions. Slammer smiled at the sight of Spike and Lolly speeding ahead of him, followed in close pursuit by Roxy. Slammer and the rest of the crew stopped because they had to go over their escape plans and it had to be done quickly.

Jane had a major pit fall to overcome before she, Roxy and her crew could escape. They needed a special round crystal to start the spaceship and to get it, they first had to get out of Happy Town and go to Evil Town where the crystal was kept.

To understand the round blue green crystal, you need to know how it works. This is not an ordinary crystal. It has properties that are hard to believe. This crystal is the only one in existence that has a perpetual source of energy. That means that this particular type of crystal can't ever run out of energy because it absorbs the energy that is all around on any part of the universe. When the crystal is put into a machine built specifically for it, like the one in the RoxyResk, it becomes activated. The machine creates certain pulses of different colored lights and at the same time different frequencies of vibrations, thus forming the way for the crystal to reach the universe's energy source.

About two years before she left planet Earth, Jane spoke to Roxy's father Frank and asked him to find out how she could get such a crystal for the spaceship that she would need to rescue Roxy. He found out through a friend of his where he could purchase such a crystal for her. They were not cheap and very hard to come by. But Frank made all of the arrangements for her. All Jane would have to do would be to pick it up in Evil Town.

Jane told Slammer that she had to get the crystal and that she would see everyone on the ship when she got back. And like a flash, she was gone. Slammer looked at Franky and told him to follow her. Then Slammer continued in the direction that Lolly and Spike had taken. Franky ran to catch up with Jane but she seemed to have disappeared. The streets were dark and not a sound was heard. He called out to Jane, hoping that she would hear him, but he had no luck. He ran for a few blocks, looking into alleyways and shouting her name. After ten minutes of searching, he decided to go back to the ship. On his way back, he realized that there was a bar that he hadn't noticed a minute before. He glanced in and sure enough Jane was walking out with a package in her hands. When she came out of the bar, Franky was there. Very concerned but trying not showing it, he said nonchalantly,

"Hi Jane. I thought I'd lost you. Is that the crystal that you had to pick up?"

"Didn't I tell you I was going to see you at the ship?"

"I know, Jane but I thought that you might need some help."

"Thank you," she replied and then there was silence.

The walk to the ship was the first time in years that she and Franky had been alone. It was a bit awkward at first. No one knew that Jane was shy. But she was and to compensate for that, she needed to keep her feelings inside her. Unfortunately, that didn't work, especially when Franky told Jane that he had missed her. She felt as if she were going to melt. At first, she couldn't move because of the emotions that were overtaking her. No one had ever told her that she was missed. Franky got to the point. "Did you miss me?" Jane couldn't speak. It took a minute before she quickly grabbed and hugged him and admitted that she missed him too. Then, she took a step backward and kicked him in the shins. "What's that for?" he asked, surprised. Jane asked him why he had left her without a word, when they still lived on the streets of New York.

Franky couldn't apologize enough. He explained to her that some men in a limo had picked him up and told him that his father was about to go on a secret mission to the planet *Astrezia* and that he wanted to see him right away. One of the men told Franky that it could be the last time that they would see each other.

"Have you heard from him since?" Jane asked.

"No. But when we're finished with our mission, I'm going to find out what happened to him."

Squeak, still wrapped around Jane's neck, whispered into her ear, reminding her that the crew was waiting. Jane looked at Franky and said, "Okay! Now I understand and I'm not mad at you anymore." Then, she grabbed him by the hand and headed straight for their spaceship. Jane and Franky didn't realize it but they would be side by side from that moment on. "Come on, Franky. We must hurry."

Somehow, when they turned the corner, the All-for-One-Man and some of his thugs were about a block behind. When they saw Jane and Franky, it gave them motivation to speed up their chase.

Slammer was close to the ship when he heard a loud noise from behind and looked to see what it was. It turned out to be Jane and Franky on the horizon, running toward him as if the devil were chasing them. It might as well have been because the All-For-One-Man, whom Slammer thought he had lost, had grown to seven foot tall, with Mr. Evil as his dominant personality. He looked like the devil himself. His other two personalities, Mr. Happy and the Brain, were hiding somewhere in his subconscious. Mr. Evil's long fingers nearly grabbed Jane by the shoulder. The fear of just the graze from Mr. Evil's hand provided Jane with the boost of speed that she needed to escape his grip.

Slammer ran to help Jane. He told Ragrezy, Spike and Lolly to take Roxy and prepare the spaceship for takeoff. Squeak popped out of Jane's pocket and wrapped himself around her neck. Spike and Lolly, with N.I.T. and N.A.T. still in their heads, went with Ragrezy. Slammer, Franky, and Jane were managing to hold off Mr. Evil until they saw some of his reinforcements appear on the horizon. Jane knew that the only chance they had to escape was for her to use Squeak as an element of fear. This would only be effective for a minute, until Mr. Evil and his thugs realized that even though Squeak was scary, impressive, and very fast, he could only catch and extract evil out of one creature at a time. She told Slammer and Franky that she no longer needed them and that they should hurry and prepare the ship for takeoff.

"And what are you going to do?" Franky asked Jane.

"I'm not going to do anything. Squeak is going to have that task."

Finding it difficult to believe and hard to keep from being

sarcastic. Franky asked,

"Just what is that little thing going to do to such a big monster?"

"You'd be surprised," she answered and then added, "Timing is important. You must hurry."

Franky wanted to help her but she insisted that her way was the best way to deal with the situation. Franky and Slammer rushed away and as Jane turned around, she saw that Mr. Evil was standing in front of her with a couple dozen of his men behind him.

Towering over her, he said, "Do you really think that you and your pitiful crew are going to get out of my town without my say so?"

Like a real smart ass she replied, "That's the idea, you big dummy."

Mr. Evil couldn't help but change back to the All-For-One-Man in front of her eyes. Mr. Happy popped out of his left shoulder, laughing and said, "She's funny, guys, isn't she?" Then Mr. Brain appeared out of his right shoulder and contradicted him, "She's not funny! She called us a dummy." Then he looked at Jane and proclaimed, "We're no dummies." He paused, looked at Mr. Happy and added, "Well, maybe he is…"

The All-for-One-Man smacked Mr. Happy and Mr. Brain back into his subconscious and returned into his seven foot Evil shaped self while shouting, "Both of you! Don't come out again. I'm in charge here."

The whole incident freaked Jane out.

Then in a very threatening voice, Mr. Evil shouted, "Tell your crew to come out."

Jane mustered up the courage to shout back, "You'd better leave and let us go about our business before any more people get hurt."

Mr. Evil responded, "You have some nerve threatening me. You have three seconds to get your crew out of the ship." Meanwhile more of his men kept appearing on the horizon.

"Don't say that I didn't warn you," Jane responded. She looked at Squeak who was squatting on her shoulder ready for dinner. She smiled and said. "Okay, Squeak. It's Din, Din time. Go and suck all those evil creatures into smoke."

Squeak drained the evil out of about a dozen of Mr. Evil's minions within seconds. Then it was Mr. Evil's turn. His remaining followers only had to see Squeak attack Mr. Evil and a second later they went running away like the wind. Squeak wrapped himself around Mr. Evil's neck. He found that he wasn't able to suck the evil out of Mr. Evil because he needed Rocky and the Changer to help him. Squeak was left with one choice. He squeezed Mr. Evil's neck tighter and tighter until he fell on his knees, almost unconscious. Squeak flew to Jane, yelling, "Run to the ship before he comes out of his daze." Squeak wrapped himself around Jane's neck and they flew to the ship as if on wings and raced through its door. Squeak couldn't have been happier, now that he was safe at home around her neck and in the RoxyResk.

Mr. Evil's lackeys tried to hang on to the ship just as its door was closing.

PART THREE
In Space on the Road to the Mine, Mine Planet

The Mine, Mine Planet

The ship lifted off while they dangled and then started to drop. Jane and her crew were lucky to have escaped Mr. Evil. Now they could concentrate on getting to the *Mine, Mine Planet* to find Lisa.

The crew put plenty of distance between themselves and the *Planet of Stolen Property*. They computed that it would take at least two days to get to the *Mine, Mine Planet* and decided to settle down and relax and get to know each other. Slammer and Ragrezy were sharing stories about bar fights and trying to impress Roxy who was watching and listening to them.

Jane was sitting next to Franky and asked, "Do you have any idea of where to start looking for your dad?"

"I really can't think about that now. We must think about Lisa and how to rescue her."

Spike and Lolly were holding hands on the floor, while N.I.T. and N.A.T. were sitting on their shoulders and talking. The two days went by without any problems.

When Jane and her crew were about two hours away from their destination, she noticed that there was an almost invisible force field surrounding the *Mine, Mine Planet*. What she failed to notice was that there were individual sparks of energy emanating from the planet and heading toward her ship. Jane had no way of knowing that those sparks were the planet's inhabitants.

Just like humans are the residents of Earth, the Spark people are the residents of the *Mine, Mine Planet*. What makes them exceptional is that they are individual sources of pure energy and that they are able to adopt any shape they wish and imitate any language that they hear. The Sparks whom Jane and her crew saw approaching their ship, were a welcoming party for Jane and her crew. The Sparks probably never imagined that the crew of any ship would interpret a cloud of energy sparks heading straight toward them as a threat.

The ship's alarm gave a warning of an attack when its sensors picked up the energy radiating from something sparkly and bright speeding toward them like an imminent threat.

"Spike," Jane shouted, "Put on the view screen. I need to analyze the force that is coming straight at us. I have to see it and read the computer output at the same time."

Slammer who was standing next to Jane, looking at the screen with her, yelled, "Don't wait! Fire now!"

"Wait a minute, Slammer. We don't even know what it is."

"All I know is that a huge energy source is heading straight for us." He paused and added, "Would you rather wait until whatever it is destroys us?"

"Of course not. I just don't feel threatened and I don't wish to make a mistake."

"Jane. I'm not taking any chances I'm going to tell Franky to fire."

Franky was all hyped up and ready for a fight. He was listening to Slammer and Jane and waiting for a decision. He wanted to hear "yes", so he shouted to Slammer,

"Well, big guy, am I going to fire or not?"

Jane instantly shouted with emphasized strength, "No! Wait!"

"Why?" Franky and Slammer asked at the same time.

Jane pointed to the screen. "Look! Look! Can't you see that?"

"See what?" They both said again at the same time.

"Didn't you notice that whatever is coming at us is slowing down?"

The view screen started to act up by flickering on and off. A single creature that resembled a field of energy with a sparkling form appeared on the screen and asked Jane not to fire. Before Jane could respond, a body of multicolored, sparkly energy was standing next to her. Jane could not believe what she saw … it was beautiful and mesmerizing…and then it morphed into a shadowy Al Capone type of figure, complete with a gangster style hat. Jane's memory went back to pictures of Capone that she had seen in history books. But this time, she saw standing in front of her what resembled a shadowy black outline with a sparkler in it. The rest of the crew was staring in disbelief. They didn't feel threatened even though they realized that the Spark people could do as they wished with them.

Jane suddenly heard a deep voice ask in a thick Italian accent,

"Allo! Are you the boss?"

"Huh?" Jane blurted out.

"Oh! *I'mma* so sorry that I startled you. Please *forgiva* me for being rude. My name is Sparky."

Jane, looking very puzzled, asked, "How in the world did you get an Italian accent?"

Sparky laughed and answered, "I worked with Italians. Most of us Spark people mimic the accents and language of the creatures we work with." Then he continued, "We are known as the Tube Spark people. We live inside a tube-shaped world even though our planet is round."

Jane smiled to herself when she noticed that as Sparky talked to her; he also lost his Italian accent. She moved away from him when strange, short sparks of energy suddenly shot out.

"What's happening to you?" Jane asked perturbed.

"Don't be afraid. I can only maintain my current shape for a while longer because my energy source reacts differently in the ship than when I am out in the cosmos. Changing forms from time to time stabilizes my energy source."

Sparky announced that he had to change his form right then and there. "Please don't freak out," he chuckled as he turned himself into a perfect glass copy of Jane with what appeared to be a sparkler inside.

"As you can see, I can take any form that I want, always with my energy spark inside."

Sparky, still a perfect sparkling glass copy of Jane, asked everyone to sit and then began to speak.

"I know that you are planning to visit my planet, but I must warn you that you might not survive in our world. It is not like other worlds, as you will soon see."

"Does anyone have any questions?"

Spike jumped up, very excited. "Are there any Entertainment Bars there?"

Sparky took on Spike's form and jumped up and down, playfully imitating him.

"Yes, there are. Oh yes, there are!"

Slammer who was sitting on one of the chairs stood up and said, "Sparky, why don't you tell us what you think is important?"

Sparky took on Slammer's form and started to explain how he and his people live and what makes everything work on the *Mine, Mine Planet*.

"In order for my people to get materials that do not exist on our planet, we have always needed to trade with other worlds. Because of our harsh weather conditions and the difference in our gravity and that of other planets, other civilizations hesitated to visit and engage in trade with us. They were afraid that they would never survive once they landed. We could not go very far from our home because of our energy issues but we were able to live with what we had. Hundreds of years ago, criminals and their families escaped a distant planet, traveled to ours and managed to survive there. Eventually their tale of survival was heard. Many outsiders wanted to trade but found our world too dangerous. It took many years for us to learn how to control the differences between our weather and gravity and those of other worlds."

"How is it possible for you to control your planet's weather and the strength of its gravitational pull?" Jane asked.

"Our planet consists of energy that communicates with energy. It's like water and steam –it's the same element but in different forms. Whatever is in it adjusts according to its movements. The same principle applies to the various forms of energy on the *Mine, Mine Planet*. My planet's energy acts like a motion sensor when an outsider arrives. Two feet of space around the individual mimics the exact type of atmosphere that is on his planet. This technology now allows all visitors to enter."

"What about the criminal element? How are you going to control it?" Jane insisted.

"The *Mine, Mine Planet* was established by criminals and they made sure that it stayed that way. No law was allowed there except for criminal law. And this has never changed."

"Hasn't that affected your world? And aren't you worried that some civilization will want to take control of you?"

"No. That could never happen. Anyone who would try such a thing would be trapped on our planet. We are too powerful and have the perfect environment. Our world is like an oven. Everything that is in the middle is what survives. And if anyone wishes to harm us, all that we have to do is focus our energy and everything in our world burns. Except for us since we would become the fire that consumes our enemy."

"When did your planet get so popular and rich?" Roxy asked.

Sparky paused, took in a deep breath, assumed Roxy's form and continued.

"It wasn't until generations of criminals realized that their world's police wouldn't follow them or even want to come near the *Mine, Mine Planet*. With time, it became populated and grew into one of the most corrupt planets of the universe and also one of the richest."

Jane, not understanding, asked, "Isn't there anything you can do to stop the criminal element?"

"Stop them?" Sparky, imitating Jane's voice reacted in surprise. "Why would we do that? If it weren't for the criminals, we couldn't have the different types of energy that make life a bit more festive for us."

"How can you be more festive than being a Sparky?" Ragrezy commented.

"I'd like to know that myself," Franky added, curious for

an answer.

"It's very simple. Just like on Earth where a drink or a cigarette makes a difference in a person's disposition, the various forms of energy that exist in certain ores and minerals affect us in similar ways when we have access to them and that is only through trade."

Jane jumped in and continued to insist, "Isn't there anything you can do to stop this criminal behavior?"

"There is nothing we can do about crime on our planet because it's crime that we depend on. Without the criminals we have no trade. Don't get me wrong," Sparky emphasized, "If the law wishes to pursue these criminals, they're more than welcome to try."

"How do the life forms that visit your world survive?" Lolly asked, to everyone's surprise.

"Good question," Sparky commented, while complimenting her.

She blushed and reacted with a smile as she cuddled up to Spike.

Sparky sparked a bit brighter to her reaction and continued.

"We have made it easier for others to do business with us but our world is an easy place to die in. We, as a sparkly bunch, have a strange history. Our people cannot go too far from our planet. The gravity in our bodies would just shrink us into nothingness."

Jane did not want to seem rude but she just had to ask, "Why are you in our ship?"

He cheerfully responded, "I have been sent to educate you as much as possible and protect you, when I can."

"Our history goes like this. Millions of years ago, a planet five times the size of Earth dried up. It was considered to be a dead planet. It had no name, but for some unknown reason, an alien race wanted the core of the planet. When they were done, there was a hole that went right through its center, which was thousands of miles wide. Its length was hundreds of times longer. The hole was big enough for Earth to go through, with room to spare. The planet got the name *Mine, Mine* because the civilizations of the universe at that time saw the aliens as greedy creatures that would mutilate or destroy worlds and then said, 'This is Mine! Mine!' For millions of years, the world was red hot in the center. It took many more millenniums until the center finally cooled off and life eventually began."

Sparky paused to allow everyone to digest what he had just said.

Ragrezy asked Sparky if he could describe parts of his world. Sparky lit up with joy and his energy shone a bit brighter.

"I would be happy to. My planet is really quite amazing. Don't forget that it's a tube inside a planet and it's a world of its own. All of us have the form of energy sparks and we can change our forms and size at will. Once you enter the center of the tube, if you look straight ahead, you will be able to see pointed mountains of ice peaks and also stars. That is the side of our plant without a sun. If you turn around and look at the place you just entered, you will see the sunlight. Gravity seems to push against the ground, away from the center of the planet. The physics of our world is amazing. There's only one ocean but there are lots of lakes and rivers and one island. This is the only planet of its kind. When you are on another world and you lie down and look up at the sky, you see stars and other planets. On the *Mine, Mine Planet,* when you lie down and look at the sky, you see a country, city, or lake across thousands of miles. There is no heaven for the Tube Spark people to see by looking up to the sky. They would have to look to their left or their right if they wanted to speak to God."

Sparky stopped, looked at everyone and asked if they wanted to hear more.

"Let's take a break and eat something," Slammer suggested, much to everyone's delight.

"Come everyone, let's eat." Jane pushed a button and out came a very tall, skillfully designed machine that was their maitre d', waiter, cook and dishwasher rolled into one shiny, bronze and aluminum body.

The crew couldn't take their eyes of this magnificently designed aluminum and bronze machine. Its eyes looked like large marbles with stars embedded deep inside. It had a handlebar mustache and patent leather hair. The machine stopped moving and lifted its arms into the air. A second later two more arms on each side of its body popped out, stretched and then disappeared. Whatever kind of a robot this was, it had on a tuxedo. The crewmembers looked at Jane in disbelief and all at once they asked, "What is that thing, Jane?" Before she could answer, a sound like a throat being cleared was heard and the beautiful bronze and aluminum robot walked toward everyone and politely introduced itself.

"Hello everyone! My name is Mr. Food. Give me your orders for today and I will serve you."

Slammer started.

Not known for his manners, he called out, "Hey you, food boy."

Very indignant, the robot replied. "I am Mr. Food, not hey you food boy."

He looked at Slammer, shrugged his aluminum shoulders, grunted 'hmm' softly under his breath, pointed a long, slim, bronze finger at him and asked, "Don't you have something you want to say to me?"

"Yeh. Get me a steak."

Mr. Food quickly rolled up to Slammer's chest, looked up at him, stretched his neck and shoved his nose as close to Slammer's chin as possible and very indignant, warned him.

"You'd better think before you speak, buddy. Remember. I'm your chef. Does that conjure up any tragedies that could occur?"

Slammer backed up and took a look at this machine that he considered not much better than a can. He couldn't believe that he had just been threatened by this contraption. But Slammer was no dummy. He knew that this food-can called a robot could get him and he'd never see it coming. He realized that he had made a mistake and he tried to save face.

He kneeled down on one knee and said, "I'm sorry, Mr. Food. Will you forgive me? And remember, no funny stuff. Okay?"

The crew was watching Slammer in amazement and wondered why he was on his knee.

"I'm a gentleman and so I will accept your apology," Mr. Food graciously answered.

Then, in a conspiratorial manner, he said, "Don't worry, Slammer. No harm will come to you. "

"Mr. Food, may I have a steak with some string beans?"

Jane listened closely and heard Slammer say, "And don't forget some nice buttery gravy on the mashed potatoes. It would be appreciated. And of course, some desert – perhaps cake and ice cream."

And as Slammer stood up, Mr. Food replied, "Right away, Sir."

Then he headed for Jane who was standing near Roxy, Franky and Ragrezy. They were talking about their different experiences since they had last seen each other. Franky stepped forward toward Mr. Food.

"Mr. Food. Look at the girls! Their mouths are watering at the thought of nice batter fried shrimp and broiled lobster. How about a piece of the catch of the day? And they have to have French fries. Right girls?" he looked at them for approval.

"You said it, Franky." Jane replied. "How did you know what we wanted?"

Before Franky could answer, Ragrezy seconded the girls' choice. "I'll have that too."

"You told me that was always your favorite food, remember?" Franky looked at Mr. Food and said, "We'll have four of those fish dinners."

"Okay," Mr. Food noted as he rolled over to Spike and Lolly who were sitting on the floor admiring each other while N. I. T. and N.A.T. were perched on their shoulders, yakking their brains away.

When Mr. Food was about a foot away, N.I.T. and N.A.T. flew into Spike and Lolly's heads and like jumping beans the two youngsters popped up and said at the same time, "We'll have hamburgers with French fries, cake, ice cream and chocolate milkshakes."

Then they looked lovingly at each other and congratulated themselves, "Good choice." Mr. Food looked at them, burst out laughing, composed himself and as he walked away, he could be heard muttering, "Whatever you say. Good luck with that order…"

Mr. Food had one order left to take. It was Squeak's. "And what would you like, Sir?"

Squeak looked him up and down and with great speed, unwrapped himself from Jane's neck and flew to sniff every inch of Mr. Food. Squeak flew back to Jane's neck and told Mr. Food that he didn't have anything that he wanted.

While walking away to get their orders, Mr. Food mumbled, "Rude little thing! No one ever sniffed me before."

Their orders took a while to prepare. Meanwhile, some very cheerful music started playing in another room where the food was being prepared. A second later, some fantastic little bugs came dancing out and started singing to everyone. Leading the dancers was a bug named Natalie. This magnificent creature looked like a tall, slender woman but in miniature form. Her body was made up of a net that flowed from head to toe, kind of like one of Cher's costumes. When she danced, huge Dragon Fly wings that were as transparent as her body spread to almost twice her size. The colors of the wings were those of a rainbow. When a light shone on her, it seemed to reflect and shine on everyone else. She had the effect of a hunger pill that wetted everyone's appetite. Whoever watched her dance found himself rubbing his stomach, in order to calm his hunger. As she danced, three colors, red, yellow and white, would appear and alternate through the net that formed her body. At times, she was striped and at other times, one color only. Her body had a shiny, glossy look when she danced. Behind Natalie were about a dozen little bugs, all miniature carbon copies of her. Natalie and her dozen carbon copies danced for a while and then began singing.

Just close your eyes and visualize. The food you want is in your sight.

There's feasts for kings and booze for queens; there's even candy, for the kids.

You must be hungry from your trip. Just visualize the food you'll eat.

The kitchen door swung open. Natalie and her buggy troops scattered out of sight as if they didn't exist.

By now, everyone on the ship was enthusiastic and excited, drooling and hungry enough to eat a cow!

Mr. Food came out with a stack of boxes in his hands and said, "Here's your feast!"

Slammer looked closely at what Mr. Food was carrying and in disbelief yelled, "Hey, Food Boy! It's just pizza!"

The whole crew looked like a mob ready to attack. They started threatening to turn Mr. Food into pizza toppings, covering him with lots of cheese and baking him into the pizza,

Mr. Food, afraid for his bronze and aluminum body, tried to diffuse the situation. "Hey, guys. Calm down. What did you expect? We're in a spaceship. You're lucky you're getting pizza and entertainment. This is not a five star gourmet restaurant on some rich planet. And use paper plates. Do I look like a dishwasher? Now, eat your pizza or no one gets dessert."

Of course, kids being kids, the pizza was just fine and the dessert – well, it wasn't cake and ice cream but a cookie in a pinch seemed to do just fine.

They finished eating and Slammer was anxious to hear more.

"Sparky, we could never have imagined such a world. Please, can you tell us some more?"

And like a friend, Ragrezy added, "Hey Sparky. I really like the way that you describe everything. That's an amazing planet you live in. I just can't wait to see it."

Then searching for the right words, he questioned Sparky. "So you mean that when you lie down on your planet and look up, you don't see the sun, moon or stars, but rather another country or whatever is on the other side."

"That's right. You understand me perfectly."

With a sparkling drink in his hand and a smile on his face, Sparky made himself comfortable and continued.

"First of all Jane, I would like to thank you and your crew for bringing us such a rare gift. You're the only one that has this particular delicacy to trade in years. You were wise to trade for information to help you during your entire mission. I will share with you information that should come in handy as you travel."

He looked at Jane and continued, "You can ask anything you want at any time. Just think of me and I will appear."

Sparky paused for a minute and then began to give more information about his planet.

"The Tube has four Weather Rings and each Ring embodies one season with its own constant and yet variable weather and temperature. There are many unusual creatures in these four Weather Rings precisely because of the extremes of their temperatures. Some like the Pond Extractors and the Ice Pick People are extremely dangerous and have to be avoided. Others, like the Moisture Extractors are cute, friendly and usually very thirsty.

"The south side of our Planet always faces the sun and the constant sunlight heats every part of the Tube, making life possible. The first Ring is the Summer Ring. The South Pole is in this Ring and it is where the sun always shines. The deeper you will travel into the planet, the darker it will get. We Spark people use our own energy to keep it light at times for some temperature control. Otherwise, the planet would close on the north side, creating an ice cone tip."

"I picture the sunny side of your planet starting with deserts. These deserts begin with small pebbles that are as hot as coal and gradually turn into sand. Am I correct in that assumption?" Ragrezy asked.

"You're pretty close. Our world begins with the hottest desert that is known to exist. Its temperature starts at thousands of degrees and decreases only as the desert progresses inwards for thousands of miles. There are areas in the middle and toward the end of the desert that only certain life forms can inhabit. As an example, there are creatures called Scale and Worm Jumpers that like the temperature to be at least five hundred degrees and they live in that particular area.

"As you travel closer to the center of the Tube, the weather and temperature of the planet become milder. The extreme heat starts to lessen. It's a gradual change into the Spring Ring. First, dew forms and the soil begins to get more moisture, making it possible for various types of moss and greenery to begin to grow and bugs and other small creatures to appear. Further inside, there are different kinds of grass and bushes with all sorts of flowers, fruits and vegetables, not like any you have seen but fruits and vegetables all the same. For us, everything is alive and so they see themselves as alive. The proof of this is that if you try to pick any of our fruits or vegetables, you will notice that they try to move out of the way so that you cannot grab them. Once you pick them off of the plant, they are only good for consumption. For them, their juice is their blood and once you slice or bite them, their blood is shed and they lose their life."

Sparky waited for a reaction and getting none, he sparked a bit and then continued his story.

"As you travel inwards, you will eventually reach the forest where even more creatures live. Some trees are as small as bonsais and others are as tall as eight or nine hundred feet. By the time you get to the middle of the forest, the temperature will let you know that you are entering the Fall Ring. As the weather continues to cool, you will find varieties of trees and plants that thrive in cool weather. Once pine trees appear, the Fall Ring comes to an end and the Winter Ring begins. This is a strange Ring - it snows lightly there for hundreds of miles, then nothing for hundreds more. Then, suddenly within an hour a foot or two of snow falls, blanketing everything and then nothing more. The closer you come to the northern part, which is also known as the starry side of our planet, the colder it gets. Eventually there is no land, only ice. This is where you will find hundreds of miles of small, icy spike-shaped mountains, varying from about a foot to ten feet in height. The Ice Pick people live here and you'd better pray that you don't run into them."

"What makes them so dangerous?" Roxy asked.

"Besides being huge and having ice picks for hair, they can also read your mind and turn into whatever or whomever you fear most. Imagine being attacked by a giant ice spider or an ice All-for-One-Man."

"I understand, Mr. Sparky but we're not going to walk there. We're going in my sister's spaceship," Roxy quickly replied.

"Just because you're in the air doesn't mean that they can't get to you. Imagine that you see a pointed ice mountain sink halfway into the ground. A second later, the tip of this mountain pops back up out of the ground with the force of a coiled spring and then shoots straight up toward your ship like a missile. This is no mountain. It is actually one of the Ice Pick Men and all it takes is one hit by any one of them and your entire crew will be gone."

"I'm glad you're telling us all of this, Sparky." Jane interrupted. "You and I will have to talk at a later time. I believe that we can trade again."

"What happens when you go deeper into the Tube, Mr. Sparky?" Lolly asked.

"Eventually, the temperature cools and more life forms become possible. This is when spring begins and the further one goes into the Tube world, the cooler it gets. The weather gradually changes to fall throughout this ring for thousands of miles and then, after tens of thousands of miles, it slowly turns cold. Before anyone could reach the northern side of the tube, he would have to maneuver through thousands of sharp ice mountain peaks that are almost impossible to fly through."

"Why would it be impossible to fly through the mountain peaks?" N.I.T., who was sitting on Spike's shoulder, shouted.

"Did you ever notice how a shark's teeth look as the shark's mouth is closing? That's exactly how the mountain peaks are formed. When you look toward the starry side of the planet, you see a perfectly round white hole. As you travel closer, what seemed perfectly round starts to take on a different form. First you see the tips of the mountains, which look like the points of the shark's teeth, and then the mountains, which complete the shape of the teeth."

"I understand that Sparky," N.I.T. replied. "But there are thousands of miles between those mountains."

"That's true. But if you don't fly in the correct currents, the gravity will pull you into the mountains, like a pin speeding toward a giant magnet. Or you could get hit by one or more of the Ice Pick People. There is no saving anyone."

Then Sparky added, "And believe me, we have seen many try to fly through those mountains."

N.I.T.'s mind was already looking to do the impossible.

"Do you have any of the escape attempts recorded, in any form? And if so, will you help us, should we need it?"

"That's very interesting," Sparky remarked. "You're the first aliens on our planet that asked to look at the possibility of how to get through our Tube world safely. All the aliens before you thought that they were invincible and believed that they were powerful enough to force their way through the middle of the mountains. They never considered the gravity and its strength. They assumed that since we didn't build things, we were limited in our intelligence and didn't know much. They never realized that we could transfer our history or any other information simply by touching and allowing the individuals to experience the answer to their questions.

"If any other aliens had asked, as you are doing now, we would have shown and told them their best options and chances for survival. And like I have said before, we are a neutral species. We don't take sides and should we be asked, the only help we can give is information."

N.I.T. flew back into Spike's head and a second later Spike jumped up with great enthusiasm. "Okay, Sparky. Lets' do it!"

The crew just watched and laughed at how clumsy and awkward Spike was when he got excited.

Sparky got brighter, which was his way of laughing and asked, "Let's do what?"

"I wa..." Spike caught himself and stopped and then continued but kind of slowly, just to make sure that he repeated everything correctly. "N.I.T. wants you to show him a safe way to exit the frozen starry side of the planet."

"Okay, Spike. Just stand still." Sparky flew into Spike's head through his ear and less than a second later came back out.

Spike put on the biggest smile that his face could carry and said, while glancing at the ceiling,

"Those air tunnels are magnificent and the sparkling colors make them easy to see."

"Don't fool yourself, Spike. One wrong move in any direction would give you certain death."

Sparky turned stern and serious. His electrical impulses crackled as he flew high enough that everyone had to look up and pay attention to the seriousness of the conversation.

"This goes for all of you. I have no idea of what you have in mind but one thing is for sure. You need information and you better have something of value to trade for it."

Franky was close to Jane and felt that he needed to express himself. "Wow! That was a quick personality change in Sparky."

Jane nonchalantly looked at him and said simply, "Hey, what are you going to do? That's business."

Then she turned back to Sparky and spoke.

"Does that mean that we can't land on your planet without something to trade?"

"Of course not Jane…Everyone is welcome for free and good luck with everything else. It's the information that costs. And believe me, we Spark people are cheaper than anyone else on the planet."

"I don't think that we have anything of value on our ship." Jane commented.

"Ah, that's where you're wrong." Sparky lit up a bit brighter, which was how the Spark people expressed their emotions…the more emotions the brighter the spark.

"You carry a very valuable commodity. We can sense or as your species would say, smell the goodies, so to speak. Do you still have that trunk in the back?"

Jane knew how business was done. She turned to Slammer.

"Go get it and take Ragrezy with you to help."

Slammer and Ragrezy went to pick up the trunk and bring it to Sparky. The trunk was filled with a material that Jane and her crew had thought was gold but turned out to be worthless to them. Slammer had planned to throw it out but never got around to it. The iron-like ore was the equivalent of coffee for the Spark people and that trunk full represented a year's worth for an entire city. Jane and Sparky concluded their business and made a deal that included whatever information she and her crew would need, even in the case of an emergency. A few minutes later Sparky told them that a shield would open and allow them to pass into his world.

"It's time to relax now because it will take a few hours to get to the *Mine, Mine Planet*."

Jane and her crew went about their business. About an hour

passed when a little adorable bug showed herself to Slammer. Just as he was ready to step on it, Sparky yelled, "Wait! Don't do that! She's harmless. She's a Moisture Extractor. Moisture Extractors are little creatures that resemble what in your world is known as a Ladybug. However, there are a few differences between the two. The Moisture Extractor is a bit longer, and instead of dots it has one elongated shiny yellow and blue striped tube on each wing. Those tubes are water pouches that swell and rise up when filled with water. Each pouch has a long antenna with an eight-finger daisy-style suction cup at its end that the little bugger uses for extracting moisture. The extractor pouches can only hold a few drops at a time but those drops fill up the pouches and can last the Moisture Extractor weeks or months, if need be. When it's time for the Moisture Extractor to fly, it unfolds its wings like a fan as it stretches them toward its head. Its wings resemble two half circles back to back."

Slammer looked at the little creature. She was about a half inch long, with long eyelashes and very large, round hazel eyes. Her nose was like a gumdrop and her tiny, pointy, bat-like ears looked almost like wings. She had full lips and a big mouth that gave the impression that she was always smiling.

Wow! She is kind of cute, he thought.

Just as Slammer was getting comfortable with the idea of a water-extracting bug, Sparky interrupted in order to warn everyone about a more dangerous water-extracting creature on his planet.

"There is a relative of the Moisture Extractors, called the Pond Suckers. Believe me! They are another story. They're twice the size of Slammer. Their legs stretch to three times their height so that their long, heavy water pouch won't hit the ground. Their large, flat, webbed feet keep them from sinking into any soft ground. When they get a hold of anything or anyone containing water, they extract it until the water pouch almost reaches the ground or the source of the water turns into dry dust."

When Sparky finished, the Moisture Extractor thanked him for stopping Slammer from smashing her. Once she gained her composure, she sat next to Slammer.

"Hi Slammer. My name is Millie. May I have a drink of water? I'm very thirsty."

Slammer looked at her and said, "Do I look like a water fountain to you?"

She hung her head very pathetically and said, "I'm sorry but I'm thirsty and you're a big fellow. I thought that you could spare a drop or two."

Then she asked him very politely if she could stay next to him and catch her breath.

"I don't care what you do," Slammer answered, swinging his arm and shooing her away. Millie realized that it wouldn't be as easy as she thought to get even a single drop of water. It was time for her survival tactics to take over. She looked around for a target and spotted Jane. Millie figured that she could sneak over to Jane's leg because she was busy reading her ship's manual and not paying attention to anything else. Mille thought that she was close enough to stretch her antenna up her leg for a water extraction. The excitement on her face was priceless because she believed that she was going to succeed and get a drink.

Jane looked at Millie as she was about to satisfy her thirst, put her hand between the bug and her leg and said, "Don't you dare try to put those suction cups on me!"

Once again, the poor Extractor failed. Millie then focused her attention on Lolly, hoping that she was different, more understanding and more generous than the others.

Lolly was next to Spike who by now was playing some computer game that he had with him. Something bumped her leg. She looked down and Millie the Extractor was there. She introduced herself and even asked Lolly if she could have something to drink and fill her water reserves. Lolly saw that Spike was glued to his I pod game and not paying attention to anything else.

She picked up Millie, put her on Spike's shoulder and asked, "This won't hurt him, right?"

"Oh no," Millie replied. "He won't even know."

Lolly looked at Spike and said, "You don't mind. Right honey?" He continued playing his game, agreeing to anything that she said. Lolly was amazed at how oblivious Spike was. He never noticed that Millie was on his shoulder and stretching for his neck because some spots of the body were easier and sweeter to extract from than others.

Millie casually stretched her antennas toward Spike with a look that said, *I'm not doing anything. I'm just sitting here, eating and protecting you from the bugs that you can't see around you.* Then, she opened and closed her suction cups, as if she were catching something, eating while resting and protecting Spike. When she felt safe, she stretched a little closer until she made contact with his shoulder. She was a few inches away from his neck and she stretched a little farther. Her suction cups attached onto Spike's neck while a chemical misted out and numbed a few inches of the surface. The area turned red and started to sweat, brining the water to the surface. Lolly was intrigued as she watched the drops of water pour through the antennas, as if they were faucets, into her colorful tubes. For a minute, Lolly thought that in a way Millie was just like a vampire. The thought disappeared as she realized that Mille was cute and nice, didn't bite or draw blood…Definitely not qualities belonging to a vampire. Millie stayed perfectly still until her reservoirs were filled. The whole extraction process was over within seconds. Just as Mille had promised, the extraction was painless, just like being kissed by the wind.

Roxy and Jane were watching how sweet the Extractor was acting. Very polite but when need be, they saw that she was also charming, not to mention sneaky and slick. After a few giggles, Jane apologized to Roxy for not getting to her sooner. Roxy, who was sobbing a bit, let Jane know how much she loved her and appreciated her rescue. Jane asked Roxy what had happened to her. Roxy, almost reliving the event, began.

"When I found out about Lisa and learned that you were also my sister, I searched for months, trying to find you. This eventually led me to the *Planet of Stolen Property*. Some men who had heard about Lisa mistook me for her and kidnapped me. That was the first time I heard about the All-for-One-Man. He was just biding his time until he could bring me to the *Mine, Mine Planet* where he could auction me off. Mr. Evil was mad at me when he realized that I couldn't fight very well. For the past year or so, he had me trained to fight. While I was in training camp, I heard about a girl my age who was the first outsider taught how to fight by the one and only creature of his kind. In a way, he was a true alien, the only life form raised on that planet from another world. Some people believed that Lisa had gained some powerful magic and strange powers from an alien named Astro Jackson."

She paused, frowned like she was thinking about something

and then continued.

Roxy pointed to the sky where the *Sphere of Tears City* was located. "Isn't that beautiful, Sis?"

They looked at each other and smiled.

"I've felt like saying that to you since I learned that you were my sister."

"I like hearing you call me, Sis," Jane replied. Then she added, "I'm curious why the city is called the *Sphere of Tears*.

"I'm going to tell you what a stranger once told me. Thousands of years ago, some criminal settlers had built a prison that housed unusual and powerful criminals. Even they didn't want to deal with such out of this world, very vicious and extremely violent characters. Back in the early years there was no city and the area was known as *The Control Town*. As the centuries passed, the super bad criminals outsmarted and overpowered their regular type of criminal guards, escaped and took control of the entire planet. They began trading with the Spark Tube People for materials from other worlds. Slaves were the most profitable and the younger they were, the more valuable they were. When the world was filled with child slaves, their cries could be heard throughout the world. And because it was shaped like a tube, it magnified the children's cries so that they could be heard throughout the universe. From that time on, all of the worlds knew it as *The Sphere of Tears City*."

When Roxy finished her story, Jane reassured her that they were going to rescue Lisa.

"Before we get there, can you tell me anything about Astro Jackson?"

Roxy, looking very disappointed, said, "Not really."

Sparky who was close by flew in front of Jane and took on the form of Astro Jackson.

Jane and her crew were very surprised at how big he was.

"Is that his regular size?" Ragrezy asked.

Sparky immediately apologized. "I'm sorry. I didn't mean to startle you." Then he took on the form of Captain Kirk of the starship Enterprise. "Everyone knows about Kirk," Sparky commented. "I hope that this look suits you better."

Jane just stared and thought. *How the hell could Sparky know about Captain Kirk? That's an Earth thing...Apparently not* was her afterthought.

"If nobody objects to this look, then let me tell you about the amazing rebirth of Astro Jackson and who made it possible. According to the records of the Cleaning Bugs, Astro Jackson was the first and only baby Cleaning Bug to be rejected by the planet's leaders and taken away to another planet to be left either to survive or die. The reason for this was that Astro at the time was the first Cleaner of his species to show any individuality by his behavior and questions. Hooty and Duty, two of the oldest Bug Leaders in the world, would not tolerate that sort of behavior. The Cleaning Bugs still had a lot to discover about themselves. They didn't understand that this child needed to learn in a different way than the others and they saw his individuality as a sign of change and chaos. Therefore he was considered to be evil and dangerous.

"There were some Cleaning Bugs that didn't want to discard the Baby Astro. Rooty was the representative for those who didn't want to kill the child.

"Your Royal Hooty and Duty, we implore you. Please save the child. We will take care of him."

"It's too late, Mr. Representative Rooty," Leader Duty shouted out. "The decision has been made. We cannot take the chance. This one child can infect all of our citizens. We must dispose of him. There is no turning back. This child has to go."

"The Cleaning Bugs traveled for days until they ran into a planet that was known for its turbulent beginnings and where there was no possibility for anyone to survive, let alone a baby. The world was called the *Mine, Mine Planet*.

"Then the Cleaning Bugs were flying in the turbulent world of the *Mine, Mine Plan*et they noticed that life was forming on different parts of the land. They didn't want to infect them with Astro so they went deeper into the planet until they saw the one and only island in its ocean. The Cleaning Bugs literally dropped him in the middle of the island and left. There was one thing that the Cleaning Bugs did not know about the island. It was a living plant-like animal that devoured anything that landed on it."

Sparky stopped talking. He took a few seconds and sparked a bit brighter as if he were taking a deep breath, and then he turned and focused his attention on Jane.

But before he could say another word, Jane interrupted. "Excuse me, Sparky. I didn't mean to imply that there is no way that you could know of all of this. I realize that there are many things that I don't understand and because of that, my curiosity is always open to new information. Please, Sparky. I need to know how your process of thinking and communication works. This will help me understand how you are able to understand."

"Jane, in order for you to comprehend who we are, you must understand that we were all born at the same time and that when one of us learns about something, we all do. When the aliens ripped a hole through the *Mine, Mine Planet*, the friction and the heat somehow gave us instant life. In the beginning we were just one big moving ocean of flowing lava. With time and cooling off, we discovered that the lava was just a liquid form of energy sparks. We developed into individuals who could unite or remain separate, if need be, to destroy any other life form that would try to use or hurt us. By some form of osmosis, we know and understand everything that grows on this planet. We, in a way, *are* the planet. So you see, we or I have existed since the very first day of the creation of the *Mine, Mine Planet*. That's why I can tell you exactly what I saw and didn't see when the Cleaning Bugs dropped their offspring onto the island. But first I want to tell you about an odd growth that I saw in the middle of the ocean, tens of thousands of years ago. It looked like a flower but turned out to be much more than that."

Sparky started getting starry eyed while reminiscing and describing what he had noticed so long ago but still seemed to him like only yesterday.

"Parts of the island were covered with a moss-like green substance. On the round perimeter of the inside of the island, just where petals had begun to grow, there was movement as though something were trying to rise out of the ground. I went back a month later and the same ground was now showing some kind of small, moving, black, pointy tentacle-like life form. I named that black five-foot thick round circle the Black Wall and called the island Bloom Island. I had wondered then how big Bloom Island was going to get because it was small and at a very young stage when I first saw it. When I went back a year later, the black circle was a bit larger and wider. The Black Wall acted as a shield that protected Bloom Island from outside intruders. It could stretch for hundreds of yards and grab any intruder trying to enter the Island. However, the Wall was already developing very strong psychic powers that sensed my presence from a great distance and stretched its tentacles toward the sky, reaching as if to grab me."

"Was it able to reach you?" Lolly asked.

"Oh no! I was miles above its reach and that's precisely what I found fascinating - it had the sensitivity and power to sense my presence. I periodically checked on the island. Many years ago I saw something that looked like a rock-shaped ship. I almost mistook it for a meteor until it stopped right above Bloom Island where it dropped something and immediately flew away. My curiosity needed to take a better look. As I got closer, what I thought was a package turned out to be some sort of new life. It looked like a rock but it was moving. There was nothing I could do but watch this Island fold up its petals, disappear underwater and devour what I thought was a moving rock."

"What do you mean petals and an Island disappearing under water?" Roxy and Jane asked at once.

"Well," Sparky responded, "if I recall correctly, on your planet Earth there is a flower called a daisy. If those petals folded on top of each other, the middle would be completely covered and from a distance it would look like a round white spot. It's the same principle with that Island. Only, it can submerge, maintain an air pocket and keep everything alive as if it were still outside. The petals, once underwater, provide a source of light and heat."

The girls nodded their understanding and Sparky continued.

"At a later time I discovered that the baby Cleaning Bug Astro consisted of materials that were foreign to this world and therefore when the Island tried to digest him, it couldn't. At that time Bloom Island looked like what you humans call a single cell amoeba. It literally became an incubator for Astro and in a way created and nurtured an alien being that actually belonged to both worlds. Astro developed at the same time as the life forms developed. As the amoeba grew into an advanced life form, it created other living parts. The best way to understand this phenomenon would be to look at your human blood and immune systems. Picture your white and red blood cells as doctors who travel throughout your body and destroy any foreign intruders or diseases that they find there. That is the equivalent of what the creatures growing on Bloom Island did. They protected Astro and the Island from anything harmful trying to land on it. In addition to the growing creatures that protected the Island, the Island also protected itself by creating different camouflage disguises or folding up and disappearing underwater. As this was happening, Astro was developing powers, speed and strength like no other creature in the universe. He was no longer a Cleaning Bug or a Spark, but both. In a way he became part of the Island and grew into an individual who could emulate any of the creatures and plants on the Island. He could never be duplicated. He had become Astro Jackson."

"Thank you for everything that you have told us, Sparky but I need to know where my sister Lisa is."

"I'm sorry Jane but I have no idea." He paused and then added. "Perhaps this will help. Many years ago, I noticed what looked like a shooting star land in the middle of the ocean. I searched but didn't find anything. About a year later I decided to go for a flight, which is the equivalent of your walk. The ocean kept calling me as though it were trying to direct me somewhere. And sure enough, there she was! I saw Lisa on

Bloom Island with Astro Jackson."

"What do you mean by - and there she was? How could you see the Island from so far away, let alone Astro and Lisa?" Roxy asked.

"Just think of our energy in the way that you perceive your eyesight. Only, even if I'm thousands of miles away, I can magnify my view and pull your image in as though you were an inch away.

"I was high enough above the island to see them, but too high for anyone to see me. Parts of Bloom Island consisted of small, low mountain-like surroundings with some type of weed grass sticking out of them. The rest of the island was sheer paradise with a countless exotic variety of flowers, plants and fruit trees. Some of these exotic flowers and plants turned out to be dangerous. One flower in particular that I saw, called the Blade-tulip had very pointy and sharp petals that pointed down toward the ground. The petals had long very striking colored stripes of red, light blue and yellow that flashed an illuminating sort of glow. The flower's stem was four feet high and consisted of dark and light green rings from the top to the ground. Any animal that walked by watched the plant's rings flash on and off in different sequences as they alternated colors. The animal would be so mesmerized by looking at the changing colors that it didn't see the petals drop down on it like daggers and pin it to the ground. Most of the time it would die and if not, then the shock of watching the roots rise out of the ground would kill it. The roots of the Blade-tulip would continue to wrap itself around its prey and disappear with it underground."

"That must have been very disturbing to see," Franky remarked with his face registering disgust and even disbelief.

"Perhaps for someone not accustomed to life on our planet," Sparky answered and then continued. "In the middle of the island was a four acre lake that was perfectly round. That was where Astro Jackson lived. The lake was actually a mirage produced by chemicals coming from any kind of light. Although it looked like a lake, it was actually solid ground."

Jane was really eager to hear about her sister and interrupted Sparky before he could continue. "I'm sorry, Sparky. I don't mean to be rude but would you *please* tell me more about Lisa?"

"I don't mind at all, Jane." Sparky responded politely.

"I had not visited Bloom Island for years and one day I learned that the Island had recently been seen above water. Bloom Island had stayed submerged for years and even changed locations but recently it became more visible than usual. I needed to understand what was causing this phenomenon. So I looked for it every day until I located it. When I did, I observed the activities of Astro, Lisa and Bloom Island every chance I could and at times I even focused my psychic energy on their conversations."

Jane and Roxy were anxious and immediately asked, "What did you hear? Is she okay? What is she doing?"

"Easy girls!" Sparky replied with humor. "I learned that Lisa liked to be outside where she could smell and absorb the powers of the ocean's gentle and at times rough winds. She especially loved to spar with her various plant friends when the rains stopped and the sun shone on the ocean. The sun's heat joined with the ocean's gentle breeze and it seemed as if a warm blanket had been wrapped around her. On such days the ocean and Island energized her like a battery. Rather than getting tired while sparring, she grew stronger and had enough energy to go on for a week without a break."

Making sure that Sparky didn't stop talking, Roxy, both curious and anxious, burst out, "What else did you hear?"

Sparky told her that on one particular day, he saw and heard Astro training Lisa.

"What did Astro say to Lisa?"

"I listened carefully and this is what I heard and saw."

'You must do better than that,' Astro shouted in a stern but loving manner when he saw Lisa pinned down by the Island's Black Wall.

'If you're going to fight the Gangia Queen in the future, you must learn how to fight in unconventional manners. First, remember that everything you cut off the Black Wall grows back. Next, prepare yourself by fighting the Black Wall's many tentacles and understand that the only way you're going to win is to simultaneously cut off at least two of the Wall's tentacles. This is also what you must do when you fight the Gangia Queen - two severing strikes with one blow.'

"A second later Lisa was facing the Black Wall and attacking it, with a sword in each hand. The Wall was only four feet high, but its tentacles could stretch for yards and even change into weapons. Lisa and the Wall were having a good work out and then Lisa got over confident. She believed that because she was only inches away from striking it, she could easily cut off one of its tentacles and perhaps even two. But before she could strike, a part of the Wall popped out like a battering ram, smacked her on the chest and threw her back a few yards. As she flew back, Lisa struck and got her piece. The Wall whimpered and moaned. Even though the Wall's tentacle would grow back (as all of them can do), it still hurt when it was cut. When Lisa landed on her feet, she was holding a small piece of the Wall's tentacle, which suddenly vanished from her hand. The Wall, as if showing off, kept waiving its tentacle around to taunt and show Lisa that it had grown back and that she needed to do better than that if she wanted to become any kind of a champion."

'Not bad Lisa,' Astro said encouragingly, 'That's enough for today.'

He paused and added, 'Think about how you were surprised today because you were overconfident. Tomorrow, you can try for the whole tentacle.'

'Thank you, Astro.'

"This is all that I heard and saw that day. But I was really surprised that day when I realized that she looked up to the sky and right at me. I knew she couldn't see me but from hundreds of miles away she was looking in my direction and what I heard next confirmed that I was right."

'Ah Lisa. I see that your senses are being heightened,' Astro commented. 'Do you realize what you just saw?'

'No. I only saw the sky and the stars but I did feel something strange.'

'Did you feel a strange sensation as your eyes looked to where your senses directed them? Those were your senses at work. Some call them psychic abilities. You will find that there are all kinds of names for things that are not understood. Your powers with time will strengthen as will your physical force. You must use your psychic powers to enhance your physical force in order to be able to cut off two of the Wall's tentacles. Otherwise, you will not have a chance in the arena.'

"What happened next?" Roxy asked.

"Astro paused for a minute to give her time to absorb what

he had just said."

'And that's why you must pay attention to your psychic powers even if you can't see them. What you felt was one of the Spark people observing us. Remember that feeling. And don't forget that they do not interfere in anyone's business unless they want to conduct trade with them.'

'Can you cut off two of the Wall's tentacles at one time?' Lisa asked.

"How did Astro answer Lisa?" Roxy and Jane interrupted at the same time.

"Well, Astro started laughing. He looked at the Wall and saw two large white eyes appear. That was when the Wall spoke."

'*Please* don't demonstrate, Astro!' the Wall pleaded.

'Ah! Come on Wall. Getting chopped up will help you put yourself back to gather faster. Besides, you can use the practice.'

'I didn't know that the Wall could talk,' Lisa said as she jumped back.

'I told you that everything is alive on this Island and although we are all as one, we are also individuals, no matter what we look like.'

Lisa was focused on learning and curious about Astro's fighting capabilities. She asked him, 'How will you be able beat the Wall? It has too many tentacles and it's way too fast. Plus it never gets tired.'

Sparky continued his narration as the whole crew listened almost spell-bound.

"I could see that Lisa kept a good distance as Astro and the Wall were sparring. Astro cut two and three tentacles at a time but they kept growing back. The Wall could not hit Astro because he was too fast. Lisa did not like the pain that she heard and felt coming from the Wall every time Astro cut off a piece. What followed really surprised Lisa in a few different ways. First she watched as the tips of the Wall's tentacles turned into huge sledgehammers, swords and even axes. Then, as quick as lightning, the Wall smashed Astro into the ground and completely devoured him.

"Lisa was in shock. She started to run toward the Wall, calling out, 'Astro, Astro!' She shouted, 'Hey, Wall. Let him go!' But before she could get half way to the Wall, its tentacles started squiggling around like they were on fire and the Wall shrieked as though it were feeling every bit of it. One of the tentacles hit Lisa by mistake and threw her back a ways. While lying on the ground she got an even bigger surprise. Parts of the Wall started flying at her. The part of the Wall that had swallowed Astro was being torn apart from the inside out and a minute later Astro came spinning out like a geyser, ripping and tearing his way out of the Wall. He stopped in front of Lisa. She could not believe it. His entire body consisted of different types of razor sharp weapons. Amazed, Lisa watched the sharp objects disappear as they withdrew back into his body. She was glad to see him but she couldn't ignore the Wall's moaning and groaning as he mended himself right before her eyes. She got a laugh when the Wall finished putting itself together and said, 'Please Astro. No more demonstrations' and then smacked him on the chest hard enough to knock him back a few feet."

"Please Sparky, this is fascinating but where and how can we find my sister?" Roxy asked.

Sparky replied very seriously, "Look here, Roxy. Don't be so impatient. There are things that you should know before entering my world. Besides, I have a feeling that you just might end up on Bloom Island. It's the safest place in the planet. You must know and understand how the Island and Astro live. Remember that any organism could mistake you for an enemy and swallow you up, if you don't pay attention."

"Astro wouldn't let anything happen to us on the Island, would he?" Lolly asked Sparky.

Sparky lit up a bit brighter, showing that he was happy because Lolly was paying attention to him.

Sparky laughingly answered, "That's a good question and I can assure you that you could not be in better hands. Astro is a very special alien. We know of no other living being that was born on one planet, discarded by his race and then dropped from the sky to die on our planet. But instead of dying, he was actually reborn and recreated by his creator Bloom Island. This new life made him part Spark and part Cleaning Bug. Because of this phenomenon, Astro has the power of two different kinds of beings and has also developed some of his own magic powers."

"How can you tell which part of him is Cleaning Bug and which part is Spark?" Slammer asked with great interest.

Sparky turned and faced him. "You can't tell by looking, Slammer because he has his own looks. You will know how different he is by his powers."

"What do you mean? What kind of powers does he have?

"Perhaps you will find out, Slammer but for now let me finish answering Lolly."

"You're right, Lolly. Astro wouldn't let anything happen to any of you. Should you end up on his Island, you would have his and the Island's protection. I can also tell you that Astro has quite an imagination. He was influenced by books that he had seen in his travels to different worlds. He liked the styles of the buildings on Earth and so he told Bloom Island what he wanted and with time he and the Island created and built a small village in a modern city style. Because he was surrounded by the ocean, he wanted to build beach style bungalows. The bungalows were made out of brass, chrome, wood and glass. They had to be twice the size of the original design because Astro was twice the size of any normal human."

Slammer, listening intently to Sparky, asked. "How in the world could Astro get such materials on his Island if no one knew where it was located?"

"That's just it," Sparky answered. "He doesn't have to bring anything from anywhere. The Island with its properties and minerals and Astro with his magical powers can recreate any kind of design with whatever materials that are required. Keep in mind that everything on the Island is alive no matter what it is made of. The bungalow city that they built is very magical. The buildings light up when dark heavy clouds turn the day into night. Usually the clouds pass over the Island within hours and the day returns. It's at times such as these that many of the Island's different creatures can be seen. One of the fastest moving creatures is the Air Speed, with six pairs of yellow and ocean blue wings, two on each side, one on the back and one on its stomach. It has cute, tiny red marble-like eyes, two flat violet color antennas and a long pointed mouth. The Air Speed, shaped like a grain of rice for better and faster flying, is two inches long and can stand perfectly still in midair or shoot forward or backwards like a rocket. It's very confident because of its speed and knows that it can escape any of the insect-eating plants around."

Franky and Lolly looked at each other and knew exactly

what they were thinking and both said at once, "Hey Sparky, are you going tell us how this creature can escape so fast? It can't just be its speed."

"You're right," he acknowledged to them and the rest of the crew; "it's not just the speed."

"Its sense of movement is so keen that before a plant can react to its presence, the Air Speed escapes its trap."

Ragrezy just couldn't contain his curiosity. "Does the Air Speed have some sort of special powers?"

"That's correct, Ragrezy. They're similar to those that Lisa used when she sensed my presence from miles away."

Sparky took a breath so to speak by sparkling a bit brighter and then proceeded.

"The Air Speed relies on sensing a plant's thoughts about its movements as it relays them to its stalk, thereby giving the Air Speed time to escape. Unfortunately for the Air Speed, there *is* a particular plant called the Bell plant and also known as the Speed Trap, which has been designed by nature especially for trapping the Air Speed. This is the one plant that the Air Speed never escapes and can't even warn his friends about."

Slammer and Ragrezy looked at each other, started laughing and said. "What do you mean by warn his friends? What's he going to do? Yell, hey you, Speed Buggy, look out!"

"Ah, I see that you two have a sense of humor; in which case you'll appreciate the cunning of this Air Speed-eating plant. Unfortunately for the Air Speed, he will experience the trap only once. The Air Speed's swiftness can't help him and he won't get a second chance with this cunning Speed Trap."

Ragrezy looked at Slammer. "Do you understand how that works? I don't have a clue."

"No, me either," Slammer replied.

Sparky looked at them, sparked a bit brighter with his own sense and sound of a humorous laugh and said, "What's the matter, geniuses? You still don't understand?"

He didn't wait for an answer and returned to explaining it to them and the rest of the crew.

"You see, this plant has a different way of catching its lunch. It's really a beautiful plant with one completely round petal that looks like a bell. Only it's upside down. Unfortunately, no Air Speed ever escapes this plant. The Air Speed likes to sit in the middle of this Bell Plant's beautiful pollen bridge in order to quench its thirst. It feasts on the sweet nectar, too busy to notice a completely clear long stem next to the Bell. It also doesn't notice the bell-shaped petal that is attached at the end of the stem or that the stem is carefully placing the top part of the petal over him and fitting it perfectly onto the red bottom of the Bell where he is sitting."

"Why doesn't the Air Speed sense that the Bell is coming down over him?" Spike and Lolly asked at once.

"Because the stem's top part is not connected to its bottom."

"Wouldn't that make it a separate and different plant?" Roxy jumped in and commented.

"Normally, as you understand plant life, I would say yes. But we're talking about things that you have never encountered, found in a different world and totally unfamiliar to you. In this case, the two plants work together as one to achieve one purpose: to get food."

"How in the world does that work?" Jane asked, now showing real interest.

Sparky smiled at her curiosity.

"The top part of the plant does the trapping and the bottom does the "cooking," so to speak. The two parts require different nutrients. The bottom of the Bell turns its prey into a sort of liquid gas. The top part absorbs the particular nutrients that it needs from this and the bottom part does the same."

"But why doesn't the Air Speed know what's happening?" Jane interjected.

"Because…this plant is a perfect example of how two can be one. Since they are separate, there is no vibration and therefore no way for the Air Speed to even sense a whisper of movement, until it is too late and the top part of the plant drops and traps its prey inside with amazing speed, which is why it is known as the Speed Trap. By the time the Air Speed realizes what is happening, it is sprayed with enzymes from the top half of the Bell. It's too late for the Air Speed but good for the beautiful Bell and the garden."

Spike, scared but curious, asked, "Are there creatures that eat peoples' brains because they're a delicacy for them?"

"That's a very strange question. Why would you ask such a thing?"

"I'm not asking for me. I don't care if someone eats that bossy brain of mine," he chortled. "N.I.T. would like to know because of all the strange creatures that are on your planet."

"There is nothing to worry about, Spike and you can convey that to your brain."

A second later N. I.T. popped out of Spike's head and said,

"Thank you, Sparky. I needed to hear that for myself and from you. Now would you please explain more about your planet?"

"All right. And if I think of any creature you should keep

your eye out for, I will tell you. Okay?"

Sparky paused for effect and then continued.

"There is another plant from the same family. Only this one works a bit differently. This one is called a Fire Bell but it doesn't have to cover its victims because once they go inside, they don't want to come out. The bell shape is much wider and deeper. In the middle there is a flat, thin pollen platform that stretches from one end of the bell wall to the other. The flower has the shape of a deep soup bowl. A bug can fly or walk down to the platform that is inside the Fire Bell. This plant allows numerous types of insects to drink its nectar. Once inside, the bugs act as if they are at a frat party and that the nectar is made just for them. *And it is*. Not only is it sweet, it is also very intoxicating. The bugs sit on the patch of pollen and enjoy the sweet nectar that is on both sides of the pretty pink platform. They drink their nectar completely unaware that they are slowly becoming drugged. Other bugs are immune to the nectar and are hypnotized instead by the movement of the Fire Bell whose various shades of red continually change like parts of a flame. A variety of bugs party inside this plant."

All at once the ship jumped up and down as if it were a rowboat pummeled by the sea. Sparky and Lolly grabbed each other, holding on for dear life. Everyone grabbed something so as not to be thrown around the ship.

Jane hollered, "Sparky, what's going on?"

"Don't worry, Jane."

Just as Slammer was about to say, "What do you mean, don't worry?" the ship straightened out as if nothing had happened

"That's *some* space turbulence you have, Sparky," Slammer remarked.

"I'm sorry everyone. Those turbulent pockets are due to various unexplainable causes and fortunately they are very rare. That's why I didn't bring them up."

Slammer put on a big smile and just had to say, "It's okay, genius. We forgive you."

Sparky in his own way sparkled and chuckled a bit.

Roxy, not wanting to seem upset about the possibility of almost dying, changed the subject.

"Sparky, can you please tell us more about the bugs on Astro Island?"

The crew agreed with Roxy's request and listened attentively to Sparky as if nothing had just happened on the ship.

"Like I said, the turbulence is very rare, and so now there is no more shaking."

Then he started to describe a bug that didn't have much luck with the Fire Bell plant.

"The Flat Head is a quiet little bug about six inches long. Its back is a solid black shell with red stripes. It has a completely flat face with eyes that pop out half way like marbles that have been cut in half. Its lips are shaped like two strings, one on the bottom, the other on top and both are just as flat as its face. Let me tell you a story about a Flat Head and a Fire Bell. One day, there was a Flat Head enjoying himself and sitting with his buddy on the Fire Bell's pollen platform. The Flat Head stuck his long slender tongue into the nectar, took a deep soothing drink, almost empting every drop out and then put his tongue back into his mouth. He took a deep breath and with great enthusiasm said in a deep voice, '*Sssheess*, that stuff is good.'

"Near him there was a Chico Bug. This bug has bright

yellow, blue and red wings that go with its surroundings and when open, stretch to three times its body length. On the wings there is a design that looks like a 1959 Chevy convertible. Every Chico Bug is very proud of this beautiful design and shows it off, because it is his family crest. The Chico was enjoying his drink while watching the Flat Head. It began complaining in a thick Latino accent.

'*Hey, mang! Jou almos drain de pool out.*'

'Don't you mean I almost drained the pool of nectar?'

'Si, Senor,' he replied.

'Don't worry, buddy,' the Flat Head pointed out. 'Look, the nectar just keeps filling up.' Not realizing that he was getting intoxicated, he added. 'I love this place. I hope I remember where it is.'

Sparky laughed as he added that before the Flat head finished saying that, Chico had already reassured him as if they were already long lost buddies.

'Don't worry. I will find it for us again,' not realizing that the fumes had already gotten him high and that he was losing his Spanish accent.

'Oh. So you've been here before?' The Flat Head commented.

'No, But I never forget, once I go some place.'

"Of course neither of them thought that they needed to be alive in order for them to remember where they wanted to go," Sparky commented.

"Any way, once all of the critters that were in the plant were intoxicated and totally unaware of their condition, it was time for the plant to enjoy its lovely guests. By the time the bugs felt the mist all around them, it was too late. Boy, were they surprised and delicious! It was just another day in the garden with its bug eating plants..." Sparky finished with a sparkly laugh.

"Are there any kinds of birds or flying creatures?" Franky asked.

"Sure, Franky. There is an odd-looking one called the Sing, Sing Square Bird. It is about four inches long and has a husky frame. Its head is almost square so that it can hold its four eyes. The Sing, Sing Square Bird has soft light blue wings with thin red stripes running from one end of each wing to the other."

Lolly, finding it hard to imagine, asked, "How can it have four eyes?"

"Picture this, Lolly. One eye is on top of its head, another on the bottom and one on each side. The eyes all work independently. The front of its face looks like it has full smiling lips, but they are only for decoration and a way to fool its prey. The Sing, Sing Square Bird has a funnel shaped nose that the bugs never pay attention to because they are always too busy trying to figure out what the bird's eyes are looking at. It is the bird's funnel nose that tilts and gives the prey a taste of its sweet potion through a mist blown softly over it. The bug goes into some sort of a trance and the Sing, Sing Square Bird starts to sing its little song. This is the last thing that its prey hears before the Sing, Sing Square Bird has its next meal.

We're so happy and so cute, hope you love our little hoot
You will love the song we sing. It will give you everything.
Problems will just disappear, we sing to you from far and near.
And if our songs should make you sleep, it's just because we want to eat.

"Sparky, are all the creatures on your planet nasty?" Lolly asked.

"No, of course not. I'm sorry that I gave you that impression. We have many friendly creatures and nice plants. But they are not the ones that you will have to watch out for when you land there."

Sparky looked at Jane and said. "Jane, you will soon have to prepare to enter the *Mine, Mine Planet.*"

Everyone looked at each other.

"All right!" Jane shouted to the crew. "What are we waiting for? Let's get ready for this rescue and a battle that we had better win."

When they got closer to the *Mine, Mine Planet,* Sparky suddenly ordered Jane to lower all of the shields on the spaceship into place.

"What's wrong?" she asked.

"The temperature is going to get hot enough that it will damage your equipment if you don't use your shields." Then he added, "Do you want to get cooked?"

"Did you hear what he said?" Jane shouted to Spike.

"I sure did!"

The ship started shaking. Spike panicked, pushed a button on the control panel and anxiously watched the shields try to move.

"Before we can get to the Spring Ring," Sparky said, "we have to travel through the hottest deserts that exist in the universe. The weather is usually very turbulent and the whole area is going to be extremely rough and dangerous. The first creatures that you will run across are the Dust Throwers. You must be aware that they exist since you can't see them. Heat sensors won't help you find them because the Dust Throwers are the same temperature as the desert. They are three times the size of a football stadium and are covered with sand, which blends into the desert, making them invisible. Even we can't see them until it's too late."

N.I.T. popped out of Spike's ear and with great concern asked.

"What would you suggest, Sparky if we run across such creatures?"

"There is only one thing you can do N.I.T. Keep a very close look out and if you see a dust ball coming at you, get out of its way, if you can."

"Is there anything else that I should know?" N.I.T. inquired, still concerned.

"Perhaps this will help. Picture a turtle whose shell is sunken in like a bowl. The Dust Thrower is like such a turtle whose shell fills up with tons of sand, which is then compressed into a dry ball. When the Dust Thrower sees a prey in the air, in this case, the RoxyResk, the compressed ball of sand pops up into the sky with such force that if it were to hit the ship, the sand ball would break up, enveloping the ship with sticky sand. On its way down, the sand would land on the ship with its full weight and knock it out of the sky. When the ship hits the ground, the partially broken up sand ball will fall and bury the ship and its passengers, turning everything into liquid and providing the Dust Throwers with their meal. Is that any help to you?"

"Yes it is. Thank you very much."

N.I.T. flew back into Spike's ear and Spike ran to the control panel a few feet away from him. He wouldn't take his eyes off the screen in front of him because N.I.T. wanted to make sure that nothing bad would happen.

It wasn't long before Spike shouted out.

"Prepare yourselves and grab on to something."

"What's wrong," Jane asked.

But before Spike could say a word, the ship shook and tilted ninety degrees to the left. A second later, it straightened out.

"What was that all about?" Jane asked, concerned.

Lolly was just yards away, clinging to a securely anchored table.

"Are we safe, Spike?"

Slammer asked Ragrezy if there was any damage. Just as he was about to answer, Spike yelled out a warning for everyone to brace themselves.

This time one of the Dust Throwers nicked the ship with a sand ball. The RoxyResk barely held together. It was lucky that Slammer was such a strong man. The way the ship bounced him around reminded Spike of a pinball machine with Slammer as the ball. Any other human or alien would have been killed by the force.

Everyone on the ship was doing everything possible to keep it afloat. The ship was going down.

"Do something, Spike!" Lolly shouted, panicking.

"The weight on the ship is too much," he shouted back, adding, "The sand is stuck and I can't shake it off."

Slammer told Ragrezy to connect some wires to the outside structure of the ship.

Meanwhile Rocky and Squeak were holding together some of the ship's panels that had loosened.

"Hurry up!" Slammer shouted to Ragrezy as other parts of

the ship started to shift.

Jane who was helping Spike on another control panel, trying to keep the ship afloat shouted. "Get those wires connected now, Ragrezy. The ship will not stay up much longer."

Some sparks from the wires covered Ragrezy as he shouted, "Okay Spike! Pull the third lever to your right."

Spike never moved so fast and it was a good thing. The ship was on its last leg, so to speak.

As soon as he pulled that lever, the ship turned red hot, the sand melted and poured off. Luckily there was no damage to the ship or its crew. In the process of saving the ship, they traveled far enough into the planet to reach the cooler part of the Summer Ring and to raise the protective shields.

But the cooler part of the Summer Ring was not like that of Earth. It was truly uninhabitable for most other species but not for those who lived on that portion of the desert.

Even though the deserts were magnificent, Jane and her crew had to be careful not to get too close to the surface. The ship had to stay at least a half-mile above it.

"Look Jane," Franky said.

"What is it?" She asked.

"Keep your eyes on that," he said, pointing to a section of the desert.

"What is that colorful plant that has water coming out of the top?" Jane asked.

"That's a giant Drip Adreen plant. It belongs to the lily family."

From the sky it looked no bigger than a tulip. But on the ground its size was really quite impressive. In the middle of this Drip Adreen plant was a beautiful white sculptured tower-like stalk. The tower looked like it had tiers with softly pleated stairs leading to small couplets containing water. This tiered structure made it more inviting for any prey to climb up and quench its thirst. There were four large petals. Two were red and two were purple; the colors constantly alternated. Each petal was about twenty feet high and ten feet wide. The plant smelled like lilacs and roses, a combination that was very inviting to the indigenous animals.

Franky looked at Jane and said softly,

"Just watch. The Drip Adreen is preparing for dinner - its petals are changing colors and glowing to attract its newest prey. It's called a Spide-Snake and it's one of the few things that can survive in a three hundred degree dry temperature. The Drip Adreen plant is another. The Spide-Snake is a weird looking creature. It has the top part of a spider with the body and bottom jaw of a snake.

"Look, Jane! The Spide-Snake has just noticed the plant, which already has its petals spread wide. It's an open invitation for it to climb the tower to reach its water paradise. The Spide-Snake really cannot resist this invitation because it sees water flowing out of the couplets into the crevasse at the very top. Isn't it interesting that none of the creatures ever wonder why there isn't any water flowing to the bottom of the plant so that they wouldn't have to climb up? They just want to get to the top where this big pool of clear water is waiting to be drunk."

Jane interrupted impatiently. "That's enough description! What happens, Franky? You have to tell me."

"Watch, Jane."

And she did. She saw how dangerous that hostile world was. She couldn't take her eyes away from watching the

Spide-Snake climb to the highest peak where the water was coming out. It was the prize that all animals thought that they were going to get. The Spide-Snake was about three feet long. It wasn't a bad trip for him to climb about fifteen feet to the top. The snake licked the tower as it climbed but every lick made it climb higher. Once it reached the top of that wonderful watery tower, trouble showed its ugly face. The water that the Spide-Snake started to drink became thicker with every drop. Before long, it found itself unable to move as that fresh water turned into a glue-like death trap. The Spide-Snake, unable to move, could only watch the petals as they slowly closed around it, until complete darkness overtook it. Then the Drip Adreen began its digestive process.

Jane noticed that the desert was shrinking as the plant life started to expand and eventually she saw docile animals roaming the land. The Summer Ring was slowly passing into the Spring Ring.

All in all, the entire trip into the Spring Ring of Sparky's planet went pretty smoothly. It was beautiful and all anyone on the ship wanted to do was to relax and look at all of the beautiful flowers and birds. They traveled for about another hour and Sparky pointed out on the screen Spark City where they had to land before arriving at the *Sphere of Tears*. Jane thought how Spark City was like the capitol of the world, a combination of New York, Tokyo, Vegas and other such places, in one beautiful circle with continuous spring and daylight. The sight was surreal. The cities that they saw on their ship's screen seemed motionless, almost floating in the sky, while actually on the ground thousands of miles away.

"Do you see the building with that house on top of it?" Sparky asked Jane.

She looked and couldn't believe that such a beautiful house still existed, let alone on another planet. She had seen such houses in magazines only. She recognized the house. It was one of the first art deco homes to be built in the nineteen twenties. Jane thought that the owner or owners of the building must have had a soft heart for that style of art deco designs and that there were probably no artists left from that era. The owner of the building had the house moved from where it was built and placed on the top of his skyscraper, surrounded by land taken with the house to create a garden and a driveway with streetlights. An elevator was constructed at the base of the skyscraper that went up to the roof so that he could drive to his house.

"Yes, I do see the house," Jane replied. "It's beautiful." She paused and continued. "Do you know who owns that skyscraper and house? What a skyscraper! It looks like it has two hundred floors."

"Yes, I do. He doesn't just own that building. He owns a good portion of the *Sphere of Tears*. I believe that you already know him. It's the All-for-One-Man. Do you really know what you and your crew are up against?"

Jane kept looking at the skyscraper with the house perched on top. It got smaller the farther away they traveled and finally disappeared from sight when they reached the other side of the city.

Jane was irritated when she heard the name of the All-for-One-Man. She wanted to search for Lisa immediately and burst out impatiently,

"Do you know where my sister is being kept, Sparky?"

He pointed to an unbelievable looking structure. It was ugly yet hard to ignore. One had to marvel at the strength that it represented with its sinister Black Walls and pointed rod iron balconies sticking out from the sides of the building. The roof had a landing pad for a helicopter. There were many guards patrolling the entire building and the roof was their central security operating position. It was a very hi-tech building with low-tech looks.

"Just how do you think you are going to gain entrance? And don't forget that the other arena warriors are almost completely programmed to obey to their masters. Instead of helping you, they would try to capture you."

"I believe all of that is being covered by Slammer and Mountain," Jane confidently assured him. Then she asked,

"Do you know where we should stay for the night?"

"I suggest the *Gimme Hotel* across the street from where your sister is staying. It's a comfortable hotel with a pool. The best part about it is that if you book a room on the sixty-seventh floor, you will be able to spy on the warriors and the others staying with your sister on the sixty- sixth floor."

"Thank you, Sparky."

Sparky once again disappeared as fast as he appeared. And no wonder…Jane realized that they were minutes away from landing.

The landing pad was on the outskirts of the city. It was a very busy airfield partially surrounded by motels, diners, gift shops and other areas with lots of slot machines and other types of games that only require a lever to be pulled or button to be pushed. And plenty of ATM machines to provide the money required to play the games. The ship slowly set down.

Once the crew landed, Jane went into her "there are things to be done" mode.

"Spike, Lolly, Roxy, Ragrezy and Slammer…take a cab to the *Gimme Hotel* and make sure to book a suite on the sixty-seventh floor."

Roxy, surprised and concerned, asked. "Where are you going, Sis?"

"Yeh! Why aren't you coming with us, Jane?" Ragrezy commented with concern in his voice.

"I have to see someone in another part of town. And you guys don't need to be worried. I can take care of myself. And I need Franky to come with me. There's an old friend of his where I'm going and he needs to speak to him for me. Once we're done, we'll come straight to the hotel." The crew hailed an air-cab and left.

Jane and Franky walked up to another air-cab waiting for a pick up. Franky stood next to it, went onto his knees, looked under it and tried to figure out what made the air-cab float. Neither Franky nor Jane had ever seen a car floating in the air with no sound and no visible way of movement.

"Franky, do you know how these cars work?"

"No, I don't. The inventor who is also the manufacturer keeps it a secret. But I have my own theory. Imagine that the bottom of the car is a magnet, with layers of a specially made material which when moved to different positions allows the planet's positive magnetic field to push against the air-cab. The cab also has a positive and negative magnetic field, which can change according to the planet's positive or negative magnetic force. All the driver has to do is push a button. If directed correctly, the magnetic field can take anyone anywhere, even over water. The speed is controlled by the amount of the special material that allows the car to be exposed to the planet's magnetic force."

She did not expect such a long answer and didn't want to be rude, but once Franky finished his theory, she interrupted, not wanting to take the chance that he might continue talking.

"Come on Franky, get in the cab. We have to go."

Once inside, Franky stuck his head through the partition window toward the driver. He asked the driver to take them to the Buzzer Bar. The old, almost blind, owl-looking driver whose name was Hoot turned around and said, "Are you trying to be funny? Do I look like a buzzard to you?" Franky stuck his face through the protective window and yelled, "No, we said that we want to go to the Buzzer Bar." Mr. Hoot trapped Franky's head between the protective window and himself, looked at him and said, "No need to yell in my ear, young man. I heard you the first time. Now sit back and relax."

Franky was choking and Mr. Hoot suddenly realized that he hadn't released him. He apologized and down came the window. Jane giggled. Franky leaned back and off they went.

About a half hour later, the cab driver dropped them off at the Buzzer Bar. The entire establishment resembled a buzzard bird. Jane and Franky got out of the cab and just stared at the bar.

"Is that a real buzzard head?" Jane asked. A second later Jane felt a breeze touch her shoulder. Startled, she moved quickly, almost knocking Franky down.

"Did you feel that?"

Franky chuckled. "Okay, Buzzy. Show yourself."

As if the wind had mysteriously blown a dark shadow out of the thin air, this amazing, never before seen colorful buzzard appeared next to Jane.

The bird was whimsical, humorous and very colorful for a

buzzard. He was shaped almost like a man but had long, thin chicken legs. His body was covered with feathers but not like the black ones on the buzzards on planet Earth. Instead, they looked a bit like peacock feathers, but with a bluish yellow tint to them. The most startling part of his body was his head, which was a spitting image of the Buzzer Bar.

Franky introduced them.

"Buzzy, this is Jane, my friend and Captain of the RoxyResk."

"What is he famous for?" Jane asked.

" Well Jane…Let's put it this way. Look in back of you."

She did and immediately jumped backwards into Buzzy's opened feathery wings. Buzzy's animal instincts took over.

"Buzzy." Franky shouted, "She's with me. Let go of her!"

Buzzy quickly opened his wings and Jane stumbled out. Franky caught her so she wouldn't fall. She bounced into a fighting position with a knife in her hand, prepared for battle.

Buzzy instantly began to apologize.

"I'm so sorry, Jane. It was just a reflex…Just like you took your stance so automatically. Please forgive me."

She looked back again and the shadows that were hidden around the bar and adjoining buildings all had peering eyes that just stared without moving.

"That's okay," she said. "I accept your apology."

Then she added, "Whose eyes are those peering out from around the bar and buildings?"

"Oh, don't worry about them. They're my buzzard buddies and let's just say that they help keep the neighborhood clean by dining with me. And since you're with Franky, you're safe.

So Franky, what brings you to this neck of the scavenger's hunting ground?"

"Jane has some business with a friend of hers."

"Ah, she's a smart one. She knew she needed you and that you'd come in handy."

"Oh yeh. You can trust her with your life once she's a friend. And you now are one of those friends "

Jane looked at the bar and curious to know about it, asked. "Who designed and built this place? It looks so real. Just like a buzzard's head."

"It wasn't built," Buzzy replied. He was very sad when he started to speak about the bar.

"That buzzard head is the only one left of all of my ancestors. It has survived through the Age of Shift until today."

Jane just had to ask. "What's the Age of Shift?" and then apologized for cutting him off.

He looked at her and then at Franky who shrugged his shoulders in a way that said, "She's the Captain. She wants to know."

"Well, Jane. The Age of Shift is the equivalent to your Ice Age on Earth. Something happened and the world shifted. The sun no longer shone on us and everything became extinct, except for the Spark people who remained in a state of suspended animation. After billions of years, the planet finally drifted back on its original axel and life started anew. Now, only the Spark people are the true inhabitants of this planet from that original Age. The rest of us that were recreated were never the same, as before the Age of Shift. A lot of other creatures were brought to this planet by one alien or another. One day I saw what I thought was an unusual and special rock.

And in a way it was calling to me. I found it irresistible so I started digging. It took my men and me two weeks to dig it up. And this is what I found: the only complete skeleton of its kind. I made it my mission to turn this building-size relative into a bar so that the whole world could see that we were at one time - the rulers of the world."

Jane who was fascinated by Buzzy's story asked, "How do you know the history of this buzzard?"

"Didn't Franky tell you anything about me?" Buzzy who was surprised that she didn't know anything answered in a smart aleck but nice way.

Pointing to the head of the Buzzer Bar, Buzzy said, "Look. That's what I would have been like if there had been no Age of Shift. My species is just lucky to have survived. But we're pretty puny in comparison to him. Just look at me and then at him," once again, pointing to his ancestor.

"Are you kidding?" Jane said with a big smile. "You look magnificent." Then to cheer him up, she continued, "He's very attractive, isn't he Franky?"

Franky and Buzzy looked at each other and started laughing as Franky said, "Oh yeh. He looks marvelous."

"Buzzy, Don't pay attention to him." Jane lifted her hand and started pointing out the similarities between Buzzy and the Buzzer Bar.

"Look at the magnificent shiny dark brown beak that Buzzy has. It looks just like the one on Buzzard bar only that one is as large as a two-story building."

Buzzy looked at Jane, then at Franky and said, "I like her. You should bring her around more often."

"Thank you, Buzzy." She went over to him and gave him a

kiss on his beak. It was very endearing to see Buzzy blush as his beak turned reddish like the color of a dark red brick.

"May we go inside?" she asked.

Buzzy replied very joyfully, like a long lost friend. "You can do whatever you want."

Jane took a minute to enjoy the idea of going into a giant bird's mouth. At first it was a bit scary walking through the door. The bar's counter and its tables were shaped from different parts of this magnificent bird's skeleton. Two of the walls that were opposite each other were made of its feathers. The other two walls were the bird's eyes. Jane found it very strange to stand in the middle of this room and have two eyes looking at her from opposite walls, as though the buzzard were saying, "I might be dead but I still see you."

"Would you like to sit and enjoy our variety of meats?" Buzzy asked.

Jane had no idea what the meat was and really wasn't interested. She looked around the bar and said, "Thank you so much, Buzzy but we're just here for business. Maybe next time…"

She suddenly saw the man she had to meet. He was in another room, signaling for her to hurry. She started to walk away while saying, "Buzzy, I hope you don't think I'm being rude. I see my contact. Buzzy and Franky, please excuse me."

Jane told Franky to wait for her and went into a back room that was about ten feet away from them. Before the door even closed, Franky could hear her talking.

"Hi Mountain! Did you make the arrangements with your men for the *Sphere of Tears* rescue mission?"

"Everything is working as we speak. Astro is setting up

arrangements with the Wall."

He paused, looked at Jane and said, "Don't you have something to tell me?"

"Yes. Slammer told me to relay this message. Put a million on Lisa losing the fight. Then, bet another million on her winning. Take five more million and make side bets that Lisa won't finish the fight. Then, see if you can make side bets on her escaping from the arena."

Jane paused and then added, "Slammer said that you know how everyone believes that it is impossible to escape from the Gangia Queen and all of her men. Not to mention the All-for-One-Man's hoodlums..."

"Is he crazy?" Mountain shouted. "They'll triple the guards and know that we set up Lisa's escape."

"Slammer said that he has this covered and then told me to tell you and I quote, 'Yes, I know that they will kill us if they catch us. But make the bets anyway.' Slammer wants to make sure you place the bets on other planets where they are taking bets on this fight."

Two minutes later, she rushed out of the back room, grabbed Franky, quickly said goodbye to Buzzy and ran out of the bar, with Franky in tow. They hailed another cab, jumped in and returned to the ship.

When they arrived, Sparky was waiting for Jane. As Jane and Franky were getting into the ship, Sparky told her that he would keep an eye on her and the crew from the distance and would help her when needed. Once everyone was in the ship, Sparky wished all of them good luck. He flew out of the ship, as if the walls weren't there. Jane and her crew were ready to go to the *Sphere of Tears*. But first they had to go to the first level of the landing pad, located in the Main Terminal where they would leave their ship and take a shuttle to the Transporter, which would take them to the *Sphere of Tears*. The ship lifted off and arrived at the main terminal. Jane and Squeak were the last to leave the ship. Squeak had to say goodbye to Rocky before he left with Jane.

"I'm sorry, Rocky. I wish you could come with us."

As Rocky said, "Don't worry about me," his mouth opened, his tongue rolled out and the Changer walked out onto his stretched platform-like tongue. In a soft voice she wished Jane good luck and told Squeak to eat lots of evil.

Squeak flew up, clung to the Changer and said, "I'm going miss you."

Then he flew next to Jane and wrapped himself around her neck. They said their goodbyes to Rocky and the Changer and left the ship.

They met up with Slammer, Franky, Ragrezy, Spike and Lolly. Then they followed the crowds that were going to where a shuttle was idling. The shuttle looked like one of the passenger cars from a nineteen fortys' train.

Only this shuttle was the size of a cruiser, with rounded wings that stretched from the front of the car to almost the whole length of its body. It had several levels that were almost full. Once on the shuttle, Jane and her crew went into their private suite with individual rooms. After they settled in, which took about ten minutes, they all met in the main room. Almost immediately, a very large, barrel-shaped creature, made of leather, appeared.

Jane knew that the planet had a very strange way of distributing water in certain parts of the world and that there were creatures that traveled and provided water for those in need, for a price of course. She was also aware that this watery enterprise belonged to the All-for-One-Man, which was one of the many reasons that he had such wealth and power.

The barreled shaped creature stood in front of Jane and introduced himself.

"I am Mr. Wet-Dry and I provide water to different types of life forms. There are millions like me who travel throughout the world. We know everything that goes on everywhere and we can change our molecular structure to adapt to everything, but not without a price of course."

Mr. Wet-Dry warned Jane and her crew not to go to the *Sphere of Tears* but he knew that it wouldn't do any good since they were already on the way. While Mr. Wet-Dry was talking to Jane, the crew noticed all sorts of bugs that were clinging to him and appeared to be drinking. This was interrupted as they watched him shrink from a two hundred pound barrel filled with water to a skinny, wet but empty, leather pouch with a human-like shape. A second later, it was like a magic faucet had turned on inside him and once again, he was filled with water. Their attention was drawn to a very noticeable bug. This cheerful, little yellow and black bug had a head shaped like a Viking helmet, tiny white antennas instead of Viking horns, two large round eyes that seemed to float in a head full of long, red curly hair, and a cute, button-like nose. It had a body that looked like a long, gravy bowl with six ant-like legs. The bug was very small and its back was covered with a stretchable top that changed colors according to its water level. This bug, like all the other bugs on this particular planet, somehow ended up in all sorts of places, like spaceships, air or ground transports and even homes. It reminded Jane and the others of another water-consuming bug, Millie, the charming little Water Extractor.

Slammer found a comfortable spot on the ground to sit with his back against the wall, to take in all that was happening, He liked sitting on the floor. Millie, who was for some reason hiding somewhere on Slammer, crawled out and climbed carefully, hoping not to be seen, on a box that was next to him. She needed to pass by him. Taking careful steps, she attempted to avoid him and in the process, she looked like she was up to no good. She saw Slammer looking at her and she hoped that he wouldn't squash her. Slammer looked at her and said, "If you try to extract water from me, I will treat you like the bug that you are." Poor Millie wasn't taking a chance on Slammer changing his mind and squishing her right then and there. She ran so fast that lighting couldn't catch her.

As Ragrezy was walking by, he observed Slammer and he asked him how he could hate such a cute creature as Millie.

"I hope you never have to find out," Slammer replied. Ragrezy continued talking and said, "When you want to tell me, we can talk."

Slammer just wanted to rest. He closed his eyes and the crew was attacked by some unseen forces. By the time Slammer reacted, the shuttle already had a few holes in it. And the creature was attacking the crew. There were claw-like tentacles all over the place. One grabbed Slammer. Jane was in shock as she watched the creature's tongue squeeze Slammer and start sucking out all of his moisture. As strong as Slammer was, he was still dragged out of the ship. The last thing he saw just before the monster drained him dry and turned him into dust was Jane reaching out to him while he was yelling, "Water, water. I need water." Then there was darkness.

When Slammer opened his eyes he was still screaming. Then he saw the whole crew looking at him. Some of them were still betting on how long it would be before he stopped screaming. Spike won the bet because he had seen Slammer have similar nightmares before.

"What were you just dreaming about?" Ragrezy asked. That was when Slammer decided to share his nightmare with his new friend. He told Ragrezy how he dreamed that his crew was attacked and that he was sucked dry of all his bodily fluids while being dragged from the ship. It wasn't easy for Slammer to talk about this.

Then Slammer whispered, "I don't mean to be nasty to Millie. I wish I could tell her that I only treat her like that because I'm scared of her."

"Why are you so afraid of Millie?" Ragrezy asked.

Slammer took a deep breath and explained to him how he for years woke up on the streets of New York City, in alleyways that were infested with bugs and that their bites stayed with him for weeks. Ragrezy understood right away how terrified Slammer was of being bitten by any bug and he told him to try to find a way to cope with his fears. Then, he decided to leave Slammer to his own thoughts while he went to move some equipment. Slammer sat down again on the floor and thought about what Ragrezy had just said about not taking out his fears and frustrations out on that poor bug. After all, Millie only wanted a drop of water and Ragrezy said that he couldn't understand how Slammer could deny someone, or something water. Slammer started feeling guilty about mistreating Millie. He found himself thinking about Millie and how cute she was. He relaxed and fell asleep. Then, he woke up abruptly. He thought that he heard some screaming. He opened his eyes, scanned the area and determined that there was nothing unusual and that everyone was okay. Then, he heard another scream but it was faint. This time, he looked down on his right and saw Millie come out from a box. She was limping and trying to run. She saw Slammer, stopped and turned to run back the other way. Then she realized that she had nowhere to run. She could either be squashed by Slammer's boot or mauled and eaten by the Grinder Bugs which were pursuing her. Millie feared the Grinders, horrible black scavenger parasites that had hard shells for bodie, nails all around their heads and three tails, each one with spiked ball on its end which smashed and ground while eating whatever they caught. As far as they were concerned, the moisture extractors existed to be their food. Slammer looked at Millie who was shaking. He didn't know that soon she would be facing monsters at least three times her size.

Millie stared at Slammer with her very large, round hazel eyes that were shaded by her long eyelashes. She was hoping that Slammer wouldn't squash her. When she saw that he was lifting his foot and raising it above her, she began to pray to Buggy, her Bug God. She couldn't look up any more because she didn't want to see herself squashed by Slammer's boot. And she didn't want to look back because the sight of the Grinder bugs would scare her again. Before she closed her eyes, she saw the Grinders just yards in front of her. She wondered how they got there so fast. She dropped her head, looked at the ground, waited for the end to come and prayed to her God Buggy. She couldn't figure out why she wasn't squashed or why she felt lighter. When she got the nerve to open her eyes, she saw that she was floating in the air and that Slammer had snatched her up in his hand and lifted her out of danger.

He said softly, "You're safe now. Would you like a drink before I put you down?

"No, no thank you," Millie replied quietly, now that she understood that he had saved her life. "I would like you to know that I'm very grateful to you for saving my life."

"It's okay. But you should thank Ragrezy." He put her down and told her to be careful.

After Slammer finished helping Millie, Jane walked over to him and just had to express the way that she felt.

"Slammer, I know that you want to keep your reputation as a tough guy and you are. But let me tell you, that was one of the sweetest things I have ever seen anyone do."

He looked at her sheepishly and said, "You didn't see anything."

She wanted to make sure that Slammer felt secure about his secret.

"Hey, Slammer!" she laughed. "How could I know anything if I was not and am not here? Do you see me?"

Slammer looked around. Jane was no longer in sight and he smiled at how fast and wise she was.

Then he heard the shuttle conductor over the intercom. "Ladies and gentlemen, we are entering the south tube connector. There will be a bit of a delay due to the traffic. Please sit back and relax. It will be twenty more minutes until we arrive at the landing pad."

By the time the twenty minutes were up, many riders were standing and waiting impatiently for the doors to open. When they finally did, the passengers were anxious and exited in a rush, nearly knocking one another over. It usually wasn't like this but the arena fights changed everything. The people around the landing pad resembled a rowdy crowd at a St. Patty's Day Parade.

Jane stepped off the shuttle, pointed Slammer toward the huge information sign that was in the middle of the Grand Ship Station. She told him to tell the crew that they would find the information about how to get to the spaceship on the sign. Then she added that they should meet her at the spaceship. Jane turned and left.

There were many transporters that carried hundreds of riders and a few special spaceships retained by small private groups such as Jane's, all going to the *Sphere of Tears*. There was one ship design that Spike found interesting, especially after he learned that it was the space ship that the Spark people designed for the aliens to use for their business trade. They had discovered that the more holes the ship had the less friction there would be and the faster the ship would travel. Spike compared their idea to fishing with a net. The larger the holes in the net the easier it would be to drag the net through water. Spike understood that the more open a space ship was, the faster it could travel through space. Less material meant less friction and more speed. The Sparks designed their space ships like round and very elongated nets that resembled the *Mine, Mine Planet*. The center of the ship was only empty space, just like their planet. Spike admired the four rings. Each ring had the height of a five story building and was about 200 yards apart from the next ring. There were four long tubes supporting the rings and keeping them from becoming one structure. The rings and tubes were completely clear so that anyone could see out of the ship from anywhere as long as no curtain or shade was in the way. Spike stopped thinking about the ship when he realized that he was separated from the crew.

Once everyone made it to the place where they were supposed to take the transporter, Jane realized that something wasn't right. She looked around and took inventory aloud.

She knew that Squeak was in her pocket.

"Okay. There's Slammer, Ragrezy, Franky, Lolly and Roxy. Hey, Slammer. Where's Spike?"

"He should be here. He told me that he had to check on something and that he would meet me here."

"Don't you mean N. I. T. had to check something? Spike doesn't check anything." Jane said with a smirk. They had no choice but to wait. Everyone's mind was on one thing or another.

Meanwhile, Slammer thought about how the transporter that they assumed they had rented for the trip to the *Sphere of Tears* turned out, not to be a transporter but instead a good solid spaceship. But it was no Enterprise. The ship was named the Assassins and it took its aerodynamic design and name from an Earth creature called the Assassins Bug. The ship had only one level and Jane and her crew found it perfect for cruising. The Assassins was designed to travel very fast and if attacked, it was built not only to withstand the attack but also to evade any enemy because of its incredible speed. If forewarned, the Assassins usually could avoid any attack. The body of the ship was black with large red dots that formed a horseshoe shape around its entire circumference. It had a protruding front and its landing gears resembled bug legs.

Slammer snapped out of his thoughts when he heard Jane shout, "What took you so long, Spike?" N.I.T., a bit perturbed, popped out of Spike's ear and yelled in the direction of Jane and Slammer, "He didn't want to leave his La, La, Land."

"Come on. Let's go." Ragrezy shouted. Then everyone entered the ship. They got ready and prepared for take-off. After the technical stuff was taken care of, they had time to spare. That was when Mr. Wet-Dry decided to educate everyone about some of the history of the *Mine, Mine Planet*.

Earlier, when Mr. Wet-Dry was in the shuttle with the others, he had asked Jane if she could give him a lift to the *Sphere of Tears* and he offered to make some form of payment in return. Jane told him that it would be a pleasure to take him and that she wouldn't accept anything from him. Instead she asked him to tell them the history of the *Sphere of Tears* once they were on the spaceship and ready for take-off.

"How does Mr. Wet-Dry know the story?" Slammer had asked Jane out of curiosity.

Jane answered with conviction. "There are creatures on this planet that are like the scouts in the Old West. As these scouts traveled from town to town, they communicated what was going on in other parts of the country. They were the information gatherers and eventually became the storytellers. Mr. Wet-Dry is just such a modern day storyteller."

Now that they were in the ship, it was Mr. Wet-Dry's turn to begin the story of how the *Sphere of Tears* had been built by the Tube Spark people.

"In the middle of the world, there are two almost invisible parallel tubes about three hundred miles apart from each other. These tubes, called connectors, are natural phenomena that stretch horizontally about ten thousand miles from one end of the *Mine, Mine Planet* to the other. Roads were built inside to allow people to travel throughout these connectors. Cities and towns were then built sporadically inside of them. The Tube Spark people built a separate connector onto the two natural ones. The *Sphere of Tears* was built in the middle of the man-made connector that now stands at the center of the world. The Tube Spark people provided the materials and the know-how while other worlds provided the slaves to do all of the labor."

"How will we get into the *Sphere of Tears*, Mr. Wet-Dry?" Lolly asked.

"Oh, that's easy. Once we take off, we will travel for about five thousand miles in the natural tube connector where we are now. Then, we will see a large opening with a thousand mile circumference. We will make a left turn into this opening and enter the man-made tube connector leading to the territory belonging to the *Sphere of Tears*. Since we all have our documentation papers, we will be allowed to enter."

As he finished his story, Jane and the crew went through their final drill for takeoff and when they were ready, Jane said very simply, "Let's go and get my sister. She's been a slave long enough!"

Once they took off and were safely on their way, Jane decided to tell her crew about her childhood and what had happened to her and her family.

"This story might not be exactly accurate but it is all I remember. One day, my Mom and Dad were taking a walk with me and Roxy and Lisa, my twin sisters who are two years younger than I. We were busy talking and enjoying ourselves and because we wanted a closer look at a toy car, we turned into an empty, deserted alleyway. My parents came after us and then two men stopped us when we tried to go back the way we had come. We were trapped. My Mom and Dad thought that the men only wanted to rob us. Dad was ready to hand over everything but the men tried to grab my sisters and me. My parents fought like the devil but were killed during the struggle. Even I tried to save my sisters. The men took Roxy to sell to a baby broker who later put her up for adoption. She was adopted by her unsuspecting foster parents, Frank and Judy. The men left Lisa for dead. When the crooks killed my parents and grabbed Roxy, I realized that there was nothing that I could do. My instincts kicked in and I ran so fast and so far that the only reason I stopped was from sheer exhaustion. And that is pretty much what I remember. Luckily, I found an alleyway with lots of debris where I could hide. I slept for days and when I woke up, I began my new life of living on the streets of New York City and sleeping among garbage bags or in dumpsters. After all, who would look for a kid among the garbage receptacles of NYC? It was the only safe place. Once I went to the *Planet of the Cleaning Bugs,* my memory slowly began to work again. That was when I realized that at least something good had happened to one of my sisters. Roxy was very lucky to be adopted by loving foster parents."

Jane seemed to have drifted off for a few minutes into her personal memories. Her crew had already heard how she remained on the street and became a kind of street warrior. But they waited patiently for her to continue with the story of what happened to Lisa - a story that Mountain had told her when she met him on the *Planet of Stolen Property.*

"Unfortunately Lisa wasn't as lucky as Roxy. When she gained consciousness, her eyes saw only the blood streaming out of our father and mother and she went into shock. To make matters even worse, the alleyway only had dubious characters passing through it. Lisa's life had changed forever in just minutes. It so happened that an incredibly ugly giant of a man who controlled some of the arena fights spotted Lisa sitting next to our parents' bodies, unable to move. The man we now know as Astro Jackson bent down to her and said, 'Hi! My name is Astro. Let me help you.' But Lisa could not hear a word that he was saying. All she saw was a big monster of a man with all sorts of bumps and a head that at times looked like a rock. He was ugly and she associated him with her parents' death even though she knew that was not the case. She was ready to fight him and she did until she knocked herself out. Astro loved her spunk and her spirit, not to mention her lack of fear. He saw her as a beautiful fighting machine from the moment he rescued her. The first thing he did was take her to his Bloom Island. When she overcame her temporary pains and various illnesses, she grew strong. In the process she didn't die but adjusted to the harsh, heavy environment. After that it was time for training. Astro's Island became an exercise haven for Lisa.

"Even though Astro was known as a fighter, when he retired he traveled to different worlds and trained many champions on the side as a business and to keep busy. But when he ran into Lisa, he decided to turn her into a project of love and admiration and along the way a champion. He was tough with his training but showed Lisa kindness. Because of that, Lisa was able to overlook some of his ugliness. But this happened only after she understood how being prejudiced could hurt another person. One day when she was training, she called Astro an ugly beast. She prepared herself for retaliation but was very surprised when he didn't hit her. For the first time, she saw him for what he was - a sensitive creature with deep emotions who suffered because she called him ugly. Lisa did a lot of thinking that night about how Astro didn't look so ugly to her once she saw the pain that she had caused him. The next day, Astro needed to be tough with her because she was training. That was when she did a lot of thinking about what hurt others. Astro knocked her around more than usual that morning and even went so far as to tell her that her hair was ugly and that she needed some…He stopped speaking abruptly because he realized that it would drive her crazy not to know what he was going to say. It was his way of relieving the pain she had caused him. After flipping her to the ground, he said that it was enough training for the day. He reached his hand out to help her stand up. Because of the events from the day before, she found herself looking at him differently, without so much prejudice and disdain. For the first time, she noticed that his smile was so sincere and caring that the ugliness that she once disliked about him was now a smile of beauty. This had her thinking how ugliness was truly in the eye of the beholder! After he picked her up, she asked him, 'How can you be a slave trader? You're too kind for that.' Astro looked into her eyes, gave her the meanest look that he could muster up and said, 'If you ever repeat what you just said about me being kind, in front of another person, you will see just how mean I can be.' Then, he smiled, winked at her and walked away. Lisa remained silent, confused by pretty much everything that had happened to her since Astro had found her sitting by our parents' bodies."

While Jane was telling her story, Slammer heard something and turned to his right. He didn't realize that Millie was sitting on his shoulders listening to the whole story. They looked at each other and she gave him the biggest and prettiest smile that she could conjure up and said,

"Thank you again for not stepping on me." Then sadly and curiously she asked.

"Do things like that really happen on her planet? Here others aren't mean to each other. They either ignore you or step on you."

Slammer started laughing. Jane stopped her story and everyone looked at him. The laughter was infectious and they all began to laugh.

"What's so funny?" Spike asked, while laughing. Lolly

looked at him and said, "Don't worry about it. Just enjoy it." So he did.

When the laughter stopped, the crew was still looking at Slammer. He shrugged his shoulders, looked at Millie, then back at the crew and said, pointing to Millie, "You had to hear it from her."

Ragrezy was anxious to hear more of Astro's story and asked Jane to continue. She did, like she had never stopped.

"Lisa knew that Astro had sold her to one of the evil Tube Spark people a few weeks after finding her in the alleyway and that her training as a fighter was part of that deal. She also knew that he now wished that he had never made the deal. Training together had made them close and now their time was up on his Island and she was due to go to an arena on the *Mine, Mine Planet.* He never thought that he would get attached to any of the people whom he sold. He realized that he was sad and wished that Lisa didn't have to leave him. He began remembering things and reliving the past. He recalled when he first saw Lisa; when he noticed that she wore a silver locket with her name on it and that her name was the same as his sister's. His heart went out to her. He didn't want to sell her but he had no choice. He made sure to be her first official trainer. A year later, on the same day that he had found her, Astro understood how terrible it was to make such a deal and then change his mind. He understood that he had made a mistake, that it was too late to change and that there was no going back. Unfortunately for Astro, he learned too late that once a deal was made with the All-for-One-Man, it had to be honored. Astro couldn't help Lisa. She had no choice and her struggle for survival continued."

"Jane, how do you know all of this?" Slammer interrupted.

Jane looked at Franky and said, "Do you want to tell him?"

"Okay. But I'm just guessing. Was it someone from the back room who told you?"

"Yes!"

"Was it someone we know?" Spike called out, frantically raising his hand as if it were a contest.

With a big smile she said, "Now, Spike, how private could the conversation be, if I tell you?"

Millie popped out of a corner and yelled at Spike, "What's the matter with you!" Then she hid before Spike could pick her up and start playing airplane with her.

Jane continued her story about Astro and Lisa.

"Once Astro finished training Lisa on his Island, he had to let her go with the Spark Trainers to the arena on the *Mine, Mine Planet*. She trained there for another two years. Her training consisted of fighting and winning and if she won, she gained certain privileges. Astro tried to convince Lisa that, in order to win, she had to fight dirty, just like in the streets. She refused to give up her sense of fairness. Because of that, most of her time was spent recuperating from her injuries. The fact that Lisa wouldn't fight dirty made her a better fighter because she put in a lot of time learning how to avoid getting hit. Once she knew those tactics, she then learned how and where to land her blows to stop, but not permanently injure, her opponent. When she mastered all of her techniques, she went to the *Sphere of Tears City*. Once there, she was placed in an academy school called "Don't Stop Fighting" where the Tube Spark people threw her and a bunch of highly trained killers into the arena where criminals throughout the universe would come to make bets and watch the fights. The fighter, who was still standing at the end of the fight, got a prize for the day, perhaps a car or a house. After six months, the strongest winners were advanced to sword fighting."

Before she could continue, Mr. Wet-Dry interrupted. "Excuse me, did you just find this out about your sister?"

"Yes," Jane replied. Then, she added, "When I'm finished with this story, I will explain what we must do when we land. Right now let's take a break. I'll continue the story in a while."

Spike and Lolly moved over to a window which was no longer shuttered now that they had been traveling in the tube for a while. It was the first time that they could really see the tube clearly even though it was almost invisible.

"Wow! Look at that, Lolly," Spike said, pointing. "The tube is almost visible and if you look all the way to the other end, it looks like a giant straw even though it's a thousand miles round and ten thousand miles long."

Lolly stared at the tube. Then she pointed, "Look, Spike. Doesn't that look like Swadun City from the planet *Swadun*?"

"Yeh, it does." He replied and then started counting how many cities and towns he could see built in the naturally created tube connector. There were sections with empty space for hundreds of miles. It was visually amazing to see what looked like cities floating and vehicles flying in the tube. Then Spike and Lolly spaced out just staring out the window.

Meanwhile Jane and Franky were reminiscing about the time they had spent together before he had to leave her in New York.

Ragrezy and Roxy were playing checkers and laughing. "I'm glad I met you," Roxy said and added, "I also thank you for helping rescue me and now helping to rescue my sister Lisa." Ragrezy was about to move closer to her when the ship shook and practically threw him on her. They both started apologizing to each other, oblivious to what was happening on the ship.

Jane yelled, "Snap out of it, you love birds. Something is pulling us down. I don't know how long we can stay in the air and there is no way to know what has a grip on us."

Ragrezy could see that Roxy was getting worried. He told her not to be afraid and not to look at him. She turned around but still peeked. When Ragrezy took off his shirt, she showed her shyness by quickly turning around so he wouldn't notice her looking at him. And it was a good thing too, because if she had seen what he did next, she would have flipped out. Ragrezy reached into his stomach and pulled out a round glass object, about 6-8 inches in diameter, and full of camera eyes. By this time, the ship was shaking violently. Ragrezy was very concerned and yelled to Slammer to get the ejector ready and open the hatch. Ragrezy ran with the object that he had just pulled out of his stomach and shoved it into the ejector as fast as he could and then closed the hatch.

"What did you just do?" Jane asked. Ragrezy told her to put on the screen and switch to automatic view. Ragrezy explained that he had just ejected the sphere with the camera eyes into space so that he and the crew would able to see 380 degrees and figure out what was happening.

The sphere lit up with very bright colors when it started recording. The whole crew was startled to see an amazing 400-foot, 5-ton bug-like creature named Tubs, hanging on to their ship for dear life. They suddenly understood that it was Tubs who was dragging them to the ground. He looked like a huge praying mantis with an extremely long, round worm-like body, fat stomach, two extra pairs of legs and three pairs of wings that were too small for flying but not too small for enabling very high leaps. At the end of this magnificent flying bug, there was a colorful sail-like tail which he used as a rudder. It lit up the sky with brilliant colors as it shifted with Tubs' movements. Although he was magnificent, Tubs could devour a house or small ship. But luckily for them, their ship was way too large for Tubs to swallow.

Slammer tried shooting the bug off the ship, but that didn't work. Jane tried to speed the ship upwards but the bug weighed them down. It was a struggle just to stay afloat. Many different maneuvers were tried but Tubs couldn't be shaken off.

Jane had no choice but to call for Sparky. She looked to the stars and hollered, "Sparky, we need you."

A second later, Sparky penetrated the ship and stood next to Jane.

"What can I do for you?"

"Are you kidding? Didn't you see that monster hanging onto our ship?"

"Yes, I did but I can't do anything unless one or all of you are involved."

"Okay." Ragrezy said. "Can you go outside and grab my camera eye sphere? And don't let it go until I tell you to."

"What does the sphere do?" Sparky asked.

"The camera eye sphere, sometimes called an eye camera or camera sphere has eight camera eyes in it. Before ejecting it into space, anyone can program it to reach a certain distance in space. When it reaches its destination, seven of the eyes come out of the sphere and surround the object from various distances - in this case it happens to be our ship. The camera sphere continues to carry the eighth eye which receives the information sent back by the other seven eyes. Any of the seven camera eyes that can see the target then shoots out lazier beams that are programmed either to stun, electrify, freeze, burn or even completely destroy the target – in this case Tubs."

"Why do you need me to carry it out?"

"Because I am in the middle of working on the ejector tube and we need the camera sphere outside the ship now."

"How does it know what to do?" Sparky asked.

"It's really very simple. Keep in mind that it's also known as a smart ball because it can identify its target and provide a three hundred and sixty degrees view of its target's surroundings and at the same time allow its designated controller to use the weapons in the ship from hundreds of miles away to hit its target. In this case the smart ball has been programmed for The Tub-bug creature."

"Okay," Sparky said. "But remember that I cannot interfere." Sparky flew to the ball and held up his end of the bargain. Sparky took the camera-ball about an eighth of a mile away from the ship, left it and returned.

"Okay, Ragrezy. It's in place." Sparky hollered as soon as he reappeared in the ship.

Jane watched Ragrezy as he played with the Assassins' control panel.

"What are you doing?" Jane asked.

"Watch the screen," he hollered. Ragrezy explained that his camera ball used Sparky's energy and that all he had to do was think of where the bolt should hit and that's precisely what would happen...Ragrezy pushed a button and an umbrella shaped invisible field of energy ignited like a bright flash bulb, only it was almost as bright as the sun. Everyone looked as the bright, colorful light exploded and small particles of the explosion hit Tubs hard enough that he let go of the ship and fell stunned to the planet. The crew watched the explosion and instinctively ducked. They didn't bother to ask what would happen if the particles hit the ship. Nothing...they soon discovered much to their relief.

The crew went back to what they had been doing as if nothing had happened. Sparky disappeared the same way that he came.

Since it was going to take a day or so to get to the *Sphere of Tears*, Jane decided to finish telling them what she had learned about Lisa.

PART FOUR
Introduction to a Very Special Planet

A Very Special Planet

"About five months ago, during a contest fight, one of the female Spark trainers flew to Lisa and assumed Lisa's glass image, as the Tube Spark people often did when they talked to residents or visitors. As far as I know this is what the Spark trainer was sent to teach Lisa.

'Hi, Lisa. My name is Sparklet. I have been watching you for a while and I see an unusual amount of empathy and remorse in what you're doing. You cannot win with such compassion. You must be fierce. You cannot have empathy for your enemy because when they look pleadingly at you, they hope that you will weaken for a split second, which would give them the chance to strike their blow and kill you. This is how they will repay you for the empathy that you so foolishly showed them. You must not hold on to this trait, no matter how honorable and kind you may be. Those feelings must be left outside of the arena or you will be carried out of it, minus your life. Our world has heard of the famous Trio Sisters of Honor. It seems that all three of you have the same traits of Innocence, Strength, Endurance and Honor. But what impresses all of us Spark people the most is that all three sisters have such innocence in their hearts. We find it hard to believe that such innocent children could survive in such violent situations and not change. This fact strengthened our belief that at least one of the sisters would be able to beat the Gangia Queen and eliminate the control of this tyrant and her controller, the All-for-One-Man.'

I think that her belief in and knowledge of our innocence is truly amazing."

Jane was a bit emotional and paused for a moment before

continuing.

"Lisa's trainers continuously reminded her that they were on her side. They explained to her that they didn't like what had been happening on their planet since the All-for-One-Man came to their world about two hundred years ago. That was when he freed all of the alien prisoners, thereby giving him power on other worlds. Sparklet told Lisa that the All-for-One-Man had already lived for four hundred years and that now even the whole universe was worried. They feared that with the evil, ageless Gangia Queen by his side, things could only get worse."

"Did you ever meet Sparklet? Did she tell you all of this?" Franky asked.

"No, Mountain told me about Sparklet and most of Lisa's history. He told me that Lisa was being prepared for a fight that the Spark people hoped she would win so that she could eliminate the evil that was controlling their planet. But let's get back to Sparklet and Lisa. Sparklet told Lisa that the Spark people had been looking for someone like her for centuries. She also told her that although she was truly pure of heart, others like her who had entered the arena sooner or later changed and had to fight dirty and without mercy. They acknowledged that she never did this during her two years of training and fighting but told her that she may have to at some time. They asked her to trust them and work with them and in return they promised that she would be reunited with her sisters. That was the last thing that Mountain told me about Lisa."

Everyone could see that Jane was getting very anxious about rescuing Lisa. Roxy wasn't any calmer standing behind her, holding some sort of ray weapon almost as big as she was, and mumbling, "Let's get her before it's too late."

Jane told Roxy and the others to relax, at least until it was time to land. Only Jane knew that at this time her sister was being taken to the main arena in the *Sphere of Tears* and that she was preparing to meet her first foe in the arena. Jane knew that she couldn't arrive in time for that fight and she hoped that Lisa would survive, so that she and her crew could rescue her before the next fight.

The trip to the *Sphere of Tears* was about ten hours away and everyone was hungry. The ship had a cafeteria that resembled a small diner. The crew sat in various places, ordered food and drinks and then continued doing their own thing. There were individual conversations. Jane wanted to speak privately to Slammer so she asked him to sit next to her at this very large table that seemed to shrink and stretch according to the desires of the people who went to sit there. If anyone wanted to have a more private conversation, the table and chairs would amazingly separate, shift and shape accordingly, either inches or feet away, until they attained the desired distance and privacy. Slammer and Jane did just that and then they ordered some burgers and sodas.

Their waiter turned out to be one of the Mr. Food robots. He rolled and at times even floated from table to table taking orders.

"I remember when you, Spike and I first met," Jane told Slammer. "I'm really glad that both of you aren't meaner and nastier than you were when I first met you. In fact, both of you have really changed."

Then she asked, "Is there anything that I should know about you and also about Spike?"

Slammer needed to explain himself to Jane so he quickly replied. "Okay! When I was six years old going on seven, I borrowed some lunch from a kid I convinced wasn't hungry because *I was*. After I let him up, I thanked him. When I turned the corner, his buddies came out of nowhere and beat the heck out of me. I was only six and as big as a grownup but I was getting beaten up and bullied by kids my own age. I looked like a teacher who was fighting with kids and losing the fight. They used garbage can lids and anything else they could find."

Then Slammer told Jane that when he looked back at what had happened then, it was a good lesson for him. Getting beaten up because he had been heartless and stolen from another kid showed him exactly what it felt like being bullied. Many years later he finally understood that just because a person was bigger than someone else it didn't give him the right to be a bully. And with those thoughts in his mind, he decided that he should tell Jane a few things about Spike and himself.

"Jane, I need to tell you about Spike and our relationship and I really want to apologize for his and my behavior when we met you for the first time. Perhaps if I tell you a bit about us and how he and I met, you will understand and hopefully forgive us."

He began by explaining how he found Spike in a garbage dumpster looking for food. Spike was so helpless and funny looking that Slammer started laughing and instead of picking on him, he protected him. From that time on they stuck together like glue. One day after a heavy rainstorm, Slammer was abruptly awakened in his comfortable cardboard box. Spike was freaking out, stretching his arms up in the air then slowly lowering his fingertips until he felt something he knew was not there the night before. When he saw his reflection in the rain puddle, panic struck. He ran to Slammer and grabbed him by his shirt while hanging off his neck.

"Look at me! What has happened?" He franticly asked.

Slammer pulled one of the nails on his head and asked if it hurt. "No," Spike replied. Slammer pulled a bit harder and tapped some of the nails with a pipe that was on the floor next to him.

"How about now? Did that hurt?"

"No. But my head is itchy."

"So you have nothing to worry about Spike. I'm sure that you'll find out what those nails in your head are all about sooner or later."

Then Slammer asked him if he felt any different. Spike said that he felt smarter.

"That's good. Then you can help me earn some money and buy a spaceship."

"We bought our ship. For a while we made a good living and eventually as you know, we had to sell it. It was about six months after that when you saw me at the Bull Bar, and you know the rest."

"Thanks for sharing, Slammer. I not only understand but I forgive you both. Don't forget. I also had to do things that I preferred not to. But when faced with situations such as we have faced, we did what we had to do. Besides, our similar experiences in life should only serve to bond us closer together."

They were still hours away from the *Sphere of Tears*. The first set of fireworks were decorating the skies, informing people that the fights would begin within a few hours, which usually meant longer. The fireworks were so big and spectacular that they could be seen in the sky from the ground throughout the world. Even though the *Sphere of Tears* couldn't be seen from the ground, the fireworks were another story. They were very special. Imagine looking into the darkness of the atmosphere from the ground. Anyone watching would have sworn that the *Sphere of Tears* had exploded into nothingness. Then from all sides of the city, rocket shaped explosions flew everywhere toward the inner world. Every few miles, more sparkling explosions went off, making the sky brighter and more colorful than ever before. It was fascinating to watch thousands of Tube Spark people turn into sparkling rockets that exploded every few miles without blowing anything up and without destroying themselves.

Franky and Jane wanted to watch the fireworks and catch up on all that had happened during the few years when they were apart.

"Jane, I'm not sure that you want Squeak to see this room. From what I understand, he's more of an indoor kind of creature."

"What do you think, Squeak?" He popped out of her pocket and told her that he would not come out again unless she told him to.

In order to have the best view of the fireworks, Franky took Jane into one of the most amazing rooms on the spaceship. He had been in only one other ship that had such special rooms. He wanted to apologize to Jane in a very majestic way and this was the only kind of a room that would allow him to accomplish that. He hoped that this special experience would make her happy. Franky took her by the hand and said,

"Come on. I want to share something with you."

They walked down a hallway until they saw a sign that said View Room.

"Open the door and go in very slowly," Franky whispered.

She turned her head toward him as she opened the door to the View Room and at the same time put one foot forward. But when she turned to enter the room, she looked in and flew backwards into Franky's arms. She quickly grabbed him by the neck.

"Are you trying to kill me? What kind of a surprise is this?" she screamed, half out of her wits. "That door leads to the outside of the ship. If you are trying to be funny, you're not."

Franky was so taken-aback by her reaction that he couldn't stop laughing.

"I'm sorry, sweetheart. I thought that you knew about this kind of room. Besides I told you to go slowly."

He took her hand and she pulled it back.

"Oh come on, Jane. I'm sorry but if you saw your face, you also would have laughed."

She looked at him and realized that he was probably right.

She finally smiled and said, "Okay, let's try this again."

This time she held his hand very tightly, with her nails digging into his wrist.

"I'm sorry, Jane" he said, trying unsuccessfully not to show the pain. "I should have told you that everyone who opens the door to this room for the first time instinctively jumps back. It *is* difficult to walk into a room, where it feels like you are walking out of the ship and right into space, and not *be* startled. It's as if the View Room were a square glass box placed on the side of a building or in this case, the side of the ship."

Franky was holding the door open and once again encouraged Jane to enter.

"Don't be afraid, Jane. The room is empty and no one will see your fear. Just put your foot through the doorway and when you step down, you will feel the invisible solid floor."

But Jane was no dummy. "You go in there first." He joyfully did and then Jane closed her eyes and gave it a shot. But she wouldn't let go of the door until she was all the way in and the ground felt solid. Jane just stood there for a minute and slowly began opening her eyes. Franky had never seen them open so wide. She couldn't stop staring at the universe. The view was breathtaking. It literally took her breath away. The planets were never clearer and so close to her. The sky had planets that resembled illuminated marbles and twinkling stars scattered throughout its black background. Shooting comets seemed to pass close to Jane even though they were hundreds of thousands of miles away.

Franky grabbed and shook her. "Breathe, Jane. You must breathe." She didn't even realize that she had become breathless because she was so engrossed in and enveloped by visual excitement. Franky was standing in front of her, already inside the View Room. She snapped out of her trance-like state and was embarrassed at having been caught in a weak moment. She straightened up and let go of the door. She nonchalantly gazed at the sky and slowly walked toward the stars in the universe. She took about twenty steps forward and asked Franky how far away they could walk before bumping into an invisible wall.

She got her answer after taking four more steps.

A voice was heard throughout this ballroom-size invisible room.

"Warning…You are three feet away from the wall. Please be careful and have a nice day."

Franky could see the surprise on Jane's face and he put on a big smile.

"Pretty cool, *huh*, Jane?"

"It takes a bit of time to get used to, doesn't it? This beauty could become habit forming." Jane answered.

They started walking slowly from one side of the room to the other, mesmerized by how much bigger and brighter the planets, stars and comets looked when surrounded by darkness.

Franky and Jane found it playfully magical and colorfully bright when they looked at the spots of light, which reflected the beauty of a planet. When a group of comets passed by, showing their tails of energy, it was as if heaven gave the two friends a special Fourth of July spectacle to enjoy.

Jane was looking at another clear View Room to her left and it felt strange to see some of her crew floating just yards away. Then she thought about the strange sensation that she had while traveling in this spaceship that was silent, pollution free and flying inside a tube. Jane felt like she was in a glass straw with cities in it. Then she wondered if microscopic bugs looked at life inside their glass tube in the same way she did in the tube connector. As she continued looking into space, she took a step to her right and activated something. It turned out to be a telescope that had been provided for them.

Franky was surprised and remarked,

"I didn't know this feature was available on our ship."

He grabbed the telescope and then caught himself. He took Jane's hand, pulled her toward the telescope and said,

"Tell me how the view is."

Trying not to show her excitement, Jane said, "Thank you" and then gave him a big smile. She opened her eyes as wide as she could, looked in the direction of the *Sphere of Tears* for a few seconds, adjusted the telescopic sight and then began imagining the different ways that things worked in the other worlds.

The outer part of the *Sphere of Tears* was about 500 miles in circumference. Jane could see that many of its buildings had roofs with movable solar panels that rotated like weather vanes. She remembered from what Sparky had told her that the solar panels captured the sun's energy and that when the winds passed through the panels, they rotated and captured the wind's energy.

She noticed that parts of the city looked like huge mirrors from far away. They were blinding but all she had to do was put on reflection glasses, which were near the telescope, and that took care of that problem.

Franky put his arm around her shoulder and said, pointing to the city. "Look at that. What do you think?"

"It's beautiful," Jane replied as she moved the telescope toward the center of the city.

"It's amazing how the buildings fit together in a circle with the Fight Arena in the middle. Their architecture recalls that of different international cities, like Paris, Tokyo, New York, and even Rome."

Then Jane asked Franky, "What do you think?"

Franky, deep in his own world shrugged his shoulders and answered,

"Ah, to me it just looks like a humongous combination of an indoor and outdoor shopping mall."

Spike announced on the intercom. "One hour before we land."

Jane immediately said, "Come on, Franky. We have a job

to do."

They stepped out of the View Room into the hall, which led to the Control Room. The rest of the crew was already inside, waiting for Spike to land the ship. Jane noticed that the closer the ship got to the city, the more fear Squeak exhibited.

All of the landing pads were on top of buildings that were only blocks away from the Arena. The only delay was the heavy traffic. Extra pilots were required to take the ships away once the clients had exited and went on their way. They waited their turn to land and finally a pilot was available to take the ship away.

Lolly and Spike had never been to an arena fight before. They were so excited that they nearly flew out of the ship once Spike landed it. They both carried binoculars that magnified automatically with vocal commands and they rushed to the end of the roof where they began looking at the magnificent arena that was shaped like a football. At the same time, N.A.T. and N.I.T. each popped out of one of their body's ears and sat on one of their respective shoulders. They looked like Rorschach inkblots, constantly changing their forms. This time they were holding hands that were stretched as long as monkey arms from one shoulder to the other. The two brains would retract them only when they decided to pop back into their bodies.

Somehow they had created their own binoculars for a closer look at the arena. Meanwhile the rest of the crew took a while to get out of the ship.

"Look, Spike." Lolly said, not knowing whether what she was looking at was real or not. "Is that real?" She asked, pointing at the seats.

Spike explained. "Yes, those are various groups of different colored seats scattered throughout the stadium and they are made of gold, platinum, silver and other valuable ores."

"Aren't the Spark people worried that the criminals will steal it all?

"No way!" Spike said with great confidence. "The priceless material on this planet is why this is the richest planet in existence.

"I don't understand. How does that prevent thieves from mining this planet into nothingness?" Lolly asked, looking confused.

"Trust me. I know it for a fact."

Spike was certain because he had heard that when the All-for-One-Man first came to this planet, he had decided to have some of his men load up a spaceship full of gold, platinum and diamonds. The Spark people warned him not to attempt such an evil act. The All-for-One-Man didn't care what happened to his men since he could always hire more. So with this in his mind, he decided to give the theft of the planet a try. As his men attempted to escape from the planet with the riches, the Spark people warned them a few times. First, the thieves were warned verbally. When they wouldn't listen and turn back, they were fired upon with powerful energy bolts as a warning. But when the thieves fired back, the Spark people in the area united and created a ball of fire with the thieves in the center. They were incinerated and instantly became ashes.

That was when Spike learned that the whole *Mine, Mine Planet* was made up of the priceless ores and that various types of Spark people lived throughout the planet and actually made up the planet. It was a difficult concept for Spike to understand but he finally realized that everything on this planet was Spark energy shaped into various forms. The Spark people had grown accustomed to different luxuries that they received by trading with other worlds and the All-for-One-Man really understood that if he provided the materials to hook the Spark people to their pleasure needs, he would gain the kind of power that he wanted over them. The Spark people didn't know how to deal with the All-for-One-Man. While he had three personalities, they all agreed with Mr. Evil and the Sparks never saw the other two. Mr. Evil promised the Spark people that he would make sure that no one would steal their precious materials as long as he was in power and that in return for this protection, they would allow him free access to trade with them. Two hundred years later, the Spark people realized that the deal that they made with Mr. Evil was the worst mistake that they had ever made. They hadn't understood just how evil the All-for-One-Man really was.

"Is Lisa fighting for the Spark people?" Lolly asked Spike.

"A while back Slammer and I ran across Astro Jackson and he told us that he was training someone to help the Spark people get rid of the All-for-One-Man. This fighter did not have much of a choice and she agreed, with one stipulation: that if she won, she would be freed. I guess that is a yes to your question Lolly. Lisa has two reasons for winning."

Once everyone exited the ship, Squeak asked Jane if he could come out of her pocket. He wanted to wrap himself around her warm neck and watch what was going on since they were out in the open again.

"Sure, come on." Squeak jumped out of her pocket and instantly became large enough to wrap himself around her shoulders. And for a few minutes, everything was fine. But then, Squeak, uncontrollably and unconsciously, started to squeeze Jane's neck with his tail. Squeak was frantically looking around as if he expected to see someone. Jane thought that he was looking for something or someone but definitely not a friend.

Jane grabbed him and asked, "What are you doing? "

Roxy said, "Look Jane. Can't you see that he's terrified?"

"How could I see him? I was too busy trying to stop him from choking me? Besides, he's not supposed to be afraid of anything."

"What's wrong, Squeak?" Slammer, who was standing nearby, asked.

"It's Mr. Evil," he replied.

Ragrezy looked at him and reminded Squeak that Mr. Evil was left behind with the rest of the All-for-One-Man.

"Oh no, he was not! He's in there," pointing to the *Sphere of Tears*.

Jane told the crew that Squeak was probably right and that her friend had warned her not to be surprised if the All-for-One-Man got there before they did.

Jane gently said, "Squeak, remember that I told Rocky that I wouldn't let anything happen to you. Just hold on to me. Okay?" That seemed to have comforted Squeak.

Then she asked. "Why are you so afraid of the All-for-One-Man?"

Not wanting to face the situation, Squeak answered, "Because he's the only one I have ever run across that I couldn't drain the evil from."

Trying to make him feel better, Jane said, "Yeh but look at the situation. Normally it wouldn't be a problem because Rocky and the Changer would be with you. You can't go after such an enemy on your own, especially against such a very powerful trio."

Squeak calmed down while Slammer called Spike and Lolly. Then Ragrezy instructed the attendant where to bring their luggage and everyone began walking to the hotel, which was a couple of blocks away. It was a visually interesting and informative walk to the hotel for Jane and her crew. The streets were crowded as if it were New Years Eve on Times Square.

"Can you feel the energy all around? Jane asked Squeak. "Maybe that's why you think Mr. Evil is nearby."

"Oh no, the energy in the street has a nice feeling. The one I'm picking up feels more like it belongs to Mr. Evil."

The crew was only a block away from the hotel and Squeak started uncontrollably wrapping his tail around Jane's neck again. She pulled him off and held him in front of her face.

"What's the matter, Squeak?" She saw him staring in the direction of the hotel but she couldn't see over the crowds. A second later Slammer came over to her and started talking, trying to calm Squeak down.

"Don't worry. I know it's not your imagination. I just saw the All-for-One-Man. He won't hurt you. I'll make sure of that." And to make him feel even more secure, he added, "Plus, Jane and the rest of the crew will be watching out for you."

Jane was very anxious and grabbed Slammer's arm. "Where is that evil man, Slammer? I want him. He has my sister."

"No! He doesn't have her. Lisa is in the arena cages like the rest of the fighters waiting for their next battle. The All-for-One-Man is just checking into one of the hotels. And it looks like he's in the same building complex as we are."

Jane started walking very quickly toward the complex

hoping to see Mr. Evil but Slammer slowed her down and pointed to the entrance that they needed to use.

"We cannot start trouble now, Jane. Mountain and Astro have everything set up. Our best chance of success is to go with the plans that have been made."

They entered the south part of the building onto the second floor and Roxy just had to stop once she walked through the door. Looking down two flights from the inside of the structure that held multiple hotels, the lobby looked like New York's Grand Central Station. Only it was at least ten times larger and instead of people taking walkways leading to different subway and railroad trains, they ended up in a hotel of their choosing.

The crowds of people in the building were greater and more chaotic than in the streets. Some carried banners; some wore hats, shirts and sweatshirts with all forms of advertisement supporting one or more of the fighters. Many of the shirts and sweatshirts had pictures of Lisa, presenting her as the hero and champion of the arena fights.

Jane and her crew eventually checked into their hotel and agreed to meet in the center of the lobby about a half hour later, so that they could go to the fights.

While all of this was taking place, Slammer went to room 73S on the seventy-third floor where he was to meet his friend, Mountain. He knocked on the door and heard a voice say, "It's open" and he walked into the room. Slammer was startled because he didn't see Mountain *but rather* a room full of black figures in black raincoats and hats, all leaning against the walls, trying to look like shadows. Slammer braced himself for a fight.

Mountain came out of another room in the hotel suite and

said, "Welcome, Slammer. It's good to see you again."

The next words out of his mouth were, "Did you make the bets, Slammer?"

"Of course I made the bets! Now tell me. Who are your friends who look like shadows plastered against the wall?"

"Ah! Let me introduce you to my friend. Hey Astro! Come on out. I want you to meet an old buddy of mine," he hollered toward another room,

This monster of a man came out and walked to Slammer. Slammer was considered a very large man but in comparison to Astro, he was the size of a big child. Astro stuck out his hand and that was when Slammer realized just how big this man was.

He said, "It's a pleasure Astro. I have heard plenty of good things about you."

"Glad to hear that, Slammer. Your buddy Mountain has told me about some of your adventures together. And by the way, what you are looking at that is leaning against the walls is my friend from my Island. Say hi to the Black Wall."

Slammer didn't know what to do. The next thing he knew, there were arms stretched out to him from the coats and hats leaning against the walls. They turned out to be dozens of spike-like hands ready for him to shake as voices kept coming from the shadows and repeating, "Hi Slammer, Hello Slammer." He just kept answering and saying hello to the hands without touching them.

"Come on, Slammer" Mountain said. "You too, Astro. Let's sit and make sure that we have our jobs coordinated."

Astro waved his hand and one of the shadows floated over to him and handed him some kind of map of the arena and the city's layout. They spent another few minutes together before Slammer had to get back to his crew.

Meanwhile anyone looking at the holding rooms where Lisa and the other gladiators were being held would have given an arm and a leg to have such accommodations. These were not just holding rooms. They were what people on Earth would compare to a Fifth Avenue high rise with a spectacular Central Park view. Imagine a specially built room that offered all of the comforts anyone could want from whatever world he came from. There was even a window in every room that had a view of scenery from each gladiator's planet.

The Spark people believed that since their great warriors were a profitable business, then they were to have the best of everything. Unfortunately, the greedy slave owners did not agree because they did not want to pay the extra expenses that came with such a belief. The Spark people didn't care. They were good businessmen and in addition, they knew that it was the right thing to do. They thought that the gladiators should be treated like gold because in effect they were.

The area of holding rooms had an unusual formation. There was an inner circle that had circular configurations of small rooms whose interiors were very deceptive. The rooms were fantastic. They were so large that it was difficult to figure out how such small-looking rooms could be so large and luxurious on the inside. This size displacement technology invented by the Spark people was quite amazing and hard to figure out. Each room expanded in a way that made it turn into the room that the gladiator wanted. The rooms had no doors. A force field kept the gladiators in and apart and strangers out.

A guard was patrolling the halls of this holding area. He liked watching Lisa spar and since he was told never to interfere with the gladiators, he just watched.

Lisa was in her cell practicing moves with different holograms that actually damaged her if she were struck by its blow. Lisa liked to practice dodging such attacks. She had learned that no matter how big or fast her opponents were, if they couldn't hit her, then they couldn't hurt her. Oddly enough, if a truck ran into her, it would smash into pieces because of her amazing density, power and strength.

At this time, Lisa was sparing with a hologram called the Nail Man. He was tall, thin and basically resembled a six foot steel pole. Nail Man had a flat head. His cheeks, nose, chin and ears were made out of different shaped nail heads. His hands were long and extra pointy, and yes, very sharp. His fingers were thin with points that would not bend or break.

"Come on, tooth pick boy!" Lisa would call out, motioning to the Nail Man. She knew it riled him up.

"I told you. I'm Nail Man." Then he would lift his hand up and his four-sided, scalpel-blade nails would fly toward her with the speed of a bullet. Lisa avoided them while charging and just as she was about to strike, he sparked off and on, disrupting her practice. Lisa knew to look toward the invisible shield wall.

A fighter named Chingo periodically smashed into his room's energy shield wall in an attempt to break through into Lisa's room. This was one of those times.

"Why are you banging on the shield wall?" Lisa shouted, very aggravated. "How many times have I told you not to bang onto it?" Lisa knew that he was merciless and very mean and violent. There was absolutely no beauty in this monster of a beast. Lisa was aware that he made mistakes while fighting when he was angry. So, she began antagonizing him.

"I promise not to hurt you. I heard that you asked the East Poll fighter not to hurt you because you don't like pain."

Chingo shouted, with unbelievable rage. "How dare you speak to me like that? You wait until I get my hands on you."

He continued hitting the shield. The shock didn't seem to bother him. He was so big that the wall shield was the only thing stopping this humongous creature from attacking Lisa.

"How can you, a puny Earthling be compared to the great Chenango people? I can squash you with one hand."

"You should watch your temper, Mr. Chingo. You can't squash what you can't catch."

This really frustrated him and he just kept banging at the wall shield with greater fury and tenacity yelling, "I'm going to rip you apart."

Somewhere in the inner workings of the arena there was a central control chamber for the shield doors and where the guards sat to keep an eye on the gladiators.

A new guard named Hage was watching the computer screen and noticed how out of control Chingo was getting.

"Hey, Gugy," he shouted to another guard sitting across the room in front of another screen. "I think this Chingo is going to penetrate the shield if he keeps on hitting it. What should I do?"

Gugy lifted his head from the computer he was looking at and with a big grin said as he walked toward him. "Oh you're going to love this." Then he told him to get up. Gugy took Hage's seat and said, "Watch the screen."

By this time all of the other guards had gathered around the screen as if an event were about to take place. And for them it was an event.

Hage watched the screen intently as Gugy pressed a button and when Chingo hit the shield wall again, sparks flew and the electric shock threw Chingo back onto his butt, nearly knocking him unconscious. The guards laughed and watched him struggle to get up and then fall down again.

The idiot guards were basking in the power that they had by hurting this big beast who in his world was considered royalty.

Lisa looked across the shield from her room and shook her head mumbling, "That beast is not going to stop fighting until he's dead."

By this time Jane, Franky, Ragrezy, Lolly and Spike were waiting for Slammer to arrive. Jane knew that if he were not there on time, they couldn't wait and that he would have to find everyone at the arena.

Jane heard that Lisa was going to have her first fight in the main arena. For many of these warriors, it was a chance to escape the arenas of other worlds whose owners practiced torture and barbaric ways against those who were to them just slaves. For many gladiators this was their chance to gain their freedom. For others it was the big time but for some it was the road to death. But for the ones who did survive, they were able to gain and enjoy fame, fortune, and perhaps even freedom. Some who survived gave up their freedom and chose to remain and fight as long as they could fight on the *Sphere of Tears* where the conditions made them feel special and as if they were vacationing in Las Vegas.

The tunnel hallways leading to the arena looked like those of the Taj Mahal; only they were hundreds of yards long and at least one block wide. The arena's lobby and hallways were so large and so long that many transportation services could be provided. There were small electrical baggage carriers and other vehicles such as electric wheel chairs and small six passenger open motorcycle cars with two wheels in the front and two in the back. These held three couples in a row, each row elevated a few inches more from the back to front so that every couple could see in all directions. The driver was in his own seat in the front, holding the motorcycle-like handlebars.

The fights that had been delayed for a second time were now scheduled to start in a half hour. Even though Jane and Roxy were anxious to get the plan to save Lisa underway, they also realized that they just had to wait. They had heard that the arena lobby and hallways were magnificent and they decided to be tourists and enjoy themselves by walking to the arena.

The design of the tunnel walkways might have been like those of the Taj Mahal but the stores and their windows were just like those in any mall that could be found on any world. They were full of merchandise ready for every type of buyer. Lolly dragged Spike to a window that had caught her interest. The shop was called "Stones and Bones." She just stared in amazement at the display in the window.

Jane and the rest of the crew knew that it would take a while for the two to absorb what they were looking at, so she suggested that she and her crew go to the coffee shop next door and wait for them there.

Displayed in the window were different types of jewelry. There were gold bracelets and diamond, gold, ruby and even pearl necklaces. After staring at the display of jewelry for a few seconds, Lolly and Spike put their hands on the windows and gasped and held their breath. They pressed their faces against the glass like excited children, squishing their noses to the window as their mouths dropped open. This was definitely something they had never seen before. All of the jewelry came to life and formed dancing shapes. Then music started to play. Spike turned around to see if anyone else was looking at what was happening. No one was. He turned back and continued staring at the jewelry that was now dancing to the music.

A second later a diamond necklace started to sing:

> *You can rent me, even lend me.*
> *Then a golden bracelet sang:*
> *I will shine, the glimmer's mine.*

Then everyone joined in:

> *You can wear us, use our Status.*
> *Wear with clothes or even naked*
> *But one thing you cannot do*
> *Is steal these jewels, 'cause we'll get you.*

When the jewelry finished singing, they returned to their places in the original display, looked at Lolly and Spike, then waved, 'Come on in.'

Lolly jumped up and down and grabbed Spike by the arm. "Come on, Spike. I want to go in." And she did with Spike firmly in tow.

A magnificent woman came floating out from behind the display counter. She wore diamond high heel shoes. Her legs and arms were gold. Her head was made of silver and her hair of unusually thin strands of gold. Her eyes were emeralds and shaped like those of a cat. Small rubies formed her delicate yet full lips. Her nose and her cheeks were very tiny light peach colored topazes. Her dress was like a nineteen thirties ball gown, made of platinum mesh and decorated with pearls, opals, aquamarines, bloodstones and corals.

"Hi," she said to Lolly and Spike in a sparkly voice. "My name is Bony Jewels. I am the owner of this establishment. May I help you with anything?"

"We're not here to buy, Mam. We just want to enjoy this fine art and we are curious to know how these jewels come to life." Lolly said.

"They never died, dear. And they're not for sale, only for rent. We are part of the Spark people and we are always alive and under their protection."

"Well, that explains part of this." Spike thought.

"We would really like to know about you. Do you mind telling us about yourself?"

"Not at all, dear. It's nice to know that someone cares enough to ask. My father was a mad scientist who was born on the planet called Moist-Cal. We were developed from one mineral, Calcium. We are made of what you Earthlings call bones. At the beginning, like all life forms, we also died. But when my father's experiment was ready, he said to me, 'I have decided to honor you by trying out on you a theory of mine that will let you live forever.' He really hoped that his theory was right and he couldn't wait to try it out. My father reassured me, 'If anything happens to you, sweetheart, I will make you live forever.' And then he mumbled, 'I think. I sure hope so.'

'What are you going do, Daddy?'

'If anything happens to you, I will try out my theory.' I knew right then and there that my father was crazy. And oddly enough, the next day I died mysteriously, from who knows what."

Lolly who was confused by what she had just heard asked,. "I don't understand. Are you saying that your father killed you just to dump you in another world as an experiment? Why would he do that?"

"He was a mad scientist who wanted to leave his mark. Before he shipped me to the *Mine, Mine Planet*, which was actually a good thing for me, he developed my D.N.A. so that it could retain information from one chemical change to another. In other words he made me, through my D.N.A. like a memory bank. He realized that on this marvelous planet my structure in a way would integrate into the chemical structure of the planet, thereby restoring my life because everything on this planet is alive. That is why my arms and legs are gold and silver and the rest of my body and even my joints are made of semi-precious and precious stones and ores. I think that these jewels give me a nice look. What do you think?"

"Yes, they do." Lolly said. "What do you think, Spike?"

"I think she's gorgeous. I wouldn't mind polishing her jewels!"

Lolly smacked him on his head and said, "I didn't ask you all that."

And they both shouted "thank you" as Lolly grabbed Spike and ran out of the shop, holding on to him by his sleeve. Then they held hands and went next door to the coffee shop where Ragrezy who was sitting with the rest of the crew said sarcastically with a smile, "It's about time. Can we go now?" Everyone stood up, left the coffee shop and started walking toward the arena.

Along the way Jane inquired with great curiosity, "Ragrezy,

do you know how the arena is laid out? I'd like to have a better idea about the arena and its surrounding area."

"Okay. Imagine that you are looking down at the *Sphere of Tears* from the sky. You would see a city that stretches for hundreds of miles and in the middle of that city, there is a two mile circumference dedicated just to the arena. There are many tunnels leading into the arena as well as open roads leading to it. And all along those tunnels and roads to the arena, there are many businesses. All of the hotels and buildings that face the arena have specially constructed balconies. Each balcony unfolds to hold at least two dozen spectators in order to give other tenants who cannot see the arena from their apartments an opportunity to view the fights."

"How are they able to collect the fees for the fights?" Spike asked Ragrezy.

"Oh, I know that one." Franky interrupted.

Ragrezy could see that Franky wanted to impress Jane, so he said,

"I'm glad that you know. I could never figure that out."

And then Franky showed off his knowledge.

"First of all, because the event lasts for eight days, the rules for being in the city temporarily change. The entire city actually turns into a special kind of business. The buildings surrounding the arena have some of the most expensive seats in the area because of their view."

Franky paused like the ham he could sometimes be and then continued.

"There are hundreds of thousands of balconies in that two mile perimeter and they hold millions of spectators. And that's just the outer rim of the two mile circumference. The fees for the fights are automatically added to the rent bill which basically states, 'As long as you live in the city, whether you watch the fights or not, you will still pay.'

"Anyone who wishes to come into the city must pay an admission fee. The city is treated like a night club. If you don't pay, then you can't come in. The residents don't mind paying extra, neither do the outsiders. Most of them are criminals and one way or another, they get their money back. Then there are a few who figure out a way not to pay at all. This really never surprises anyone. After all it *is* a planet built on dishonesty by criminals of every kind."

The fights had been going on for a while but often with first time fighters. By the time Franky finished his story, the loud speakers were announcing the two gladiators who were going to fight next. What came across sounded like very clear radio announcements, only with advertisements in between the names of the fighters.

Jane knew that Lisa wasn't due to fight yet but she wanted to get to her seat in plenty of time.

She called Lolly, "Hey Lolly! Grab Spike and follow me!" Then she looked at Franky and Ragrezy and motioned with her head, "You too!" She grabbed Roxy's hand and rushed toward the arena.

Spike was panting because Lolly was dragging him at an unbelievably fast pace.

"Boy, you girls sure like to rush."

"Rush," Franky commented, walking just as fast. "This isn't anything. Wait until a woman takes you to an eighty percent off sales day. That's when you'll truly understand what rushing means. Even a freight train can't compare to some women running for a sale, especially on shoes."

After a few minutes all of them were standing in front of their seats.

The crowd was pretty quiet for now because these were just preliminary fights. The most important fighters were yet to appear. This gave Jane time to relax. Meanwhile Roxy was admiring the design of the whole place. She thought that the arena was probably a bit like the one in the time of the Romans, only many times larger and with added features that the Romans had never dreamed of. There was one particular section of the arena that stood on its own and even moved. It was about twenty feet high and held at least a hundred men. In front of it there was an elevator large enough to hold a truck, reserved for extra large fighters. The section was made of gold. On top of that section there was a tent-like open room with a chair made out of platinum covered with all sorts of gems.

Roxy stopped daydreaming and asked Ragrezy, while pointing.

"Do you know who sits on that throne-like chair in that section of the arena?"

"Oh sure. That chair is for the most powerful and influential person who rules the *Sphere of Tears* and whatever else he can manage as a business. That is the All-for-One-Man's chair."

"Where *is* he?" Jane who was listening to the conversation asked.

"Don't worry, Jane. He'll be here. The fight won't start without him."

"Why? Does he have Lisa with him?" Jane asked Ragrezy.

Meanwhile Roxy kept looking for their sister who was not in sight. There were some new fighters in the arena, who still had to prove themselves at this time. The crowds didn't care very much; they were still waiting for the main event. Even though this was Lisa's first fight in this arena, she was also the only person to have challenged the Gangia Queen for the championship. This made her event the top draw.

Franky who was sitting next to Jane pointed to the place where the big boss of the city was to sit before the challenge could begin.

"See, that is where the All-for-One-Man is going to sit."

"I heard that when you told Roxy."

Jane looked at Franky and then at Ragrezy.

"I don't understand something. How can my sister be the one to fight this Gangia Queen?"

Franky shrugged his shoulders and answered with an "I don't know" grunt.

Ragrezy who knew the story volunteered.

"I'll answer that for you, Jane. You see, one day when Lisa was fighting on another planet, she heard that Astro had retired and she took the opportunity to challenge the Gangia Queen who was considered unbeatable now that Astro was no longer fighting. The rumor is that the All-for-One-Man gave Gangia some sort of power so that she couldn't be killed.

"It is believed that when Astro started to train Lisa, he gave her similar powers and that because of his Island her body adjusted and developed the same strength as Astro's. Lisa made it her mission to train and fight so well that she could defeat the Gangia Queen and gain her freedom. Then she would be able to reunite with the sisters she had heard so much about but could barely remember. If Lisa wins, she will become the ruler of the *Sphere of Tears*. As far as the story goes, she has no interest in this. All she wants is to win so that she can be with her sisters. That's the way the story has been told to me. The rumor also goes that no one will challenge the Gangia Queen because no one wants to die. Well here we are, making sure that Lisa lives and we can all get out of here alive and go home."

"Thank you, Ragrezy. I hope everything works out as planned."

Then Jane looked around the arena and said,

"I still don't see Slammer. Where is he?"

Franky put his arm on her shoulder. "It's okay Jane. Slammer is always on time when it comes to his job. The main event hasn't even started yet."

Then a loud sound pierced the sky... It made the crowd as quiet as a church mouse. A minute later this was heard coming over some sound system.

"Ladies and whatever the rest of you are. Welcome to the three hundred and seventy fifth anniversary of the Power Fights. As all of you know, the champion of this battle will rule the *Sphere of Tears* until a new champion dominates the arena."

The crowd kept shouting: "Long live the champion!"

Then all sorts of military music began to play. The section that held the great throne-like chair was lighting up like a Christmas tree. All those seated or standing in this section looked like ex-fighters from one planet or another because Mr. Evil, the dominant side of the All-for-One-Man, believed in surrounding himself with protection and not in taking any chances.

When the music stopped, everyone was standing throughout

the arena and not a word could be heard. All of a sudden Mr. Evil came sliding out from behind the throne. The crowd was cheering like never before.

Mr. Evil spoke to the audience in a very commanding voice.

"Today we have a challenger who believes that she can beat and yes, even kill the Great Gangia Queen. My Queen. It has been over a decade since such a challenge has been made. And my Queen is looking forward to the exercise."

The crowd once again roared. Some looked like they weren't sure who they wanted to win. The others didn't care. They just came for the blood.

"Thank you very much." Mr. Evil's voice shouted out over a loudspeaker to the crowd.

"I realize that all of you have come to see the championship fight. And you will see it. But first! There are some new fighters from another universe who want to compete for the chance to control the *Sphere of Tears*. Look up at the sky!" Mr. Evil yelled as he pointed upwards. Everyone immediately looked up at the sky and their eyes filled with a look of amazement at what they saw.

There was a long, triple-level rectangular-shaped spaceship with a scull-shaped globe attached to each end. Each one was four times the size of the end of the ship that held it. A second later two humongous creatures came floating down, one from the bottom of each globe, about three hundred yards from each other. One had a body as large as the platform reserved for the All-for-One-Man. He had four arms. Each arm had the dimensions of a thick tree trunk and to make matters worse for his opponent, his hands had claws the size of a four foot blade. His fingers fired a type of chemical that would momentarily paralyze his opponent if he breathed it in. It would only last for a second but that's all he needed to kill his opponent. He was named Fatara from the planet Fatapry.

The second creature named Long'ha came from the Longy Planet. Long'ha was three hundred yards opposite him. She was a weird-looking, extremely hairy creature, very thin and about ten feet tall and half the size of her opponent Fatara. She did not have arms, hands, legs or feet. She had something better: six tentacles, each with a six-fingered claw, that she used to grasp, tear and put food into the tentacles which functioned both as her mouth and breathing system. The tentacles and their claws also functioned as her hands, allowing her to grab onto and hold things and as her legs, allowing her to walk, jump and even roll like a ball. Her hairy rounded torso held her six tentacles - two on the bottom; two on the top; one centered on the front and one centered on the back. Long'ha had a head that looked like an unshaped lump. It had four eyes that were back to back, giving her three hundred and sixty degree eyesight. Her head swiveled whenever her body moved thereby insuring that it would always be in an upright position on her body.

When the creatures landed on the arena, they looked up and down and sized each other up. Fatara had a good idea of what Long'ha was going to do and sure enough, she did just as he thought she would. She was so fast that she literally bounced like a ball and landed on Fatara's back and started to feed on him. His fatty flesh was so intoxicating to Long'ha that she didn't notice that she was so high up off the ground. She also didn't foresee the trick that he planned to play on her. Just as he was to hit the ground, which was the equivalent of a fifty floor drop, he intended to turn over so that when he smashed into the ground Long'ha would now be under him and would be squished as he landed. He just knew that he would be the winner.

Unfortunately for Fatara, Long'ha was much tougher than he imagined. When he hit the ground, it shook like a mountain-size boulder had crashed. Fatara was on top of Long'ha, just as he had planned. But Long'ha just threw him down like a fluffed up pillow. She stood up, brushed herself off and said, "Is that all you've got?" As big as Fatara was, when he saw Long'ha get up like nothing had happened, he realized that he had to eliminate her quickly or it would never happen. He immediately attacked her but she was too fast. Compared to her, he was moving in slow motion.

The fight lasted for a while. Fatara couldn't get to Long'ha's head in order to chop it off because of her speed and Long'ha couldn't get to the soft part of Fatara's underbelly because of his bulk and his unexpected speed. Both of them were getting tired and neither seemed able to kill the other.

Fatara foolishly thought, *Even though Long'ha moves so fast, all I have to do is paralyze her for a second and that will give me enough time to finish that skinny thing off!*

Well! Fatara was in for some surprise! They fought a few minutes more and when Fatara got close enough, he enveloped Long'ha's body with his enormous arms and used his fingers to spray her with his paralyzing gas.

Just as Fatara lifted two of his arms to chop off Long'ha's head, she stuck him in his underbelly and sides with every six-fingered claw that was free. Just before he fell to his death, he asked in disbelief.

"Why didn't you get paralyzed?"

"Because my race is immune to your gas…My people have studied you for years and we know all of your tricks. We need to eat and you are the tastiest dish in our universe. We have always taught our children how to hunt and kill you. So, I will compliment you on your skills and thank you for feeding my family."

And Fatara closed his eyes for the last time.

Long'ha slowly got up and despite all of her injuries she smiled and waved to the crowd as they cheered her on.

The spaceship that was hovering above the city had her children watching everything on the screen and when Long'ha signaled the ship, it only took a second for a box to come down from the sky and land next to her. The crowd hushed instantly.

Mr. Evil's section lit up once more so that the crowd would know that he was about to speak. He looked at Long'ha and said.

"Oh, is that a tribute for me?"

She looked up at him and smiled.

"No, it's not," she replied as she touched the box. "It's for my children."

All of the sides of the box fell open. Dozens of tiny Long'has climbed on Fatara and before the crowd could react, they devoured him like piranhas and not a drop of him remained. Mr. Evil didn't like the fact that Long'ha didn't pay him a tribute but like all businessmen, he knew that when the crowd loved what he hated, it made profits for him and so he overlooked her petty indiscretion.

Long'ha watched her children and as soon as they finished eating, they got on the box and it folded back up with them inside. They all floated back into the ship and disappeared into space. During all of this, the crowd was going wild, but the initial effect wore off, a second after the ship lifted off. Mr. Evil realized what had happened and thought, *That's a very inventive way to feed a family.*

Once that thought left his mind, he realized that the roaring crowd was demanding that the main fight should start.

"Gangia, Gangia" was repeated over and over

Mr. Evil shouted over the sound system which was loud enough to drown out the crowds.

"All right, you beasts and whatever other ugly thieving things are out there." The crowd laughed. "I'm sure that you know my Gangia Queen." The crowd went wild when she came out from behind the chair.

She had a body that resembled that of a seven foot tall praying mantis. Her head was elongated and her eyes green, unusually wide and slanted. Her mouth was bigger than that of a piranha and it opened and expanded to such a size that she could inhale most of her adversaries whole as her five rows of razor sharp teeth ground them to a pulp.

The Gangia Queen walked to the front of Mr. Evil's platform and stated,

"It is time for me to put an end to this child's dreams and aspirations of capturing my crown and ruling the *Sphere of Tears.*"

Then the crowd watched her jump, twist and spin in the air like an acrobat and make a perfect, twenty-foot drop landing into the arena.

She was prepared to fight. The Gangia Queen truly deserved her name. Her elongated head was literally shaped like a crown. This was due to the fact that her entire body had pointed nails sticking out of it. The crown and the nails were made out of one of the strongest materials known in the universe, A.S.M.S. or Atomic Strength Molecular Structure. The Gangia Queen may have been built like a praying mantis but she fought like a bull. She had pointed horns that popped out randomly from different parts of her thin body and she could use those horns like daggers or like grenades that exploded upon impact and instantly grew back. This was definitely to her advantage since there was no way her opponent could know when or where her horns would appear or how they would strike.

"Roxy, do you see Lisa?" Jane asked, leaning forward.

"No, Jane. But I think that she might be coming out next."

And sure enough, Mr. Evil stood up, took the microphone and started talking again.

"As I have promised you before, I have with me the only challenger for the Gangia Queen's throne to arrive here in over a decade."

The crowd went wild. Once the crowd stopped roaring, Mr. Evil continued.

"Do not be deceived or disappointed by this challenger's appearance. You will be able to place your bets up to two seconds before the fight begins. And without any more delay, say hello to the challenger." Mr. Evil looked at the crowd and just said, "Here's Lisa."

The crowd fell silent and then started laughing because Lisa looked like a sweet young thing. The Gangia Queen was many times larger than she and looked vicious. There was definitely nothing sweet or young about her.

Jane couldn't believe that she was seeing her sister. Lisa was five foot ten and had a very healthy physique. She didn't resemble her twin Roxy. She wore silver shoes laced up past her calves, a pleated yellow skirt an inch above her knees, and a one piece, tightly fitted, light blue leotard and tights that was comfortable for fighting. She had long blond hair braided into two pony tails. Each ponytail went past her shoulders and then divided into two more pony tails. These ponytails were braided scissor-style. And at the end of each of those four scissor-style braids, her hair formed a dangerous, chemically created multi-colored pointed diamond tip.

Lisa's face was very pretty. Her eyes were big and blue like the ocean on a sunny day. They were kind and soft, which gave the impression that she understood whatever someone was feeling. She certainly didn't look like a gladiator. Yet she had a certain strength to her that could be felt.

Lisa was standing next to Mr. Evil when he was speaking. In order to show up the Gangia Queen, she jumped from where she was, instead of going to the edge of the platform. Then she did all sorts of twists and turns, landed and was ready for action.

The crowd laughed and roared in disbelief. "Is she kidding? Gangia will finish her in a minute!"

They both decided to start their battle with swords, just to test each other out and get a feeling for their respective techniques.

Mr. Evil didn't like to be mocked by the crowd and warned Lisa. "If you want your freedom, you have to earn it".

Lisa did not like that and even before the crowd could react, she leaped so fast at Gangia that she was able to cut her neck enough that it hung off her shoulders. The Gangia fell to the ground.

Lisa looked at her and wondered why she hadn't moved. She could have avoided her but she didn't. She noticed that the crowd was stunned and that they just stared at the Gangia Queen.

Lisa thought that she was free and started looking into the crowd for her sisters. She was too busy to notice what was happening. Lisa thought that because she had partially severed Gangia's head from her shoulders, it would stay off. But Lisa was aware that something wasn't right. And sure enough, her instincts were correct. Gangia's head was back securely on her shoulders and as if she had gained some magical powers, she seemed to fly straight up from the ground where she lay and to swoop down on Lisa with her sharp knife-like claws ready to strike and shred her apart. The crowd went wild. Mr. Evil never looked so happy. But that did not last long. Lisa moved out of the way with lightning speed and attacked Gangia before she could react. The fight continued.

Meanwhile, in a front row tier of seats, Jane and Roxy were getting very impatient. Lolly and Spike were in their own world. Ragrezy and Franky were just doing what they had been told to do: watching the fight until time for the rescue.

Roxy, Jane and Squeak, who was sitting on Jane's shoulder, were ready to get up and help Lisa, but Slammer had not yet gotten the signal from Mountain. So he put his hand on her arm and with a bit of force stopped her from standing up.

Meanwhile Lisa was putting up quite a fight. She had already stabbed Gangia many times and she had even cut her head off more than once. But it didn't make a difference. The Gangia just put her head back on her shoulders before it was half way to the floor and closed her stab wounds. As the fight continued, Jane was getting more impatient and noticed that her sister was getting a little tired.

"What's taking Mountain so long, Slammer? My sister is in real trouble. Lisa is no match for that she monster."

"Jane, we must wait." When she heard that, she turned

around and asked, "Is Mountain in trouble?"

"No. Jane. There's no trouble. But you must be patient."

"But look at my sister. She can't last much longer. That monster just won't die. There is no way to kill her."

Mr. Evil started talking over the sound system as if a new fight were about to begin.

"We are going into the second phase of this fight. Since we didn't think that Lisa had a chance and the sword play had no definite result, we will go to the power play of the game. Are all of you ready for the shields to rise?"

The crowd went out of control yelling, "Yes, yes! It's about time."

Suddenly it was as if the sky were exploding. There was a crash and an Earthquake-like tremor. It was as though two mountains were rubbing abrasively against each other. The crowd stayed silent as it watched a wall of energy encircle the arena so that none of them would be hurt. The almost invisible wall rose from the ground to about fifty feet above the tallest buildings surrounding the arena. While this was going on, Gangia was watching Lisa start to change into her preparation mode. Gangia just couldn't help herself and when she raised her arms to strike, the crowd watched her as she intently and intentionally kept striking the ground with some sort of whip. It created havoc, tearing apart whatever it hit, like a lighting strike during an electric storm. She didn't touch Lisa as she continued in her preparation stage, even though she desperately wanted to attack and kill her. When Gangia finished beating the ground out of frustration, she leaped onto Mr. Evil's platform and expressed her desire to kill Lisa. This was Mr. Evil's reaction.

"Gangia, you cannot attack and kill Lisa while she is in this state, no matter how much I would love it. The Spark people will not stand for that."

"What is she going to become?" she asked.

"I have no idea," Mr. Evil replied and then added, "Why are you concerned?"

"Ha!" she answered with a forced laughed. "No matter what she becomes, I will kill her anyway."

While this was happening, Jane kept repeating, "Is that our sister? What is going on?"

Slammer said, "Don't worry. What is happening now is a good thing. Mountain explained the fight process to me."

"Well!" Roxy, very anxious, asked. "What is happening to our sister?"

PART FIVE
THE REBIRTH OF LISA

Lisa

"Look. The best way I can put it is that Lisa is like a caterpillar changing its form. Your sister is temporarily changing into a fighting machine."

A blue cocoon had developed around Lisa and it began to glow, periodically growing brighter and gradually changing from blue to red.

All of a sudden the crowd started to cheer. The bright red shining cocoon lifted up about five feet from the ground. About a minute passed and the cocoon started to swell; a second later it turned into red dust and drifted into the wind, leaving an amazing woman floating in its place. Lisa had become a fighting machine with golden legs and arms and a silver cybernetic titanium torso. Her head, hair and face, basically remained the same but they had acquired an enhancing, metallic quality. Her new body was able to form a variety of weapons upon her command as well as an endless variety of ammunition. She also seemed larger and taller. Lisa slowly floated to the ground, walked in front of Mr. Evil's platform and said.

"Thank you for giving me the time to prepare for this battle."

Gangia was sick and tired of all the politeness. Just before she jumped off the platform, she simply said, "Come on sister! Let's see what you've got."

She landed close to Lisa. Because Gangia was so tall and fast, it was hard for Lisa to keep her in one spot so that she could chop off her head and try to take her eyes out. With Gangia blind, Lisa would have time to figure out how, if not to kill her, to at least contain her. Before Lisa could even think another thought, Gangia was on her like lightning and knocked her down. She was hacking away at Lisa but her weapon did not seem to cut her. Lisa was back on her feet a second later. What happened next was quite a surprise for Gangia. Lisa needed to run and put some distance between the two of them. She knew that while she was still running, Gangia would leap for her back.

One of Lisa's powers included the ability to replace any part of her body in an instant when necessary. Lisa turned around knowing that Gangia would be in mid air and heading straight for her. She pointed her fingers at Gangia and all of them shot out from her hand just like little rockets. Before the fingers were even an inch away from her hand, another set had already grown back. Meanwhile the fingers that were flying toward Gangia were interweaving with each other like magic, creating a wire net. Once the net wrapped around the Gangia Queen, it kept squeezing Gangia so that by the time she hit the ground, she was diced up like sushi. The crowd went wild and Lisa once again scanned the arena for a sign of her sisters. Then an even louder cheer came as Gangia's body somehow started putting itself together. By the time Lisa noticed the crowd's excitement, Gangia had already thrown something at her. It exploded and when the smoke cleared, Lisa was trapped inside a dome creature made of some invisible yet glowing material. A second later, the inside of the dome was giving birth to some kind of drill-like creatures. Lisa noticed that the creatures were actually part of the dome itself.

Well, I see that the Gangia has some tricks of her own, Lisa said to herself. Then she thought how weird it was to think this at such a dangerous time.

The almost invisible dome creature was actually a part of Gangia. It had two eyes inside its top. Each dome drilling creature had a mouth with three jaws. Each jaw was at least a foot long and came to a point that looked and functioned like a drill. The teeth were shaped like drill bits and when the jaw opened, the teeth twisted and grabbed at whatever enemy the dome had captured.

Roxy and Jane were in the stands just watching because they realized that there was nothing that they could do. The protection shield was a complete surprise for everyone. No one could penetrate it. Jane's crew, full of anxiety and frustration, could only watch.

"Oh no!" Jane and Roxy, both rising to their feet, screamed out, as they helplessly watched the dome creature.

"Oh my God," Jane and Roxy yelled, "those teeth are drilling into Lisa. We have to stop this."

Slammer said very calmly, as if he knew something that they didn't, "Relax, it's not over yet."

Jane turned away from the arena and straight into Slammer's face.

"Are you blind? Do you not see that those drilling monsters are making dozens of holes into my sister and that some of them are already completely through her?"

"Jane, they're not drilling into her. Lisa's body is making room for the drills to pass straight through. Otherwise, why would she be smiling and waving to the crowds?"

Jane quickly turned around to look and saw that although her sister was still getting drilled, she was definitely smiling.

Meanwhile Lisa had been scanning the arena to find her sisters and sure enough she did, when Jane turned around. When Lisa saw that Jane and Roxy were looking at her, she waved to them and they waved back. Lisa decided to show her sisters some of her powers. She looked at the top of the dome where its two big eyes were staring down while it was drilling away at her. Then with a big smile, she waved goodbye to the dome eyes and turned herself into some sort of corrosion liquid which instantly filled the whole dome. As the dome started to dissolve, the Gangia who was just watching began to scream as she realized that part of her body was dissolving. An instant later, the dome turned into a heavy mist and flew into the Gangia's piranha-like mouth. Gangia found it impossible to believe what she saw.

There was Lisa standing good as new and taunting the Gangia with, "Is that all you can do?"

"You're not doing much better," she replied and then added, "Although I must admit, you're doing better than I expected."

Then the fireworks began. Gangia lifted her arm as if she were signaling "stop" and five two-inch horns shot out of her forearm and hit Lisa, exploding like ten pounds of T.N.T. Lisa was blown a couple of hundred yards into the sky. When she came down, she smashed into the ground. About five hundred feet of ground flew up as if a meteorite had hit and created a crater that was about fifty feet deep. The crater filled back up like magic with earth. The explosion threw the Gangia up against the force shield and flattened her.

Gangia sprang away from the shield. From that moment on, there was a back and forth battle between the two, trying to blow each other up. The crowd loved it, especially when they thought that the explosions might penetrate the shield and hit some of them.

Jane was getting out of control. "Slammer," she kept insisting. "We have to attack. My sister needs us. And where is Mountain? I haven't seen him."

"Mountain is here but we must be in position before we can attack."

Jane was watching when the Gangia Queen cornered Lisa. A minute later Lisa was on the ground with the beast towering over her and about to run her through.

"So you think that you can beat the great Gangia Queen! You shrimp of a human!"

"Maybe I am," Lisa said proudly, "But my heart and soul are larger than you can ever hope to be and that is why I *will* beat you..."

This angered the Gangia so much that she raised her sword to give her final blow and continued to repeat, "So you think that you can beat the great Gangia Queen."

The beast was very talkative, which turned out to be a good thing. It gave Lisa the chance to act.

The Gangia closed her eyes while still yelling in rage as she struck and hit the empty ground. By the time all of this happened, Lisa had already cut off the Gangia's head. Once again she watched it fall to the ground and saw the Gangia Queen stumble while trying to catch it as it rolled away. Lisa took the time to rest and tried to figure out why the Gangia Queen couldn't be killed.

Astro, unseen by everyone, had been watching the fight for a while. He wanted to help Lisa but certain rules would not allow it, until now. He had figured out why and how he could justify his behavior. He did not want the Gangia Queen to keep the power she had because the All-for-One-Man owned her. And since the champion of the arena world would become very influential in the world of the *Mine, Mine Planet*, he wanted Lisa to be the champion even though she didn't want to rule the *Sphere of Tears*.

The Gangia Queen was too vicious and sadistic and couldn't be killed because of Mr. Evil's magic. Only the Spark people knew her weaknesses, including Astro and Lisa because they were part Spark people. Even though Astro knew Gangia's weak spots, he was never to use this knowledge against her. But it didn't matter if he beat her with his magical powers.

Since Astro was an alien to the Spark people and at the same time a part of them, he was chosen to represent the Spark people. He became the planet's ambassador because of his understanding and the fact that he was the most powerful being that had ever lived in their world. However, there were certain rules that had to be followed when it came to the arena fights. Once Astro retired, he could not interfere with the fighters while they were in battle. Astro could not help or fight on behalf of anyone. That's why there was nothing that he could do to help Lisa.

Then he realized something. Because Lisa was living on his Island, some of what had happened to him also happened to her, making her part of the Spark people.

Once he thought of this, he also decided that he could let Lisa know how to defeat the Gangia Queen.

Astro had to quiet down the crowds that had filled the arena. There was only one way to do that. He stood up in a specially built section in the front of the arena where everyone could see him. Representing the Spark people, he stretched his arms toward the sky and a split second later, the eyes of the crowds followed the two streaks of Spark fire coming out of his hands that shot into the sky. Normally the crowds would have panicked and scattered but they knew that Astro had awesome and even unbelievable powers. They realized that those explosions could have killed most of them but they knew better and began applauding and cheering when the two city-sized explosions turned into a magnificent umbrella-style colorful rainbow that covered the sky over their heads. The variegated sparkles floated down for a couple feet and then exploded into puffs of colorful smoke. Then seemingly out of nowhere, Astro jumped into the arena and stood next to Lisa, knowing that he could not interfere with the fight itself but could give Lisa advice.

Everything and everyone stopped on the dime. Mr. Evil immediately stood and hollered.

"What is this about, Astro? You'd better have a good reason for being down there."

"I just need to give an urgent message to Lisa about her sisters."

"What need?" Mr. Evil responded. "Her sisters are going to try to help her escape. You think that I am not aware of such things?"

Then, he said with great confidence, as if whatever message Astro had for Lisa wouldn't make a difference, "Hah. Go ahead and tell her what you have to. The Queen is about to chop her head off and hand it to me anyway. And her puny human head doesn't go back together like my Queen's does. Now hurry up. The people are impatient. They want to see blood."

While Astro was talking to Lisa, the Gangia was looking for her head which had rolled a foot to her left. When Astro finished whispering something to Lisa, he leaped out into the crowd and walked away. He didn't want anyone to figure out what he had said to Lisa, so he shouted over the crowd's roars, "Don't forget what I told you. Look to the Mountain, two make one, and timing is critical."

As soon as Astro rushed out of the arena and into the

crowd, Lisa commenced with the "do or die" segment of the fight. She lunged forward to run her sword through the Gangia Queen who had already put her head back onto her shoulders. Lisa was not prepared for what happened next. The Gangia kicked her five yards back and she slid and sank into the ground, forming a crater. But once again the ground evened itself out. It seemed like the whole arena could be destroyed and like a rubber band, go back to its original form. Lisa was not thrilled that the Gangia had surprised her. This Gangia Queen was faster than she thought.

And she didn't like the fact that the Gangia got close enough to knock her on her butt.

At the same time Jane was growing very impatient.

By now everyone was standing. Jane was in front of Ragrezy, "What is happening with Mountain?" she asked Slammer.

"I think he's just about ready. He's waiting for a signal from Astro."

"What signal?"

"Look!" Slammer answered, pointing. "Do you see those black figures that are fifty feet apart from each other throughout the arena?"

"Yes. What about them?"

"They are on our side. And the guys with Mountain are almost as big as mountains."

Jane just couldn't wait anymore and neither could Roxy.

"You do what you want because we're not waiting anymore."

"How are you going to penetrate the shield wall?"

"Don't you worry! Rocky and the Changer are taking care of that."

And just as she finished saying that, the ground shook, a bright red light covered the sky for just a second and then the shield wall was gone.

Jane shouted with great urgency, "Now! Squeak! Do what we planned."

It happened so fast that Slammer couldn't react. Squeak had instantly grown to four times Jane's size.

He picked her up from the ground, held her in the air and before she knew what happened, he dropped her on top of the Gangia Queen's head. Jane landed on the Gangia's neck and like a crusader on a stallion she plunged her sword straight through the top of her skull. The crowd was cheering like never before, especially when the Gangia threw Jane off and into a wall. Jane was stunned and just sat there, shaking her head

The Gangia pulled the sword out of her skull like it was a tooth pick. By this time Lisa had gotten her momentum back and grabbed the sword that the Gangia had just pulled out of her head and plunged it right back in again. When she did that, she looked toward Mr. Evil. And once again, Gangia pulled the sword out of her head and tried to plunge it into Lisa's back. Jane had already gotten up and gone to help Roxy who she saw was fighting some guards who were attacking her.

Gangia had another trick up her sleeve or rather her chest. When Lisa attacked the Gangia, she knocked her down and sat on her chest, holding her sword against her neck, trying to cut her head off. A second later Lisa was ejected from the Gangia's chest. The Gangia had a thin layer of some special material on her chest. It wrapped itself around Lisa and shot her up to a certain height and then exploded with Lisa in it. Unfortunately for the Gangia, the explosion did nothing to Lisa. The wrapper was gone and Lisa floated back down and began fighting with the Gangia once more.

By this time the arena was in a bit of a chaotic mess. When the main shield was destroyed, so was the rest of the security shield and equipment. By now the gladiator prisoners were fighting with the guards and many of the crowds were fighting with each other, just for the sake of fighting.

Jane needed access to Lisa so she could help her.

Lisa and the Gangia Queen were firing all sorts of weapons at each other and since the shield was down the explosions were seen all over the arena. While firing at each other, they even blew up some of the buildings. Then Lisa hit the Gangia with a very powerful dust ball which sent her all the way up to the roof of one of the buildings. This gave Jane a chance to reach Lisa and tell her that she and the crew were there to rescue her and that Astro and Mountain were also with them

Lisa looked toward Mr. Evil and saw that Astro was there.

She turned and said, "Excuse me Jane but I must accomplish a very difficult task and it must be timed properly." And just as Lisa was about to say something else, the Gangia Queen flew down from the roof and landed on top of her. They continued fighting.

At this time Mountain and Astro were chopping through all of Mr. Evil's men so that Slammer could chop of Mr. Evil's head at the very moment that Lisa cut off both of the Gangia Queen's feet. Mr. Evil thought that no one knew his secret so he wasn't concerned about what was going on behind him. He was too busy enjoying the destruction of the arena. Astro and Slammer eliminated all of Mr. Evil's bodyguards but by then it seemed that the crowds had divided into two different forces. Mr. Evil pretty much owned everyone in the city in one way or another. And at least half of the people who owed him money figured that it would be good to see him dead. In that way their debts would be gone. The rest of the crowd had the same interests as Mr. Evil and wanted him alive. The fighting was very chaotic. Getting to Mr. Evil was not as easy as it seemed. Franky, Ragrezy, Jane and Roxy were now watching out for each other. Everyone was fighting, except for Lolly and Spike. Lolly was in a corner of the arena watching over Spike while he was moving and staring at everything that was going on and speaking in some strange language as he played with the nails in his head.

It wasn't long before Jane's crew noticed that when they were outnumbered or in a bad situation, black tentacles would appear, changing into different shapes, ready to help by smacking their enemies on the head with a hammer or some other object that these pieces of Astro's wall could turn into in a moment's notice.

Jane's crew thought that Astro's Black Wall which wore black hats and long raincoats sure came in handy.

The Wall was fighting side by side with Jane and her crew. Lisa was watching for a signal from Slammer just like Astro told her to do. She was trying to figure out how to watch the Gangia and for Slammer at the same time. Lisa changed her position with one leap and before the Gangia could figure out what Lisa was up to, Lisa spun the Gangia around with a blow so that her back was facing Mr. Evil and Lisa could see Mr. Evil and watch for Slammer as she fought with the Gangia.

While all of this was going on, somewhere inside the planet the Spark people were having a meeting. Just visualize different size stars gleaming in the darkness of some meeting room resembling outer space.

Dim-Star, one of the more burnt-out Spark people said,

"Didn't we tell Astro that only the Spark people are to know about Mr. Evil and the Gangia Queen's secret?"

"Yes, you did, your Sparkyness," One of the Sparks replied and then continued.

"Please remember that Astro is not interfering with the arena fights. This disturbance is considered by everyone to be a free for all."

"Perhaps it is." Dim-Star replied. "But Astro told Lisa how to kill the Gangia and you know that we cannot allow that to happen."

"First of all your Sparkyness…"

"My name is Dim-Star," he shouted, very unhappy about this unknown Spark's nonchalant attitude.

The Spark replied, "Do you realize that even though Astro was not born on this planet, we have integrated him into our world? He is physically and mentally a part of us and in a way, even better than we are. He can travel to other worlds while we, the Spark people, are bound to our planet. So, he had a right to tell Lisa and Lisa, being part Spark like Astro, had the right to know."

Then, another voice from some other Spark commented.

"We never told her not kill the Gangia."

Then he looked at Dim-Star and said, "You know that what they want to do is impossible. No one can time three strikes as one."

"Perhaps improbable," Dim-Star answered angrily, "but

not impossible."

Lisa and the Gangia were still fighting and destroying the arena. By this time parts of Lisa's body were turning into all sorts of fighting machines that bombarded the Gangia who just wouldn't stay down. Lisa had to keep fighting until she saw Slammer.

It took him a while to fight his way there. When there were just two bodyguards left near Mr. Evil, Astro took care of them while Slammer positioned himself and waited for Lisa to notice. As soon as their eyes met, Lisa went into action. The Gangia Queen never saw it coming. Lisa's pony tails thus far were used for striking, like a knife-whip. They had remained one size and she even used them like propellers for chopping up her attackers.

This time Lisa leaped into the air and landed on the Gangia's shoulders, doing a hand stand. When the Gangia looked up at her, Lisa was already looking down. Their eyes were only inches apart. Lisa with a Cheshire cat grin, said, "Hello."

And just as Gangia was about to say something, she painfully grunted and fell to the ground, screeching. The Gangia had not noticed that Lisa's ponytails had a life of their own and that they now stretched down to her ankles. The ponytail braids turned into very sharp scissors. Lisa had timed the cuts perfectly and just as Mr. Evil's head was flying off his shoulders, the Gangia Queen was folding like a deck of cards that flew into a world of destruction.

The Sparks were having their meeting about what to do about Astro and how to control him. When they heard the horrific screeching, they understood that Mr. Evil and the Gangia Queen were being killed. Their plans had to change and quickly. They knew that they had a catastrophe on their hands. They could no longer be bothered with Astro's helping Lisa or her escape with her sisters. Astro had not broken any of their laws or his promises.

One of the Sparks commented, "It doesn't matter now anyway. The world has to be cleansed – again."

When Slammer chopped off Mr. Evil's head, he experienced something totally unknown to him before this moment. He freaked out. But then, he never had a chopped off head look at him before and say,

"Thank you. I've been waiting for this for hundreds of years."

Then the head hit the ground.

To make matters worse, he knew from the way that Mr. Evil smiled that he and Lisa shouldn't have killed those two. And sure enough, they found out why a minute later.

The Gangia and Mr. Evil started to turn into some sort of dark smoke. Mr. Evil was up on the platform, melting. The smoke that was coming out of him, as he was getting smaller and disappearing was flowing down to where the Gangia Queen's body was lying. She was also melting and turning into smoke which then proceeded to travel upward to Mr. Evil. The two dark clouds of smoke and soot joined up in mid-air in the middle of the arena.

Slammer watched this as it was happening and so did the whole arena. The two trails of smoke were turning into one humongous monster-like creature. As they combined, the creature grew to the size of a twenty-story building. Its head was formed from a combination of Mr. Evil's head and the crown of the Gangia Queen. Its body took the shape of a thin bull with horns and its legs became the same as those of a praying mantis, only thicker. As they watched, it developed two tails; each one had four fingers that functioned like claws and grippers. Once the transformation was complete, the creature started destroying everything in sight. And to make matters worse, it kept firing its horns, which were as large as small missiles, on the surrounding buildings trying to kill everything. The *Sphere of Tears* was smart to have provided itself with the newest structural technology. As the creature destroyed one part of the arena, the other side of the arena was already returning to its original shape. Jane and her crew were really fighting hard and holding their own against their enemies.

Astro had commanded his Black Wall to surround, envelop and contain the creature long enough for them to make their getaway.

Meanwhile the Spark people were planning what they had to do. They knew that this bizarre combo-creature that used to be Mr. Evil and the Gangia Queen could not be contained for long.

"Are we going to give the warning?" Dim-Star asked his colleagues.

The Sparks lit up even brighter as they answered.

"There is nothing else we can do."

It took only a few words announced to the whole planet and then panic struck. Every man was for himself everywhere throughout the *Mine, Mine World*.

The combo-creature was still fighting Astro's Black Wall just so it could escape and kill Lisa.

The amount of time left before the planet was to start anew, so to speak, was repeated every five minutes throughout the planet.

"You have six hours to evacuate the planet. This is not a drill," resounded everywhere.

Astro ran to where Lisa was. By this time Jane's crew had joined her. Jane said that Squeak was telepathically arranging things with Rocky who would be there in a minute with their spaceship.

There was great destruction everywhere around them.

Spike was pulling the nails on his head as Franky asked,

"Squeak, where is Rocky and our ship?" And just as he said that a bright light and a slight hum made him look up and there it was.

The ship landed and when the door opened, Rocky was right there ready to do what he loved best. He saw Squeak and opened his mouth. As soon as Squeak saw Rocky, he jumped off Jane's neck and ran straight into the rock's mouth.

"Let's get it, Rocky," Squeak hollered as Rocky's mouth closed. By this time, the combo-creature had escaped the Black Wall's grip and was headed for Jane's ship.

Rocky grew larger than the combo-creature and swallowed it.

Meanwhile Jane, her sisters and her crew, Mountain and Astro included, were getting into the ship.

Rocky was looking ill as if he had just swallowed a plate of poison.

Jane was at the ship's door as she hollered, "Come on, Rocky. We have to leave the planet."

Rocky took a look at Jane, faced the other way and literally spit out the combo-creature with such force that it flew straight through the buildings, knocking them down. The combo-creature slid about a half a mile, taking everything with it and creating a two hundred foot deep crater. The creature stood up, shook itself off and charged for the ship. It took only two leaps and then it was just inches away from snatching the RoxyResc.

Jane and everyone on the ship were looking at the creature that was heading straight for them. Then the most unexpected thing happened. The creature just stopped in mid flight and the next thing they saw was it being sucked backwards into the planet. It was as though the planet had become a vacuum cleaner. A spiral cone, made out of Spark people, was pulling the creature into some sort of gold and silver veined box where it would be safely contained for the moment.

A second later Sparky materialized in front of Astro and very seriously said with great urgency:

"Astro, you know what the Spark people have to do now. You also know that you will be safe in your Island and that because of the development that Lisa has had, she can survive with you. Both of you must decide now since we probably won't see you again for thousands of years."

Astro looked at Lisa. Lisa turned and looked at her sisters and then looked at Astro again. "I'm staying with my sisters."

Everyone looked at Astro. He could see that they didn't want him to leave the ship with Sparky.

"Thank you, Sparky. Give my best to my people. I will stay with Lisa and travel the universes. We will see each other again."

As he disappeared out of the ship and into space, Sparky was heard saying faintly, "Good luck."

Jane ordered Spike to raise the shield so that they would be able to see what was going on. At first Spike saw a few hundred spaceships heading toward the dark, icy part of the planet. But then he saw that most of the ships were heading toward the sunny side of the planet and he followed them. There were thousands of ships that were thousands of miles in front of the RoxyResc. Spike sped up to catch and then pass them. But not more than ten minutes passed before Jane saw a bright explosion light up the sky in the far distance.

Jane very sternly commanded, "Spike, magnify the screen." And when he did, it was a sight to see. Everyone just stared at the screen in amazement. The spaceships heading toward the sunny side were blowing up in mid-air as if they had hit a wall.

"Spike," Astro shouted. "Turn this ship around immediately."

Astro looked at Jane and said,

"This is what is happening now and what will happen later. The Spark people can only destroy the combo-creature by incinerating the whole planet. I never understood why. I just know that every now and again, the *Mine, Mine Planet* has to be incinerated because of the different types of creatures that are created by the negative side of the Sparks."

Lolly asked, "What do you mean by the negative side?"

"I was coming to that but things are a bit sketchy."

"Does that mean that you don't know," Ragrezy asked.

And just as Astro was about to reply, Sparky, like magic and as if listening to everything, once again appeared next to Astro.

"I'll tell you what it means in a minute," Sparky said speaking to the crew.

Before starting, he turned to Astro and in his own Spark fashion quietly made it clear to Astro that he needed to understand the damage that he had done by telling Lisa how to kill Mr. Evil and the Gangia Queen. Then Sparky told Astro in no uncertain terms that he could *only* contain and *never* kill another time-developed Spark creature again.

Roxy was in ear shot of what Sparky told Astro and her curiosity made her ask, "What do you mean by time-developed?"

"You see," Sparky replied, "when Astro was dropped on Bloom Island by the Cleaning Bugs, he was a baby and over time he acquired part of our atomic D.N.A. structure, making him part Spark. A similar thing happened to Lisa when Astro brought her to train on his Island. She was young enough and spent enough time there to develop a part of the same atomic structure, thereby making her also a part of the Spark people. They both spent enough time in the place to develop this D.N.A. structure. That is what is meant by time-developed."

"But what about the All-for-One Man and the Gangia Queen? How did they come about?" Roxy asked.

Sparky was pleased to provide the explanation.

"When the All-for-One man came to the *Mine, Mine Planet* over four hundred years ago, he gained a great reputation for being evil. Somehow the evil that exists on our planet integrated itself into the All-for-One man and he in turn created the Gangia Queen. What makes him so powerful is that he has become total Spark evil and he does what the good Spark people will not do. We worry that someday he will be able to escape from this planet and dominate the entire universe like the *Everything Is Ours Planet* tried to do."

Then Sparky turned toward the crew.

"You need to understand why it is impossible to destroy this creature. It is because the Combo-Creature is actually *now* a part of the Spark people, as odd as that may seem. Only, he is our negative side."

"What do you mean?" the crew asked almost in unison.

"Give me time to explain. There is good and evil in everything, just as there is positive and negative. This negative side of ours has developed its own personality and needs. It wants to be on its own and yet, at the same time it wants company and a way to keep itself entertained. In order for our negative side to enjoy itself, it has to have a different sort of physical structure, one that can feel and enjoy pleasures which otherwise would be missed. Unfortunately, through the millennia, good and evil have become unbalanced and evil has started to increase its power. Every time this particular type of combo-creature, which represents our negative and evil side, is killed, it is reborn more powerful and then given a different name. We cannot destroy this evil but we have discovered that as long as it remains alive, in one form or another, it cannot get any stronger or do any more damage."

"Why does the planet have to be incinerated?" Roxy asked.

"Because it is the only way to destroy the Combo-Creature and in a way separate the unity of what creates it. Unfortunately the destruction of the evil creature is only temporary and does not eliminate evil from our planet. While the incineration is going on, the evil Sparks get mixed in with the good ones. Once the planet cools off, the evil Sparks eventually begin to search for each other. It takes a long, long time for them to find one another. While that is happening, aliens from other worlds start to land and colonize the barren planet. While the *Mine, Mine Planet* redevelops, the Sparks will continue to live with whatever happens, according to the kind of aliens that land, colonize and eventually trade with them. The evil parts of the Sparks gradually form a new and ever more powerful creature. But rather than just stay as one creature, it at times separates into a few different characters such as Mr. Evil and the Gangia Queen. In this way, it can have more fun and do more damage. The creature, whatever form it may take, uses the corrupt and evil aliens who come to the planet as servants and elements of entertainment."

"I still don't understand," Lolly said. "What happens when the evil Sparks find each other?"

"They gather in some hidden crater and slowly form into another creature or whatever you want to call it, more powerful and evil than the previous one. Unfortunately, it always grows stronger when it is reborn. That is why it is so important not to kill it again. And why it must stay in the next form that it chooses. Do you understand now?"

"I think so," Lolly replied, looking directly at Astro.

Sparky who was really in a hurry to leave continued.

"Because it takes us a while to recuperate from the incineration and even longer to develop some form of civilization and trade, we would like to keep whatever we get again. Do you understand that we can't enjoy any of the other worlds' goodies, if nobody can survive here? It takes thousands of years before anything can develop again after the incineration. In any case, I must warn you that the Combo-Creature is still very powerful and you must escape this world before that thing gets lose. It could stop your escape and trap you in this planet and you will be incinerated. Your only way out of here is to go through the dark, Winter Ring of the planet."

"I thought that it was blocked with ice," Mountain commented.

"That's not your only problem." Sparky replied, as if he were saying, "You guys are screwed."

"Do you have any suggestions?" Jane asked.

This was where Sparky showed a bit of his disappointment in Astro.

"I'm sorry to say but since Astro is the one who created this mess because he allowed his emotions to rule, even though it was not illegal or wrong, he is the only one who can help you. We the Sparks cannot interfere in the process. We will be too busy trying to contain the sort of beast this negative side of us will develop into."

Then just as quickly as Sparky appeared, he also disappeared but not without his words "good luck" fading in the distance.

The crew looked to Astro for instructions.

"Why are the ships blowing up or melting in mid air?" Roxy asked.

"Wouldn't a better question be - Why isn't this ship heading toward the dark icy side of the planet?" Astro responded.

Jane immediately shouted, "Spike, you'd better turn this ship around now!" Then she looked at Astro and said, "I'm sorry but he doesn't listen to anyone except me when it comes to the ship."

A second later everyone had to grab on to something because the ship was like a car trying to make a U turn while traveling at a thousand miles a minute. Once they turned around, Astro told them that the process for the incineration was beginning and that was why the ships were melting. Although there was no visual fire that could be seen in the sky, it was getting hotter and the all of the other ships had shields that could no longer protect them. The ignition of the incineration was to start from the Summer Ring and shoot straight through the Winter Ring. Because they were still turning around and the ignition had already begun, they had two hours to get as far away from the planet as possible.

Jane and her ship were one of the last in line even though they were going as fast as they could. It did not look good for them.

"Why don't we use the warp speed on this ship?" Mountain asked.

Slammer, to make sure that he was heard shouted at the top of his lungs, "Because Spike didn't check to see if the ball of atomic thrusters was in the engines…"

For a second Spike put the speaker on its highest volume, and all that could be heard was,

"How many times do I have to tell you that I'm sorry? I'm sorry, I'm sorry."

They were just leaving the Spring Ring and entering the Fall Ring. They had been speeding through the planet for at least an hour and during that time, they did not know about the threats that were to come, only about the one that was behind them.

While they were busy figuring out how to speed up the ship, the box that the Combo-Creature was trapped in began to expand and turn red hot like a piece of coal. At first the box was about a foot square but within a short amount of time, it grew to be the size of a house with cracks all around. A short time later, the creature exploded out of the box and immediately sped in the direction of Jane and the RoxyResc.

By this time Jane and her crew were entering the part of the planet's weather ring where it started to get windy. Out of nowhere, a snow storm appeared and a few minutes later it disappeared. Then the sky got dim, giving it a sinister look. Oddly enough, it dropped five feet of snow within the five minutes that it snowed.

When the weather cleared and they looked at the screen, they saw that for thousands of miles in front of them there were now only hundreds of ships left that were trying to get through. They watched helplessly as some spaceships crashed into mountains that were not there a minute before and others were crushed when the mountains suddenly created multiple peaks that butted each other like rams' horns.

They still had a distance to go before they would enter the Winter Ring where the sun never shone and the mountain peaks periodically crashed into each other.

Spike got on the intercom and asked Jane to quickly look at the screen again.

Hearing Spike say something urgent like that, the first thing that the crew wanted to do was to look at the screen and so they did.

"What in the world is that? It's coming straight at us."

A minute later the alarm sounded on the RoxyResc.

"Spike! What's going on?" Jane shouted.

"It's the Combo-Creature. It's following us. It's at least ten times larger than the ship and it sure looks mad."

"Put the shields up!" Ragrezy commanded. And Spike did.

Astro very calmly said. "I want all of you to just stop what you're doing and only think about that beast out there. I will conjure up some magic that will hold it back for at least five minutes."

The crew all stood still, closed their eyes and visualized the creature. Everybody except Mountain....Astro looked at him and could almost read his mind like a book. And sure enough, a second later Mountain said,

"Why don't I just go out there and beat the crap out of it?"

Astro responded with, "All right tough guy. Just close your eyes and concentrate before that beast beats us all to a pulp."

It would have been on the RoxyResc in seconds. But just as the creature was going to grab the ship, it pulled back in surprise as it began fighting the air that was surrounding it.

The crew didn't understand.

"Astro," they all asked almost at once. "What did you do to it?"

"Well! There is, however, one thing that the Combo-Creature cannot fight." Astro responded, chuckling.

"What is it?" Ragrezy asked.

"Magic! The Creature cannot fight magic. Its mind is weak and very open to hallucinations that are as real to him as they will be to you in a second."

He waved his hands and some sort of a light mist passed through the ship and when they looked at the creature again, they saw two Combo-Creatures fighting one another. They were turning into a faded image as the RoxyResc sped further away. The further away they were from the creature, the closer they were to the cold threats that were soon to show themselves.

They were only a few thousand miles away from the Ice Mountains. It was only minutes before they saw the ships that were in front of them. A second later Spike came over the intercom

"I hope that you are all sitting for this, because I see a

mountain coming straight up towards us."

It was a good thing that the ship could maneuver fast. It had a great technology built into it. Spike was doing some fantastic flying, avoiding other ships and avoiding being smashed by some mountain. And it was pretty amazing that none of the crew bounced around and smashed into the walls or any other part of the ship. A minute later all they saw was empty space in front of them with mountains all around. The mountains were so beautiful that they looked as if an artist had carved out cities on them. It was a magnificent sight for all of them. They had never seen such beauty. It only lasted a short time and then the Ice Pick People decided to show themselves. They were leaping on to most of the other ships and driving their pointy ice pick bodies through them. They were shaped like humans; only they were made of ice and their head and all of their appendages were pointed and sharp.

Spike and Lolly were in the Control Room looking at the wall size screen and into space. Lolly had her arm around Spike's neck and with their heads together they were both enjoying the beauty of the trip. Jane, Roxy, and Lisa were sitting at a nearby table just a few yards away, getting to know each other while glancing at the screen.

Mountain was in the Engine Room with Ragrezy, Franky, Slammer and Astro about a hundred feet in the back. Jane never understood why it was called an Engine Room since it was connected to the Control Room. Actually, it was just a huge room with some separations. There were partial walls and columns; everyone could see and hear each other or use the built in sound system. Or they could just look at the smaller screens that were strategically placed throughout the whole area. Mountain was doing just that; then he looked toward the Control Room and shouted out to Jane.

"Tell that pin headed pilot of yours to climb before we hit something."

Jane looked at the screen and repeated to Spike what Mountain had just told her. Spike said calmly,

"Take it easy! Look closer. We're above the mountains and we've escaped the Ice Pick people. We're safe for now. But when we enter into the part of the sky where the Air Current Tubes have to be ridden, it will be like riding a surf board. The difference is that if you make one mistake on the board, you're wiped out but you can still get back on. Only with this situation there is no getting up again. On this ride the danger will be in trying to enter the Air Current Tube."

It was a very peculiar scene that they saw through the screen. The ship was in the dark and yet the sky was bright because of all the white snow and ice that surrounded them. In some parts of the sky, they could see tubes of currents that could only be identified by their finely colored particle rings. Some of the tubes were miles wide and others just wide enough for a couple of ships to fit into one at a time in order to have hundreds and sometimes thousands of miles of easy flying.

Spike turned to Lisa and asked, "What are the dangers in trying to enter the Air Current Tubes?"

"Remember this, Spike. Entering the Air Current Tube is the riskiest part of the trip. You cannot hit or even graze a part of its ring when you enter or you will blow up. However, once you're in it, you can decide to leave at any time. But it would not be recommended."

"Why not?" Spike asked.

"Well. First of all, the drastic change of the air pressure and currents would kill you. And secondly, Lisa paused and put her finger to her lip and said sarcastically,

"Oh that's right. There is no secondly. But I have something better."

She pointed to the screen. "Look! Do you see what's going on?"

Spike watched as some of the ships tried to enter the tube at the same time and he thought that sooner or later someone would miscalculate. Well, he was correct. There was a spark, a puff of smoke and it was Sayonara baby for that unfortunate ship.

After seeing that, the crew knew that there was no way that Spike was going to go near that tube and let something like that happen to them.

There was a loud explosion behind them. Spike quickly adjusted the screen to see what had happened.

"Astro, Astro," he shouted. "The creature is behind us again and right behind him is a huge ball of fire."

Even though this was all happening thousands of miles behind the RoxyResc, the creature would be upon them within twenty minutes.

Ragrezy who was preparing things in the Engine Room shouted,

"Spike, I am going to eject one of my camera balls in front of the ship so that we can see the RoxyResc and everything that is happening around us for thousands of miles."

While he was doing that, Astro surprised everyone. He walked to the Control Room and pulled out a piece of the Black Wall from his pocket. It instantly formed itself into a raincoat and black hat. Astro and the raincoat walked back to the Engine Room as they talked. Spike was occupied with avoiding the creature behind them.

Lolly grabbed Spike and screeched, "Oh no! We're going to die! Look! The Combo-Creature is catching up to us and it's swallowing up the ships that are behind us as it's approaching us."

Lolly grabbed Spike's arm, put her head on his shoulder and very dramatically said, "We're going to get burned to death."

By this time Astro and his Raincoat had come out of the Engine Room and found Jane. She looked at Astro and asked, "How are we going to escape? It's at least another two hours before we can be far enough away from the *Mine, Mine Planet* to survive, and from the looks of it, we only have ten minutes left before the Creature gets us. Do you have any ideas?"

"Before we do anything," Ragrezy shouted, "let me launch the camera ball."

Slammer thought, "if only the ship could travel as fast as that camera ball." He still couldn't figure out how it developed its own thought processes which allowed it to identify the exact location where it had be or how it got in place so quickly.

The monster was just minutes away from grabbing, destroying and swallowing the RoxyResc.

"Hey, Astro," Mountain said, kind of bossy yet jokingly. If you and that Wall are going to do anything, don't you think you better start?"

The crew was looking at them and wondered why they were so calm. They acted as if they had been in similar situations before. And they had.

Lolly couldn't take her eyes of off the screen. The creature was almost upon them and the fire ball was right behind. The weather kept changing. It was as if there were waves of constantly altering temperatures. One minute, the mountains and the Ice Pick people were popping out of the ground; the next minute they were leaping to attack a ship and then melted in mid air. What was fascinating was the way new mountains and Ice Pick people formed so quickly. It was like shutting a light on and off. One minute the sky was filled with mountains of ice and the next it was a clear sailing sky.

"Hey, you two," Jane said, not showing any panic and understanding how men are. "Do you think you two macho men can get us out of here before we burn to death?"

Slammer and Astro looked at her and then at each other and started laughing. Mountain said, "You'd better listen to her, Astro or she will give you a beating before we burn up."

Astro looked at Spike and said, "This is critical for your escape. When you see the ball of fire in front of you, press the warp speed button immediately."

"The warp speed doesn't work," Spike stated and then added, "Don't you think I would have pressed it already, genius?"

"Look here, you spiky pin head. My friend, the Black Wall is inside your speed warp machine and it will provide the energy that you need. The timing is crucial. If you press it too soon, you might not get out of the planet. The Wall can only provide this energy thrust for a minute and a half."

"How are we going to get through the ice wall?" Franky asked.

"You leave that to me. Just remember that you're going to travel at warp speed through a hole that shrinks as quickly as its opens. So you must time it perfectly. And don't push that button until the creature is about to snatch you. Remember that even at warp speed it will take you four minutes to get out of this mess. The way I see it, you have to avoid the creature for three more minutes. When you see the fire ball in front of you, press the button."

Lisa was calm like Astro and Mountain and so she observed the crew. While getting to know her sisters as well as she could, given the circumstances, she had never been in such a situation with others.

She thought, *There certainly is a lot of concern about burning to death and the crew is sure getting snippy.*

"Astro!" Slammer shouted, "What the hell are you waiting for? Will you get going already?"

"Keep your shirt on, tough guy." Then Astro whispered in Lisa's ear, telling her to take care of the crew and then kissed her cheek as he said, "See you when you come out of this mess." And just like Sparky, he disappeared.

For the next two minutes Spike was occupied maneuvering the RoxyResc through the mountains, like a surgeon doing precision work, while avoiding the Combo-Creature, which was a just foot away from grasping the ship. The heat from the incineration explosion was melting the ships that the Combo-Creature had missed as he passed by chasing the RoxyResc.

The closer that the Combo-Creature got to the RoxyResc, the more Jane noticed that the Combo-Creature's butt was catching on fire. The incineration explosion was catching up with him. Meanwhile the RoxyResc was getting to the thickest and deepest part of the Winter Ring where the mountains almost closed the opening of the planet and became a wall of solid ice. Meanwhile Astro was speeding ahead of the RoxyResc and had to burst into his own ball of fire. He melted a clear path, creating a tunnel for the RoxyResc to pass through. As soon as the hole was created, Spike pushed the atomic warp speed button. The escape out of the planet was close and hairy but took place without a hitch. And within five seconds, the ship cleared the planet and was far enough away that everyone inside should have only felt its shock. But when she didn't feel any vibrations, Jane was surprised. The entire crew was not aware that they had just escaped within seconds of being incinerated or that the creature was still alive speeding to escape its own incineration. The RoxyResc shut down and could not go any farther because the Black Wall's energy source was completely used up. It would take a while for the engines to start up again. So there was nothing that they could do but watch the planet and wait.

Ragrezy told Spike to magnify what was on the screen. They were in for some surprise.

The vision of what they saw was fantastic. The *Mine, Mine Planet* had what looked like a fiery sparkling tail coming from its sunny side. It resembled flames shooting from a rocket ship on lift off. The planet was starting to crack and expand; it looked like it would explode at any second. It kept getting redder and a second later it was as though a million bombs had exploded out of what was a second ago was the icy dark side of the planet.

"Look at the smoke that is coming out of there," Franky commented.

"Something is not right." Mountain immediately replied. "Clouds like that cannot exist in a vacuum."

"What do you mean?" Roxy asked.

"Clouds require oxygen for them to exist."

"So?" Roxy flippantly remarked.

"So this!" Jane exclaimed as she pointed to the screen.

And when they looked, the surprise that they got was something that they did not expect.

The cloud was speeding toward the RoxyResc like it had a score to settle. As the cloud was getting closer, it began dissipating and within minutes the Combo-Creature showed itself. "Oh no," Lolly gasped, once again clinging to Spike.

"Why won't that Combo-Creature die? It's even bigger than before."

"Get us out of here, Spike!" Jane ordered in a very anxious tone.

"I'm sorry, Jane. I can't. The ship just won't start. What are we going do?"

Lisa immediately said, "We don't have a choice. In another ten minutes, that creature will be upon us. I have to do what Astro's Wall did."

"But you can't." Jane and Roxy responded at the same time.

"We just found you. We can't lose you again."

"Listen, sisters," she said gently but hurriedly. "We don't have time to argue... Either we can all die or I can hopefully give all of you another chance to survive."

There was nothing they could do. Jane and Roxy kept her company for as long as possible. The Combo-Creature was gaining on them. They had about five minutes left before it would destroy them. Spike was not going to push the warp speed button until the last split second, in hopes that some miracle would take place.

For Lisa and Mountain, the fact that this Combo-Creature was still able to attack was nothing new. But they certainly would not be surprised if Astro were hiding somewhere in space, watching everything. There was no way to know for sure and there was no Black Wall left for them to use to start the RoxyResc again. Mountain and Lisa could not look to Astro for help and so they were on their own. Lisa wondered if she could imitate what the Black Wall had done. She didn't know for sure if she could fuel the warp speed drive because she was only part Spark. But she didn't care; she was going to take the risk anyway and perhaps die, trying. Mountain and Slammer said that they would stay with Lisa. And since Jane had to be with Spike, the three sisters said their goodbyes but remained together until the last second for support.

Just as Lisa's sisters were leaving, Lisa floated upwards and came down feet first right into the warp speed hatch. Before she went completely inside, she looked at Mountain and said, "It has been an honor to have spent all this time together. I hope that we can do it again."

Mountain looked at her and responded with a big smile. "Of course, you're going to see me again. You're a Spark and indestructible."

And then he closed the hatch.

The Combo-Creature was just moments away from destroying the ship. Spike had his hand on the button, ready to push it.

Jane and Roxy kept hollering from the Engine Room. "No! Don't push it! Wait until we tell you to."

"We have only seconds," Spike yelled. "But don't worry.

I won't push the button without your okay."

And then he added, as if talking to himself, *It's been nice knowing you.*

Jane rushed to the Control Room and stood over Spike, staring at the screen and watching the Combo-Creature who was just seconds away from crushing them. She just couldn't say the word "push." But within that few seconds, Jane had to face the decision of saving her crew or watching everyone, including her sister die.

Jane was agonizing over having to tell Spike to push the button and the time to say it was now. Jane was about to give the order but just as her lips were forming the word, Spike tightened his muscles and prepared to push the warp speed button that even he didn't want to push. Just as Jane was going to say "Now," Spike pushed the button and at the very same time a bright flash of light appeared. A piece of the sky seemed to mimic a very flat and large Astro as it instantly glided in front of and over the RoxyResc, installing a shield of energy that the Combo-Creature could not penetrate. Astro had been watching everything from a part of space where he couldn't be seen. He knew what the Combo-Creature intended to do. What he didn't expect was how much stronger it was than the last time and how much farther it was able to travel away from the *Mine, Mine Planet*. Another second more and the Combo-Creature would have grabbed Jane's ship. Jane realized that the ship had not moved even though it had made a lot of noise. She was shocked to think that her sister was probably dead. Everyone was looking at the screen and watching as the Combo-Creature smashed against the shield. About ten seconds later, they saw the creature start to stretch from the back and as it was being pulled, it stretched again and a second later sprang backwards like a rubber band into the *Mine, Mine Planet*. After a few minutes, another explosion came from the planet. It was as if the Spark people wanted to make sure that the incineration worked. It wasn't long before the dark side of the planet started cooling off.

The first thing Jane did was grab Roxy's hand and run to the warp speed hatch to see if her sister had survived. To their great relief and surprise, Lisa had already been taken out. Mountain knew how important Lisa was to Astro and Lisa to him. Mountain had a sixth sense about everything and just as he felt Spike's emotions while he pushed the button, he also felt Astro's energy. He pulled Lisa out simultaneously as Spike pushed the button. Slammer and Mountain were next to Lisa when the shield appeared. Slammer wasn't sure if he would have known to pull her out, when the order to push the button was given, making Mountain the savior and the hero of the day.

Lolly started to jump up and down, relieved that the ship once again had power and that they could go wherever they wanted to.

The shield disappeared and Astro appeared, standing close to Jane, Roxy and Lisa.

The crew was relieved to see Astro.

"What great timing!" Mountain commented

"Hi girls," Astro said with a smile and then he looked at Jane.

She looked right back. "Hello to you," she responded. "Thank you for saving us, Astro but are you all right?"

"Of course I'm all right. I was just thinking about things when I was in the heavens a minute ago."

The crew thanked Astro for saving them and their ship.

Then he humbly asked Jane, "Do you mind doing me a favor?"

"Anything you want is okay with me," She said and smiled, happy to see him.

"Ah! Thank you, Jane. May we just travel for a while? I'm sure everyone wants some time to get over this mess and figure out what they would like to do."

"That's a great idea. I could use some time to talk to my sisters."

They were standing next to her and acknowledged what she said with a smile and a bob of their heads in agreement.

All of them liked the idea of taking time to gather their thoughts. After the work of checking the ship was done, most of the crew began to exchange ideas about their plans, unlike Franky and Ragrezy who didn't care what they did… and if it was nothing, then they were doing something that they wanted to do. The crew members checked on one another.

Jane felt a tug. It was Rocky. She had not wanted to bother him since he was still not feeling great and so she had just kept him in her pocket. A second later, Squeak popped out, grew to the size of a rabbit, sat on her shoulder and whispered in her ear, "Rocky said that he wants to go home and that his mother is calling for him but she won't come and get him unless Rocky tells her to."

Squeak changed his shape and draped himself around Jane's shoulders and neck and gave her a special hug as if he knew that he would not see her for a long time. Then he gave a long sigh, wishing that he could stay but needing to go in order to help Rocky. Rocky came out of Jane's pocket, adjusted himself to her size, looked at her and said sadly,

"Jane, I'm sorry but swallowing the Combo-Creature has over loaded my system with evil and my Mom is the only one who knows what to do. Only I cannot call her to get me, unless you tell me that it's okay."

"Of course it's okay. Why didn't you tell me this sooner?"

He said simply, "Because you were too busy."

"Oh thank you, Rocky. That was very sweet of you but just don't do it again." Then she added, "Have you telepathically communicated with your Mom?"

"Yes! She will be here in a minute."

Squeak actually appeared on and disappeared from everyone's shoulder within seconds, saying nicely to each one in a deep, deep voice.

"Nice knowing you."

Then he flew over to Jane and hugged her again. When he was done, he went back into Rocky's mouth. Jane and whoever was with her accompanied Rocky into the Engine Room. Once inside, Rocky floated in the air toward the warp speed hatch and said to Ragrezy,

"When I go into the hatch, pull the ejection lever."

Everyone watched as Rocky floated into the hatch and was then shot out of the ejector.

It was quite amazing to see. Rocky started to expand and change his shape. In a way he began to resemble a spaceship that looked like a flying squirrel. The crew looked at the screen and pulled back, when a second later another spaceship appeared with his mom in it. The ship was at least a hundred times bigger than the RoxyResc. Rocky headed straight for it and before he even l got near it, he vanished leaving a trail of energy leading toward the ship. After that, a bright flash was seen and the ship was no longer visible. Once that was over, everyone went back to business.

Jane asked Franky, "When are you going to look for your father?"

Franky was smiling from ear to ear. This was just the opportunity that he needed.

"I was just about to ask if you wanted to help me rescue him."

Jane, pointing her finger toward his chest, said, "Wait a minute."

She walked to Roxy, who was two feet behind her and asked,

"Do you want to come with me?"

"Yes," was her immediate reply.

Then Jane turned around and asked Lisa if she wanted to go with them.

Lisa wanted to but knew better than to say yes. So she just said exactly what was on her mind.

"I have never forgotten you two. I love you and I always will. From the first time that I saw the two of you in the arena, I have relived this wonderful memory from when we were children. Do you remember when we used to walk in the botanical-like park in N.Y.C?"

They both shook their heads yes, with tears in their eyes.

Lisa continued. "I have always dreamed of how someday we would see each other again and we would live close to each other, get married and spend our lives together. I have come to the realization about who I am and how I want to stay. I realize that my life belongs in the wind. The freedom to drift is all I know. Astro has raised me and to me he is my father. I am an arena fighter. I don't know any other way of life and I would feel like a trapped animal in the lifestyle that I just described or in any other life style other than my own. I am a Spark but I will always be your sister."

They hugged each other and started talking about whatever three sisters in their particular situation would talk about.

Ragrezy and Franky were content to discuss plans to rescue Franky's father and to travel the universe with Jane and Roxy.

Mountain looked at Slammer and asked, "Where are you going to be? I need an address to get your winnings to you."

Slammer looked at him deep in thought and sighed.

Then he looked at Spike, who was busy making goo-goo eyes at Lolly and almost floating in the air.

Slammer looked back at Mountain and then at Lolly and Spike and said, "It looks like they're going to settle down or something. What are you going to do Mountain?"

"I will be busy for a couple of years collecting our money and you know the kind of dangerous situations that collecting can create, especially when the losers don't want to pay. But it keeps me in shape and it's lots of fun, sometimes."

"You know something, Mountain. That sounds good. Now that I don't have to watch over Spike, I could use some exercise, like in the old days. Besides, the guys you can't take care of, I'll take care of for you."

Mountain started laughing. "Are you kidding? You'd better stick to lifting bulls."

"Yeh, and you're the full of bull that I'm going to lift up and believe me, you're a lot fuller of bull than the two I picked up."

They started cracking up and showing off and play fighting for a few seconds. Then Slammer maneuvered himself to be by Spike, stopped playing with Mountain, and looked at Spike who was busy talking to Lolly. Slammer smiled and then said. "Hey Spike. I'm going to hang out with Mountain for a while. Okay?"

Spike stood up and very surprised asked. "What do you mean hang out? The last time you and Mountain spent time together, you two weren't allowed back on the planets that you and I used to do business with."

"Spike," Slammer replied, "We're not soldiers of fortune anymore or out to start any wars. Besides, it looks like you'll have company of your own for now."

"You're right, Slammer. And I hope you don't expect a big goodbye. You know how I feel about the unknown and I want you and Mountain to be careful."

Spike realized that Slammer was right and that Lolly was important to him, for now. And he figured that it was only a matter of time before he and Slammer would run into each other again. Spike began romancing his lady, as if Slammer and Mountain were not there. Lolly started stroking the nails on Spike's head. As Spike oohed and aahed, he whispered into her ear and she began laughing.

Then he looked at Slammer and Mountain and with a big smile began his "I'll see you later" type of goodbyes. But before he could finish, Slammer cut him off and responded.

"Take it easy, pin head. We're not leaving yet. We're not like Astro, Rocky or Lisa. We need ground or something solid to walk on. Wherever Jane makes her next stop, that's when we will get off. We probably have a collection to make there anyway... meanwhile I'm going to look at the warp speed engine."

"Hold up, Slammer," Mountain said. "There's something about that engine that you need to know."

"And I'm sure that whatever it is, Mountain, you're going to know all about it." And they walked away laughing.

Epilogue

Meanwhile nearby, Lisa and Astro were deciding on what they were going to do next. Lisa was telling Astro that she wanted to fight but not for the sake of fighting but to help different worlds with the kind of trouble that only they were known for being able to address.

"You know, that's a good idea, Lisa. I see a great profit in such adventures."

"Astro, this will not be a business. We're not gladiators for profit".

She paused, looked to the skies and a minute later came to a conclusion.

"But of course, we will need money."

Then she sighed, "Oh well, I guess a little profit wouldn't hurt."

Astro asked Jane to let Lisa off at a nearby planet called the *Cloud Tree Planet*.

Jane looked at the planet on her screen and asked Astro. "What kind of world is it?"

"Do you see that three thousand mile wide road that goes completely around the world? It separates the planet in half. On one side there is a forest; on the other side there are only clouds. This 3000 mile wide road is where the cities are built and the creatures of the planet live. The way that the world works is really weird. You would not believe what exists under those trees and clouds. It's like there was a war between them. It rains sideways there. 'How can it possibly rain sideways?' you may ask. Well, one day I will explain it to you. And there are even creatures that live in the clouds as if it were an ocean.

And at times the cloud creatures come popping out, trying to get to the tree side of the planet, and in the process create havoc on other parts of the world. But that's another story for another time."

Lisa who was very confused looked at Astro and said. "I thought we were going to help worlds that are in trouble together."

"We are," he assured her "but I have to make a stop in my Island for a minute and calm it down and let it know that you and I are okay. And I will meet you on the *Cloud Tree Planet*.

"Do you know how long you're going to be?" Lisa asked, a bit disappointed to go alone yet excited about the adventure.

Then she added, "I have no idea about where to go or where to meet you."

"Just go to the Green Smoke Hotel Bar and ask for Chester. Tell him what we are going to do and that you're waiting for me to come and get you. Chester will give you whatever you need. And when I see you in a day or two, we will begin our new adventures."

Lisa smiled, told everyone goodbye and then vanished through the ship and headed for the *Cloud Tree Planet* which was just minutes away from where they were.

Mountain was sorry that Astro had to go. He walked over, gave him a big hug goodbye and said.

"Tell you what, pal. In five years the Frigatey Planet is going to celebrate its emperor's two thousand and sixty-seventh birthday with arena competitions. We can make some good dough with that, so I'll be seeing you in five years."

"I'm looking forward to it," Astro replied.

Slammer who had come out of the Engine Room was

watching all of this. He went to Astro and while shaking his hand said, "It was nice meeting you, Astro. See you in five years". Then he went back into the engine room

Jane was next to Astro and couldn't contain her curiosity. She just had to ask. "Astro, how can you go back to your Island? I thought that the world was incinerated."

"Don't worry, Jane. Only things that are not from the *Mine, Mine, Planet* have been incinerated.

"What do you mean?" Franky who was listening asked.

"The fire that exists consists of the Sparks. So for us, it's like going for a swim but instead of in water, it's in molten Spark lava."

"Now, that's some interesting stuff," Franky commented. Then he grabbed and shook Astro's hand.

"I never did thank you for helping us and for the many times you directly and indirectly saved my life, not to mention pretty much that of everyone else in the crew."

Then he added, "Thank you. Have a good trip back home and maybe we will see each other again. "

"You can bet on that, Franky," Astro answered as Franky left to join Mountain, Ragrezy, and Slammer in the Engine Room.

Jane looked at Astro with great admiration and began to speak.

"I don't know how I can ever thank you for what you have done for me and my crew. I almost don't want to say it, because I know that when I do, it will be goodbye and you will be gone forever."

"That will never happen. I'll tell you what, Jane. I am going to give you something that no one else has."

He took her hand and placed it on his chest which held his multiple hearts. Then he looked at her and said.

"We will see each other throughout the years. But when we're apart, I have given you the power so that no matter where you are, all you have to do is call for me from the depths of your emotions and I will come to you…Otherwise you can just think of me and we can communicate telepathically. Jane, it is time for me to leave."

"But where will we see each other again?" She reacted in panic.

He looked at her and said. "The answer to that will be on your screen."

Astro turned into a Spark light and shot through the ship like a rocket.

Jane ran to the screen and just as she looked at it, she saw Astro shoot out of sight like a comet whose tail had already written in bright star-like fashion.

SEE YOU IN THE PLAYGROUNDS OF THE UNIVERSE.

Would you like to see your manuscript become a book?

If you are interested in becoming a PublishAmerica author, please submit your manuscript for possible publication to us at:

acquisitions@publishamerica.com

You may also mail in your manuscript to:

**PublishAmerica
PO Box 151
Frederick, MD 21705**

We also offer free graphics for Children's Picture Books!

www.publishamerica.com

PublishAmerica